The Robot Army Trilogy, Part 1

The Hub

Beth Schluter

W & B Publishers
USA

The Robot Army Trilogy© 2015. All rights reserved by Beth Schluter

W & B Publishers

For information:
W & B Publishers
Post Office Box 193
Colfax, NC 27235
www.a-argusbooks.com

ISBN: 978-0-6923569-7-5
ISBN: 0-6923569-7-5

Book Cover designed by Dubya

Printed in the United States of America

PART ONE

THE HUB

Chapter 1

The Hub

Star opened her eyes to the gloom of distant lamplight and gathered her thoughts as the faint sounds of voices earmarked the start of a new day in this afterlife. This half-life of scavenging and making do and surviving mankind's greatest defeat, the"Apocalypse," as everyone called it, which happened over forty years previously. It would have been better if she had not woken and slept on in her glorious dreams of a different existence, where she could stroll in the open, feel sun on her skin and enjoy the laughter of children splashing at the riverside. All images she had stolen from an ancient storybook from the Hub library, none of which she had ever truly experienced in her sad life of living underground in this old mine.

Star was seventeen and had been born in the mines, she had never known the Earth that her parents had grown up in. That Earth was only to be found in the stories they told around the fires in the evening for those who wanted and craved to hear. Star was orphaned after her parents succumbed to a fever some years previously, probably the result of living in this mine through the cold wintry years gone by.

The outside world had been bitterly cold for long periods of time during Star's childhood. However, of late the temperature outside had been tolerable. Star knew this because she was one of the few allowed out into the polluted land surrounding them. Star was one of the scavengers. Searching through the remnants of the civilization that once lived here on Earth, now reduced to rubble and scattered in a war-torn burnt-out land, the scavengers looked for anything that may be of use to the community they lived in.

"Star! Get up! Time to get ready!" Finch's voice boomed in her ears.

Finch was a couple of years older than her and he felt that gave him the right to boss her around, but everyone in the Hub knew she was a better scavenger than him. She tolerated his ego because he had earned her respect when he saved her from certain death when a wall almost collapsed on top of her as they were both out scavenging last year. He literally had flown through the air to push her away from danger just in time. He never bragged about it, not once and that sealed it for her. A friend in need was a valuable asset. Besides, he was quite a looker these days. Taller than her, handsome, with dark features, very strong and capable , but best of all he had his eye on Star.

"Coming Finch, keep yer air on!"

Star slowly crept out of her bunk, careful not to stand on Chaff's fingers as she climbed down past the lower bunk where Chaff slept.

Chaff slept on regardless, but then she didn't need to scavenge yet. She was only eight and not allowed out into the polluted air. Her job was washing the pots, along with the others in her age group. Today was her day off, so she slept on.

The dorm was filled with bunk beds, all labelled with the owner's name in some form or other. Here eight girls slept—aged from age eight to nineteen. Next door to the dorm was another one where adults slept. Robyn, Chaff's mum was one of them, her other daughter Wren slept in the bunk next to Star's. She was seventeen too and also a scavenger.

The men's bunks were across the way to the adults, separated by one of the many tunnels stretching through this old mine they called home. All the new born in the mines were named after birds that lived on Earth a long time ago. It was Travis' idea, he was one of the elders of the community. He didn't want everything to be forgotten of his previous life, so this was a way of remembering the birds.

Star was named after Starlings, Bull after Bull-finches, then there was Merlin—Gale her mother—who was named Nightingale. There was Wren, Robyn, her other daughter Chaff, named after a Chaffinch, Finch himself and many others of a similar nature, a veritable Bird community!

Crackers and Milk

Star pulled on her oversized jacket to keep out the chill until she reached the fire. Two other scavengers were already around the fire eating their breakfast, a few crackers Robyn had made and some goat's milk to wash them down.

Here in the mines, now called The Hub, home to around seventy people with some animals that had been saved and bred post "Apocalypse" they shared equal space with their human companions. A few goats and chickens kept the survivors alive, along with the indoor farm that grew supplies which were once found only above ground. Underground streams kept them watered without the inevitable pollution of lakes above ground. It was quite basic, but it had kept the community alive for forty- five years. Everyone had their own jobs and responsibilities, no one begrudged them.

Bull, at twenty five, was the biggest of the scav-engers, named after his size. He could always be relied on if trouble came your way. Muscular, fair-haired, level-headed, perceptive, and strong; the kind of back-up you could wish for in times of danger. Next to him at the fire sat Wren, seventeen, the same age as Star but the two of them couldn't look more different. Wren had long, fair hair and a dreamy look in her eye .She was prone to imagining things and could not always be relied on to give accurate accounts of things she witnessed.

Star, on the other hand, was quick-witted and keen-eyed, with a tough veneer that belied her age. Wayward dark hair that had a mind of its own and dark eyes that engaged you like a magnet draws steel. She, like Finch and Bull, was expert at using a bow and often wore one strapped to her back whilst out scavenging. This was more for protection than for hunting as they hadn't seen a living creature in years.

"Not crackers again is it?" moaned Star, her least favourite of breakfast offerings.

"Sorry, love, you got up too late to have the cereal and toast, I ate it all" smirked Bull.

At that Star had to smile and get over her moaning. She'd never experienced such foods, Bull had heard of them from his Mum, Mary, described in such exquisite detail it made him drool. Nowadays you were lucky to eat at all. At least there was food in the Hub.

Star and the others ate in silence then prepared themselves for their role for the community.

Each scavenger put on their safety masks ready around their necks, shouldered large rucksacks for carrying any supplies they found, then armoured themselves with an array of weapons salvaged at the Hub. There were knives, bows and arrows and a couple of handguns—just in case of trouble—available for anybody who needed them. Trouble had a habit of finding scavengers these days as supplies dwindled and the good stuff had become scarce.

They knew there were other survivors somewhere because one of them had spotted signs of disturbances amongst the wrecked buildings when out scavenging last year. Nobody knew where they lived though – maybe it was best that way.. Buildings had also become more unstable over the years, crumbling into pieces without notice, another peril for the scavengers to deal with.

"Make sure you stay safe." Robyn said to her daughter as Wren began to wrap herself in layers to keep out the chill.

Here in the breakfast hall it was nice and cosy because of two fires heating the space. But outside it was a different matter. The polluted air had blocked out the sun's rays for decades and made the scavenging a cold affair.

"I know, mum," Wren smiled. "I'll be careful, don't worry." She kissed her mother on the cheek and hefted her rucksack and weapons over her shoulder.

The four scavengers, dressed in their warm clothing and protective masks headed out of the warm hall into the long tunnel that took them out towards the entrance to the mine. The four were used to working as a team and knew each other's strengths and weaknesses. Bull generally worked with Star and so Wren and Finch worked together mostly.

Into the Grey.

Once through the outer tunnels the scavengers emerged via a rusting steel door into the gray light of the new day. Masks firmly in place they, squinted against the half light until their eyes adjusted and then made their way to the vehicle shed. A few motor bikes, scooters, bicycles and battered jeeps were all that remained still working from around twenty vehicles salvaged in the first months of the new era of this post war existence.

Star looked carefully into the distance where Bull was focused. Had he seen something? Or was it simply Bull being careful as usual? They had not seen a soul for nearly a year, so they did not expect to encounter anyone, especially here. The Hub was well hidden, but you always had to be careful. Dwindling supplies meant everyone would become more desperate and that could spell trouble.

"Let's go!" barked Finch, eager to get going.

He staggered over the frozen rocks towards the shed, keeping his eyes sharp on the horizon as he went. It wouldn't do to give away the Hub, the safety of all the community depended on the scavengers' vigilance.

In the shed they selected two motorbikes as they needed to go further afield this time. They donned full-face helmets to further protect themselves from the air pollution. Wren rode pillion with Finch and Star with Bull. Off they set into the grey.

***

All around them nothing grew. All plant life blackened and petrified was covered with a coating of frost-laden dust. Buildings lay in ruins mostly, with an odd few left half intact, but shells of their former selves.

No animal life was to be seen or heard, no birds in the sky. Nothing could survive in this grim, frozen environment. Roads were littered with shells of cars, deep craters and cracks here and there. It would have been impossible to drive the jeep this way, the gaps were very narrow in places. but the motorbikes at least could squeeze through where it became tight.

The terrain was difficult to cover, but Bull and Finch had become expert riders by now. Navigating carefully past broken remains of rusty shells of vehicles had become the norm. Miles of rough terrain passed by

Star's vision. The whitened bones of dead creatures littered the open land to their right and Star wondered what they had looked like. She had never seen large creatures alive. The goats and chickens were all she knew. The library in the Hub had shown her larger animals that had lived on what was called a farm but now all that was gone, gone forever; pulverised to extinction by an alien species who destroyed their planet.

A while later Bull pulled to a halt to check out his map. He unfolded the tattered and worn paper and checked a few landmarks.

"Are we going the right way?" asked Finch worriedly.

There were no longer any kind of road signs to help find the way. They had been burnt out or blown apart long ago.

Bull checked the map, then gazed towards the horizon.

"The old road leads over to the ridge over there. It should be beyond that." Bull replied, folding the map back into his pocket. "Follow my lead!" he called as he revved up the bike and set off in the direction of the ridge cross-country.

Minutes later, "Look out!" he shouted to the others and swerved to one side, pulling up short. Just in front of him, partly hidden by the lie of the land was an enormous crater where the land had simply disappeared! Star held her breath as she held on tightly to his oilskin

"That was close!" she remarked, letting out the breath she was holding onto.

"I think a change of speed is required, as well as a change of direction!" Wren dreamily exclaimed. "If we'd have been going a bit faster that would have been it!" she added.

"No kidding! I'd never have thought that!" retorted Finch, turning the bike to circumvent the crater.

"I think I'll take the lead for a while, Bull, if you don't mind?" called Finch as he rode at a more dainty pace along the edge of the crater. Bull made no reply but simply followed at a more leisurely pace, still scanning the horizon vigilantly.

Fallen, burnt out trees and crumbling skeletons of animals littered their route over the fields, blackened and pitiful in this dead world.

"I wonder what animals they were?" asked Wren, more to herself than anyone.

None of the youngsters in the Hub would have any experience of animals apart from the goats and chickens they saw at home.

At the crest of the hill they had been aiming for they pulled up and looked down at the valley below them.

"There it is!" Bull exclaimed enthusiastically.

He pointed to a large shell of a building, sur-rounded by other smaller buildings, torn and blackened in the valley below. There was no sign of life or move-ment anywhere, but as usual the scavengers headed cau-tiously down to the valley, keeping to whatever shelter they could find en route.

Chapter 2

The Building

This had once been where people lived and worked, where animals had roamed in the surrounding hills and fields. But now, there was no living being apart from them for miles. As they rode along what had been the main thoroughfare into the town, dodging obstacles on their way, Wren imagined living here, having a school and friends to hang out with and everything complete and pretty and alive again. *It must have been pretty,* she thought to herself. There must have been colours, not this black and grey...

The world she lived in had been deprived of sunlight and fresh air for decades. The alien invaders had not only pulverised whole towns and cities into oblivion, but they had also ravaged the globe by fire-bombing it incessantly until the skies had been filled with toxic fumes and the sun's rays had been obliterated by the airborne dust of ash floating from the decimation of everything on Earth.

They dismounted their bikes and hid them in the shelter of a ruined building at the side of the road. Weapons at the ready they set off in pairs to hunt for anything worthy of scavenging.

Bull headed straight for the large broken building in front of them, with Star in tow. Each scanning the perimeter in different directions. Deeper into the ruin they went, climbing over obstacles on their way. After a few minutes Star could see why Bull targeted this building. There were stone stairs, steeply leading down into the darkness...

Torches on, they continued their descent into the unknown. The steps wound down like a spiral towards another level, then another set of stairs also covered in dust and debris.

"What was this place?" asked Star, sniffing the air below ground cautiously, despite her mask.

She was surprised to see Bull all of a sudden remove his bike helmet and he was about to remove his face mask...

"No" Bull, no!" exclaimed Star desperately. "It's too dangerous! You can't breathe in this air!"

But Bull merely hesitated a couple of seconds before revealing a mischievous glint in his eye and removed his mask. He looked her in the eye as she gasped disbelievingly. He took a quick breath, scanning the dark with his torch as he did so, then he took another breath, deeper this time. He immediately fell to his knees and Star was beside him in an instant ready to rush his mask back on.

"Oh no! Bull! Please don't die on me! Not like this ! You stupid...!"

Star desperately tried to grab his mask from his hand and lift his head up to replace it when his body started convulsing. Star was beside herself, she didn't know what to do, when suddenly Bull lifted his face and in her torchlight revealed that he was laughing!

"What?" Star stepped back on her haunches, falling sideways in the dust.

"Star. It's okay! I'm fine! Take your helmet and mask off. We're far enough below the surface here, the air is not bad. I can breathe fine!"

He helped her upright and convinced her he was breathing easily.

Star gingerly took off her helmet and mask and took a shallow breath and was surprised to find it was true. The air was breathable! She looked around without the hindrance of the helmet that had given her a blinkered vision. The place was huge.

"What is this place?" Star demanded again.

Bull shone his torch around and headed for a railing in front of them, pulling Star with him. The light from their torches revealed below them in the gloom lots of what looked like little caves with glass fronts. There seemed to be chairs dotted around the floor space in front of the caves, caked in layers of dust. Near Bull and Star there seemed to be metal stairs leading down to them.

"What are they?" Star whispered. She had never seen anything like them before.

Bull smiled and looked at her. "Those my dear Star are what are known as shops!"

Star looked bewildered. "Shops? What are shops?"

Bull laughed again. "Star. Before the war this is where people bought goods, with money. We are in the lower level of what my mum calls a shopping mall ! She recalled there used to be one in this town, but was sure it wouldn't have survived the Apocalypse. Looks like it did, well, at least some of it did! Come on!"

Bull placed his mask and helmet on the floor by the balcony then turned on his heels and headed for the metal stairs with Star following in disbelief.

"There are big steps on these stairs!" Star remarked. "I bet people found it difficult to go up and down them!" She shone her torch down at the treads while Bull shone his torch around them carefully, still vigilant as ever.

" I think these stairs used to move on their own, mum told me about them. They are called scullators if I remember right. You just stood on them and they'd take you up or down. Easy!"

Star looked disbelievingly and shook her head. She wasn't about to fall for that one!

"Yeah, right! You won't catch me out twice, mate!" she retorted.

Bull said nothing but smiled to himself. He wondered if there would be anything left here after all this time. Minutes later they had descended the steep escalators and found themselves in a circular space, with corridors heading away in different directions from the circle. The glass in the caves were mostly cracked or blown inwards revealing dust covered mannequins or empty boxes strewn inside.

Glass Caves

Once at the foot of the stairs the two scavengers stopped to listen for any activity and when none was found they moved quietly towards the nearest "shop". The window front was trashed and dust laden mannequins were strewn across the door and window space.

Stepping over them carefully they both entered the premises to find empty boxes and overturned shelves covering most of the floor space. There was nothing of any value to be seen. Star tried to imagine what the "shop" had looked like before the war but couldn't quite imagine it. Just before turning back to the entrance Star's light caught another door at the back of the vast room and she headed for it.

Star tried the handle and pushed. Locked. She pushed harder with all her might but it wouldn't budge. Before she could ask Bull for help he was already beside her, pulling a crowbar from his rucksack. He levered the door until it opened with a mighty crack!

***

At the same time back at the Hub a little six year old girl, Merlin, or Lin, a friend of Chaff's began to chatter excitedly. The Hub community deemed Lin a little strange, wild-eyed and dark-haired. She often talked to her "imaginary friends" and was convinced these friends were real. Chaff however, found nothing strange in her at all and defended her valiantly whenever other children tried to be mean to her.

Lin's mother was called Nightingale, she'd only been seventeen when Merlin was born. She refused to name the father, insisting that she had not slept with anyone. People gave her a wide berth generally, deeming her a bit strange too. Her own parents had died not long after she'd been born, nobody was sure what they had died of but thought that the pollution had caused their lungs to collapse as they had wandered for weeks through the ravaged world looking for a place to live before one of the Hub's sentries found them and brought them to live in the community. Now Nightingale and her daughter Merlin were tolerated but feared by many. Robyn felt sorry for the child and encouraged her daughter's friendship with her.

Robyn puzzled over Lin's latest outburst as she played with Chaff in the kitchen area whilst Robyn prepared a meal.

"The lights are coming! The lights are coming!" Lin called out with glee, twirling around excitedly, arms aloft, almost as though she was dancing.

"What lights dear?" Robyn asked the excited girl.

"The lights from the sky!"

Merlin answered as though it was obvious. Robyn looked at Chaff for explanation, but Chaff shrugged and shook her head. Robyn didn't like the sound of it one bit.

***

Back at the mall they both stopped dead, still, listening....they hadn't meant to make so much noise. If there was anyone else here they would have heard that!

After a few nail-biting seconds they decided it was safe to continue. They shone their torches inside.

"Oh my god!" Star exclaimed, wide eyed!

Bull looked at her, looked at the room opened in front of them again and lifted Star off her feet!

"Jackpot!" Bull enthused. "These will certainly become very useful!"

The storeroom was filled with jackets and coats of all sizes and colours, still wrapped in clear plastic shrouds to keep the dust out. There were so many they didn't know at first where to start.

"We'll take a few this time then come back when we need more" Bull calculated quickly.

He took out a plastic sack from his pack and folded a few of the less bulky coats into it, making sure there were some for the children as well as for the adults.

If they'd had success here what would they find in the other "shops? wondered Star.

"I think we should split up to check as many of the other 'shops' as we can," reasoned Star. "We can put what we're taking at the foot of the stairs and meet up when we can't carry any more."

Bull nodded and they both headed out of the shop, each taking a different direction in this circle of shops.

After some time Star had discovered enough treasures to warrant ceasing her exploration for this particular day and headed back towards the stairs.

Bull was already there waiting for her. She was dying to let him know what she'd found but Bull was eager to get moving. He seemed a little edgier than before, but then again, it was getting late and they were near their deadline for returning to the Hub.

Bull's rucksack was heaving, it looked like a very profitable trip. However, he didn't seem all that excited any more. Before she could ask him why he put a finger to his lips and she stopped abruptly with all senses focused. Alarm pricked every nerve in her body.

There it was, in the distance, to their left, a faint sound.

The Noise

Star's eyes flickered in all directions and she swiftly pulled an arrow and loaded it onto her bow. The torches were switched off and they both adjusted their vision to the gloom. After a minute had passed a faint sound again could be heard in the distance. Bull indicated for them to slowly climb the stairs with their swag, bows ready, not making a sound.

Scanning the darkness around them they continued their trek upwards carefully, backwards, step by step, all the time scanning the gloom for any movement, but none was forthcoming.

The sound was heard again, same as before, but slightly louder this time, however, it was still below where they were.

The sound was unfamiliar, not exactly metallic, but unusual. However, they weren't going to hang around to find out!

They began now to worry about Finch and Wren. Were they okay above ground?

They both hurried, now they were near the upper part of the stairs and quickly donned their masks and helmets from where they had left them past the balcony at the top of the mall. They hurried towards the upper level, ever vigilant for any movement.

Surfacing once again they searched the street area for signs of their companions. No sign!

They headed in the shadow of the buildings towards where the bikes should be, slowly and carefully, hoping for sight of Finch or Wren. Nothing!

Suddenly, out of the side of the building they were passing they were grabbed forcefully by gloved hands .

Bull was starting to struggle when he realised it was Finch, with Wren. They released their hands and signalled to be quiet, pointing to the distance, towards where the bikes were hidden! They huddled down low behind a broken wall next to them.

Bull and Star shared Finch's binoculars and focused in the direction of the noise. The sound alternated between a whooshing noise and a semi-metallic clinking, but they could see nothing yet. There was definitely something up ahead, but what? It was a similar sound to the one they'd heard below ground they realised.

Suddenly they caught a glimpse of something white, shiny, hovering metres above ground level ahead of where the bikes were hidden!

"What is that?" puzzled Star, she'd never encountered anything like it in her life and by the expression on Bull's face, neither had he.

Before Bull could reply the white shiny object whooshed at tremendous speed past them a few metres above the ground travelling along the street . It had a kind of silvery light beaming from the front as if scanning the terrain for something. In seconds it had moved further along, with a great whooshing sound.

Just then, the scavengers were relieved to be in shadow and out of sight of the object .

All had fear in their eyes, nobody said a word. Instead their eyes followed the object's trajectory until it disappeared from view and all was silent again.

"Is that one of the aliens who destroyed our planet?" asked Wren fearfully.

Bull wasn't sure as he hadn't been alive then, but from his mother's account he didn't think so.

"No. I think this is something different." Bull offered. "But to be safe we'd better wait 'till dark before we move. I guess we're stuck here for a bit!"

They all settled in a spot near their motorbikes awaiting the cover of dark. They did not see the object return, to their relief!

Chapter3

The Hoard

They had risked travelling in the dark for fear of being seen by the object when they left the town. They had waited until Bull deemed it safe to move. They hadn't seen the object again and no sounds had been heard for hours, so they retrieved their bikes and headed gingerly back towards the direction of the Hub. They didn't risk the full beam of the headlights for fear of being spotted and had a few narrow escapes on the route home, almost crashing headlong into abandoned vehicles and fallen objects a couple of times. Hours later, tired and fingers numb with the cold, rucksacks laden, they approached the quarry entrance and headed downwards into the mine entrance sheds.

"Where on earth have you been?" a worried sentinel demanded outside the Hub shed.

A couple of sentinels had been scanning the horizon for hours fearing the worst when the scavengers had failed to reach their deadline for return to the Hub.

"It's a long story! Better told inside." replied Bull, offloading his gear from the bike and heading towards the steel entrance with the others in tow. It was far too cold to linger out here to tell their tale.

Many worried faces greeted them as they descended into the depths of the Hub, carrying their heaving rucksacks on their backs. They took some moments to warm up by the fires before facing everyone.

Robyn and Bull's mother pushed their way through the crowd to embrace the four of them, relieved to find no injuries. Chaff clung onto Wren's arm, glad to have her sister back in one piece.

Chaff was excited to see what was in Wren's rucksack and eagerly awaited the 'grand opening' of contents. However, her face fell a little as Wren produced some metal objects blackened by fire. Tools perhaps? She didn't know what they were. This didn't look exciting at all! Wren saw her sister's disappointment and slowly removed her gift from the bag... Wren always tried to find something, however small, for her sister when out scavenging. Last time she had found her a book about animals that had been hidden under some fallen debris in a house.

"Here you are, just for you, Chaff " smiled Wren, "I found it inside a metal box in one of the buildings I searched".

She produced a small dusty cloth wrapped around something which was obviously very small. Wren placed the cloth in Chaff's open palm, watching her sister's puzzled expression as she couldn't imagine what it could be.

Chaff slowly and carefully peeled open the cloth and looked stunned and enthralled by what was revealed. There in her palm was a beautiful little necklace made of golden metal, with a little angel pendant on it. She had never seen anything so beautiful! Her smile took over her whole face as she hugged her sister tightly. Robyn smiled to see her daughter so happy.

"Wow Wren! That's beautiful!" remarked Robyn. "It looks like real gold too. Well found!" she beamed at her daughters proudly.

Finch tipped out his own rucksack to reveal some wire, tools, metallic bowls and mugs along with myriad screws and bolts of all sizes. They were always handy around the Hub. The mines often needed repairs due to the infrastructure being old and worn and these would be invaluable. The crowd muttered their thanks to the pair and began to sort through the goods for what they needed.

The crowd looked to Star and Bull, who as yet hadn't begun to unpack their bulging rucksacks. They waited impatiently to see what offerings they had provided. Star looked to Bull, smiled and nodded:

"Shall we?"

"Together" Bull agreed.

They opened up their rucksacks and began tipping them out onto the large wooden table in front of the waiting crowd.

Gasps of delight filtered around the table as the people stared at the treasures unfolding. Piles of warm coats and jackets, boots and trainers, gloves, scarves and hats emerged from Bull's pack. Star's offerings were slightly different: books, medical supplies, a couple of CDs and batteries and some torches.

Bull and Star smiled proudly as the crowd showed their appreciation, hugging them, shaking their hands and eagerly trying on goods for size. This was treasure indeed!

Bull took his mother to one side and took a small package out of his pocket that he'd been saving for her. Wrapped carefully in a piece of cloth Bull placed the treasure in her hands. Bull's mother looked puzzled at her son, feeling the weight of the object.

She slowly unwrapped the parcel and smiled broadly when she discovered a large plastic bottle of "Jasmine scented bubble bath !" Luxury! The old metal bathtub which was used by his mother would now feel a little more luxurious with scented bubbles in it!

"Oh son! This is lovely, brilliant!" she hugged Bull tightly. "Now I can't wait till bath night!"

She clutched the bottle as though it was priceless and admired the fancy writing on it. She un-stoppered the lid and sniffed the contents- it even smelt of Jasmine after all these years! This was a rare find. Her son made her so proud, always thinking of her when out scavenging. He'd brought her a host of little gems over the years, all equally appreciated.

When the hubbub had died down and the satisfied crowd had allocated homes for the objects, Bull stood on the chair nearby and called for attention. They'd had their time of joy, now it would be time for the bad news.

The Object

The people lowered their voices on seeing Bull's serious face.

"I'd like to call a meeting for the elders, we have something to discuss, right now." Bull stated forcefully.

The crowd stopped what they were doing, then herded the children back towards their play area and began to settle down on the benches and chairs around the large gathering space. This is where meetings took place. The children knew the drill. Only adults allowed. Only those aged fifteen or over were allowed at meetings.

"What is it?" called out a voice from the crowd. "Is this why you were late back?" inquired another.

"Let them speak and we shall find out" uttered Robyn, calming the crowd, but herself secretly worried too.

Bull stayed up on the chair so everyone could see and hear him.

"We did have a problem today, whilst we were out scavenging" Bull looked them in the eye as he continued. "We were interrupted at the town by a strange noise. Star and I heard it below ground a couple of times, but saw nothing. Then when we came above ground to rejoin Wren and Finch we discovered that, thanks to Wren's good hearing they heard it long before they were compromised."

"We hid and waited to see what was creating the noise. It was coming from a block away from us, behind some rubble. We looked through the binoculars but we couldn't see very well. Eventually we made out something unusual, plastic-looking, shiny and white, we only saw a part of it as it was hidden by walls. It seemed to be hovering a few metres above ground.."

The crowd looked worried and began to mutter, aghast at this news.

Bull continued, "It then came towards us, well, the sound did anyway, a mixture of metallic grinding and whooshing sounds. Nothing like we'd ever heard before. We waited to see if it would be revealed as it came closer, as we were fairly well hidden. The next thing we knew the object whooshed by us, a few metres away at a tremendous speed. Too quick to even make out its shape properly. But we did see a kind of silvery beam tracing the ground in front of it, as though it was scanning it. It definitely was flying or hovering."

The crowd erupted in horror. Robyn's thoughts drifted back to Lin's outburst earlier on, was this linked to that she thought, horrified.

"How big was it?" shouted someone.

"Was it a spaceship?" called another.

Bull gestured for calm and continued:

"No, it wasn't a spaceship, it was small, I think smaller than a person. More like a globe of some sort, hovering and scanning the terrain. We waited a long time in case it came back, or there were more of them, but that was all we saw and heard. We figured it would be wise to wait till dark to return in case we'd be seen by whatever it was, so, that's why we were late."

Bull saw the fear in their eyes and the old feeling of helplessness reappear in some of the elders' reactions.

"Please no, not again!" cried out a voice in the crowd.

"Do you think it's them again, Travis?" inquired Bill, another elder. Travis shook his head grimly.

"No, the aliens in the last war didn't have anything like that as far as I can recall. This is something new entirely!"

Travis' words brought no comfort to the Hubbites. Was this the beginning of a new war? The community erupted in despair at the prospect of another invading species laying claim to their territory!

***

Lights

Far above the Earth, lights multiplied in the blackness of space beyond the stratosphere. Groups of lights partitioning off into smaller sections, gathering in a configuration that apparently served some purpose or another. At the centre of the pattern of lights a larger cluster formed, of a different colour to the others, glowing intermittently blue then red, pulsating like a heart beating. The mother ship, herding her flock into location, ready for their grand plan.

"Ceasing all thrusters. Mother ship in position, Captain," a male voice reported.

However, this was no male. He was shaped like a male and had a face with manly features, but that's where the similarity ended. The whole body was artificial, encased in a white plasticised covering, with the sleeve of one arm displaying several buttons, some glowing in different colours. He stood over seven feet tall. He brandished a gold band on his arm, denoting his rank as Gold, a supreme AI with many skills and functions.

Several other AIs—artificial intelligences—were focused on computerised screens in front of them on the bridge of the spaceship, all tasked to particular duties , in varying colours according to rank.

"Thank you, Argo" replied the captain, only one of two humans aboard the vast fleet. The other human was in the ship's lab, working with the latest models of AI.

***

Captain Grey smiled to himself at the prospect of exploring Earth, with his fleet of AIs, who were there to carry out his every wish as he commanded. It had taken a team of scientists a long time to create such technology. It had resulted in a lot of failure and even death to begin with, but now he had the power at his finger tips to create and destroy! Such power! It was a shame that only two scientists had survived the arduous journey to final success.

The spaceship was enormous, built by the AIs, even designed by the AIs. It was beyond the comprehension of the two humans aboard the mother ship how everything worked, but that was why it had been given over to the AIs to design and construct. Their intelligence was beyond any human's.

Robots with lesser intelligence performed more menial tasks for Capt. Grey and his AIs in the construction of the ship and carrying out their wishes for the grand plan. The capabilities of the weapons on board ship were also beyond anything that Captain Grey had ever dreamed. The AIs had even been involved in their own evolution, creating a super species of AIs like Argo.

Capt. Grey had travelled the universe in search of resources for his machines and had endured many battles to obtain them. Many alien species had encountered his army and lived to regret it. He had not lost a single battle but had seen the devastation of worlds in the wake of his success. Obtaining the correct resources was of paramount importance to his mission.

On board ship, the Blues, smaller AIs than the others, were the technicians and operators of the fleet. They kept the ships running smoothly and were constantly upgrading and refining the ship's weaponry and technology.

"Prepare the droids" commanded Captain Grey. "Launch at zero two five zero."

"Copy that. Launch at zero two five zero." replied Argo, waving his palm across a holographic screen in front of him.

"Droids launching!" Argo confirmed.

Scores of miniscule glowing spheres detached from the supporting spaceships and headed towards Earth.

"Prepare the transports and the cargo despatches!" Grey commanded. Argo programmed the screen to carry out the command.

"Cargo and transports ready at your command captain". Argo reported.

Captain Grey wondered whether his plan would work, looking down at the planet obscured by dust storms and toxic cloud cover. *Time will tell*, he thought.

***

The orbs descended on Earth in their thousands, ready to scan the terrain around the world in search of life, of resources and survivors. Their scanners reported back the images of what they surveyed to the ships for processing by the Bronze AIs, who would decide which materials would be required down on the planet to carry out Grey's plans.

The Bronzes were the first experimental AIs that the scientists had worked on after completing the robot constructions. The Bronzes had helped the scientists construct a walking machine capable of lifting heavy objects and they were provided with effective weaponry in their claw-like hands that would help destroy or defend, whichever was required to achieve their tasks. They were large oval-shaped mechanoids which had hydraulic arms and legs. They were used a lot in construction and had been useful in helping Grey complete his vast fleet.

The scientists had later constructed a more intelligent AI, the Silvers, who piloted the remaining ships in the fleet. They were able to make-split second decisions, unlike the Bronzes, and were invaluable when fighting battles with enemies in space. Grey's fleet was so far undefeated in battles.

From the Silvers the supreme Gold AIs had evolved. These were able to fly unaided and facially they had manly features. They had more human traits, like a sense of humour and a degree of compassion , a feature that none of the other AIs possessed. The most highly evolved was Argo, named by Captain Grey and selected as his second in command. The other Golds were named the Argonauts! They were given the task of deploying the advanced weaponry on board ships in the fleet when battles were fought. They were also able to fly in space, unaided, to bring down smaller enemy craft as required. They were extremely loyal to Grey and a formidable foe to any enemy.

***

Enemy

In the Hub the meeting had deteriorated into panic and anger from some quarters.

"After all the devastation that was caused the last time! Haven't they done enough?" shouted a woman from the group. "There's nothing left for them! What else could they take? They've incinerated everything already, what more is there?" she cried despondently.

Bull's mother raised her voice to be heard.

"We don't know that it's them. We know very little at the moment. Let's not panic just yet. As you said, there's nothing here worth grabbing, so I'm sure when whoever it is sees that, they won't want to stay!"

The crowd seemed a little more persuaded by that thought and began to think things through a bit more.

"We need to send scouts out to watch for any developments and then plan when we know more," offered Bull. "I'm volunteering for one." He added.

"Me too" said Finch.

The Hub elder, Travis had weighed up the situation and concluded, "We will all stay vigilant and the Scavengers and elders will take turns to cover the terrain we operate in, noting any activities out of the ordinary and reporting back here. No one will challenge any alien life if at all possible. Stay hidden! Observe and report! That's all, for now."

"I'll draw up a rota and allocate sections to each group to monitor," offered another elder.

"Thanks, Bill." said Travis.

Bill had been a founder of the community alongside Travis all those years ago, when they were miners, both in their twenties, working in this very same mine! They had gathered their young families and friends together with all of the supplies they could find and brought everyone down here to the depths of the mine to live. Pete, a neighbour who farmed outside the mine area, brought his chickens and goats down to the mine with him when the aliens began their destruction above ground. They had lived here ever since, scraping a life together.

Robyn debated whether she should say anything about Lin's comments to Travis, but she thought better of it. It was probably just coincidence, no need to spook the others, they're worried enough as it is.

Memories of the last war flooded into the elders' thoughts. The skies had unleashed thousands of alien craft raining death and destruction upon the whole land. Whole cities and towns were laid to waste with relentless fire bombing, even open fields and forests were denuded of life as the fires raged without control. The aliens had taken what they had valued from the landscape, minerals and rocks mainly and destroyed everything else.

Millions of people had lost their lives, no mercy was offered to the humans living here. Even the oceans did not escape the aliens' touch. Strange missiles were deployed to destroy marine life, billions of rotten carcases floated on the surface of the oceans for a long time. The air became putrid and sour, gases choking anyone caught out without a mask. The aliens certainly didn't believe in giving the human race a chance of survival! But survive they did- small pockets of survivors here and there dotted the planet, against all odds. The tenacity of the human race was a wondrous thing. But there comes a time when you wonder was there a point to surviving ?

Chapter 4

Scouting

Star wondered if she was about to encounter a new war, just like her mother's generation had. In some sense she began to feel excitement about having something different to focus on from her normal everyday mundane existence. On the other hand, the group were still trying to recover from the last war caused by the alien invasion. When they'd had all they wanted and all that remained of Earth was a burning heap, they left, abruptly, just left!

Travis and Bill used to work in this mine forty-five years earlier, so they knew it well. When life became impossible on the surface they and their friends and families had gathered resources and food and came down to live in the mines, which they later named the Hub. The community were now scared once more. They had adjusted to their new lives below ground over the decades, but now the arguments started again.

Surely they can't be back for more? There is no more here! Star reasoned with herself. *The Earth's resources are depleted already, what more can they want?*

The first day of scouting had arrived.

***

Bull joined Star and passed her more ammunition for the guns they shouldered, putting some into his own pack as well. Wren and Finch were in the next sector and had just split up from them to make their way to their allocated grid a few miles further on.

"Let's go," Bull commanded, as he mounted the bike ready for scouting their own sector.

Star mounted the bike, riding pillion again. Although she could ride a bike perfectly well, she was happy for Bull to lead. She could concentrate on scanning the horizon for any activity whilst not having to focus on dodging the many obstacles en route.

They were allocated a sector to the north of where they originally encountered the object and Finch's team were operating to the east of it. They would meet up later as they headed back to base to report on their findings. Other members of the community had different grid sectors to survey, all worried about what they may find.

The terrain of course remained difficult, so many craters and fallen trees to evade, blackened and twisted. As far as the eye could see it was the same blackened vision. Dust and ash still made it hard to breathe properly so they were glad of their masks and helmets. The air remained chill and the ground hard with frost.

***

After travelling for an hour Star suddenly tapped Bull on the shoulder hard, indicating to pull over quickly. He sped into the shelter of a ruined house nearby. Star pointed to a spot on the horizon, she guessed a few miles away. They pulled out the binoculars and looked closely.

"There it is again!" exclaimed Star, who'd spotted the silvery beam glinting in the distant gloom. The glowing globe-like object seemed to be scanning the terrain again.

"Oh my god! There's another one !" pointed Star to the east of the globe. Both were doing the same, scanning, backwards and forwards using the beam.

"What on Earth are they looking for?" Star puzzled once again.

"Beats me!" Bull replied, putting the binoculars back into his pack.

Suddenly the familiar noise of grinding metal and whooshing came close, very close to where they were. A globe had appeared from behind them! They ducked down low to avoid being seen as it moved slowly at first backwards and then forwards behind them.

They didn't dare move and held their breath for what seemed like ages before the globe passed by then suddenly whooshed at great speed to scan another sector.

"They're everywhere!" Bull sighed despondently. "I think this is what we're gonna find wherever we go now. Is there any point in continuing further?"

Star thought carefully. "We've been given a task. To scan the whole sector. We've only done half of it so far. We need to finish the job. We can't assume it's the same everywhere!"

Bull reluctantly agreed and after checking the coast was clear they mounted the bike again, heading for the remainder of their sector.

"I hope Wren and Finch are ok." Star added.

Bull had been thinking the same thing.

Onwards they headed, keeping to darker corners to remain out of sight as much as possible whilst heading in the direction of the valley that lay beyond the ridge ahead. Star ever watchful scanned the skies in all directions. No orbs to be seen at that moment at least. They travelled on.

The Gathering

Over an hour later, still scanning the skies and horizon as they went, Bull and Star ventured further with care. None of the landscape seemed disturbed, all was still as usual.

Bull aimed for a cluster of broken trees high up on the horizon, which overlooked the rest of their sector, which was a valley beyond.

The closer they got to the ridge the louder it became. Metallic grinding and clicking sounds.. The sounds were coming from the valley ahead of them!

Bull pulled the bike into the cover of the tree stumps and crawled over to the ridge with Star and the binoculars in tow.

Below them in the valley beyond were vast clusters of the globes hovering in one place together. More globes zoomed at tremendous speed towards the gathered orbs from all directions. On arriving at the group they emitted clicking, grinding metallic sounds, as though they were talking to each other.

The orbs were lined up in perfectly formed rectangular groups, like army troops on parade, but hovering several metres off the ground. This went on for another hour as more and more globes joined the gathering, formed now of hundreds of orbs.

Bull and Star could only stare in disbelief.

"All those globes! Do you think they've all been scanning the land ?" asked Star.

Bull shook his head.

"I've no idea Star, but what I do know, this is only the beginning of something. Something big." Bull sadly reflecting on the evidence in front of them. They lay there watching until it began to get too cold to stay.

Suddenly, the noise completely stopped. Bull and Star looked dumbfounded as the globes hovered in silence in perfectly formed rectangles, glowing their ghostly silvery light, which reflected on the valley below.

In the blink of an eye they whooshed in unison upwards into the sky, still in formation, until out of sight, on their way to space beyond.

Bull and Star looked worriedly at each other. This was obviously the end of one stage, which meant something new was to follow! That didn't sound good to either of them.

"Let's go!" Bull leapt to his feet and started the bike up.

The Hubbites needed to know about this ASAP! This did not bode well for Earth, Bull was sure of it! He thought of their pitiful defences. They stood no chance against another invading force .No chance at all!

Off they rode back towards the rendezvous point with Wren and Finch like there was no tomorrow!

No more globes scanned the terrain, no more clicking or metallic noises to be heard, just a deathly silence like a calm before the storm! All the time Bull kept wondering what on earth the orbs were about. What was there here for them? Nothing of value was left! It made no sense. No sense at all.

***

The duo approached the meeting point but there was no sign of Wren and Finch. The frost-covered land stretched out in all directions, devoid of activity. Where were they? Both began to worry, but soon a sound was heard from a distance coming closer towards them.

Revelation

They waited at the rendezvous point impatiently for Wren and Finch to arrive. Ten minutes passed until they saw their bike appear in the distance, but something did not look right. Wren was riding the bike with Finch behind on pillion. Finch wouldn't dream of letting Wren drive normally so something was up. The two approached, veering from side to side on the bike. Wren pulled up breathlessly beside them and Finch almost toppled off the bike before Bull caught hold of him.

Finch was covered in blood, it was dripping down his neck from under his helmet, a nasty gash covered by a blood-soaked bandage on his head. His arm was in a sling.

"What's happened?" demanded Star worriedly as she tried to comfort Finch.

Finch was falling in and out of consciousness and wouldn't be giving up much information.

Wren looked petrified.. "There were hundreds of them!" she wailed. "I've never seen so many! They came from every direction."

"Did you get seen?" Bull demanded.

"What happened to Finch?" Star needed to know. "Did they hurt him?"

"It was an army of globes!" Wren gasped. "They're going to kill us all ! It's the end isn't it?" she faltered and fell to her haunches and began sobbing gently.

Star took charge and snapped Wren out of her misery. She held Wren's jacket collar with both hands and pulled her face close to hers.

"Wren! Did they hurt Finch? What happened? Tell us. We need to know, now!"

Wren looked up at Star and wiped her eyes through her visor on her sleeve. In a small tearful voice she replied: "No, they didn't see us. We heard the globes before they could get to us. Finch was driving and when he swerved to get us under cover the bike hit a rock hidden by scrub and we both fell off. I was lucky and landed in a ditch, a soft landing, but Finch's helmet hit a pole first and I think he might have broken his arm.

"You can see he gashed his head on the pole. He was quite conscious for a while and we saw all these globes gathering at speed to the left of us, then he kept passing out. I bandaged him up as best as I could."

Finch groaned in the background, trying to remove his helmet unsuccessfully in his befuddled state. Star returned to his side.

"Yes we saw the globes too, hundreds of them gathered together in the valley. Then all of a sudden they were gone!" Star interrupted.

"It's another invasion, isn't it? Another war!" Wren concluded miserably.

"We don't know that yet" Bull replied. "But it doesn't look good. We've got to get this news to the Hub quickly!"

They mounted their bikes again, strapping Finch behind Bull so he wouldn't fall off and Star joined Wren on the other bike. Star made the decision to drive as Wren didn't seem in a fit state to stay focused enough for the ride home. Star was worried about Finch, wondering if there was any permanent damage. She could not bear that! She watched him loll about behind Bull on the bike ahead, oblivious to where he was.

All along the journey back the Hubbites kept wondering what the orbs were for and what was to come next. Whatever it was it wouldn't be good.

***

Getting home didn't seem as long as the journey out, perhaps because of the urgency, both for Finch's injuries and for the concern over what was going to happen next.

When they arrived home the sentinels carried Finch inside the Hub and took him directly to Dr Charles' medical room, where all injuries were dealt with.

Bull and Star pushed the bikes back into the shed and followed Wren inside to break the news.

Chapter 5

Taking Stock

Back at the Hub the news was not taken well. All of the scouts had reported seeing the same thing happening in each sector. Globes scanning, gathering in clusters and then disappearing into the skies at tremendous speed. Women wailed and held onto their children, fearing the worst. Men tried to appear calm and tough, but inside knowing what a feeble group they made with so few in number and a limited amount of arms.

Finch had been stretchered away to treat his wounds and Star followed worriedly. *What if he's broken his arm? What then? Will he heal properly? He wouldn't be able to draw his bow that's for sure or even fire a gun!*

The Hub's doctor was an elder called Charles, he'd been the miners' medic pre-war and he'd taught his assistant, a twenty year old girl called Siskin (because of her golden blonde hair) how to do minor operations and treat illnesses within their limited resources. She had become invaluable to the community and she in turn tried to teach the younger children about hygiene and dressing wounds properly. She even started a first aid club for the little ones, which was held once a week.

Star held Finch's hand as he was levered onto the 'hospital' bed, in a room set aside for such emergencies.

"Is he gonna be alright doctor?" Star inquired anxiously as he shone his torch in Finch's eyes.

"Give me a minute girl!" the doctor puffed as he checked Finch's arm. Finch briefly resumed consciousness and smiled when he saw Star beside him, holding his hand.

Doctor Charles was nearly eighty years old but as sprightly as a fifty-year-old. He always exercised every morning before breakfast to keep himself fit. He had a white straggly beard and a mop of white hair with a bit of a kink in it. He reminded Star of Santa from the children's Christmas Story Books. He was kind and generous of his time when anyone wasn't well.

***

Back in the Hall the reports were coming in steadily. It was not good news.

"It doesn't make sense!" Travis remarked worriedly. "These globes don't sound like anything we encountered in the last alien invasion. They can't be the same invaders. But one thing's for sure, they're some kind of droids sent to find out things and report back to someone or something bigger!"

Robyn listened to all this turmoil, again debating whether to say anything about Lin, but thought better of it. She'd only be further alienated by the community if Robyn said anything, so she kept quiet for now.

Another elder responded, "Then we can be sure we'll need to arm ourselves, because something is coming. One way or another, we'll be finding out soon!"

The meeting of minds continued well into the evening, then, when all options had been explored they began to busy themselves with jobs to prepare for the worst!

The community members were each allocated jobs to prepare for the incoming invasion. Arms and ammunition sorted, guns fixed and cleaned, grenades and dynamite were dug out of safe keeping in the tunnels used as stores for emergencies.

Children filled containers with water from the underground lake, ready for boiling if needed in surgery. Bandages were wrapped carefully and first aid kits re-stocked in preparation for treatment of wounds. Tables were scrubbed and covered with clean clothes and food stocks divided up to be rationed. Nobody knew how safe it would be to go scavenging for goods in the near future. Things might have to last a lot longer than before..

The hive of activity helped distract some of the younger members of the community. Keeping them busy had been a good idea of Robyn's.

But a sense of futility was tangible among the elders and scavengers. They imagined the worst so they would be mentally prepared for it. Children no longer sang and skipped along the tunnels, preferring instead to huddle close to their families. A favourite toy held onto tightly and smiles had long disappeared. They sensed the tension too, once all the preparations had been completed. Everywhere along the Hub people walked around with worried expressions, all fearing the worst. Only one person seemed unperturbed by all the news, Lin played on happily with her toys, unaffected.

Finch had suffered concussion and remained under the watchful eye of Dr Charles for the time being. Star was banned from his bedside as she distracted Finch too much for him to rest properly! On closer observation the doctor concluded that Finch had not broken his arm, only badly bruised and twisted it and would recover well if allowed some rest from duties for a few days.

***

That evening Star laid on her bunk thinking about the imminent war. Was she going to lose more loved ones? What if Finch were killed? She couldn't bear that. The earlier excitement she had felt had quickly become replaced by the realities of war, Finch's injury was just a jolt she needed to bring her to her senses.

"You ok?" a voice of concern broke through the silence of her sanctuary.

Bull entered through the open doorway towards her.

Star swung her legs round to sit facing him on the edge of her bed. "Yeah. I'm ok, just thinking about what tomorrow might bring. " she offered sadly.

Bull leaned against the upper bunk opposite Star's and looked deep in thought. He was about to say something but stopped himself short. Star looked at him as he obviously debated what he was going to say.

"What is it? What did you want to say?" Star probed innocently.

Bull looked down at her feet as though embarrassed, then plucked up the courage to say it.

"You know, I'm always here for you if you need me, don't you? If anything should happen to Finch.... you won't be alone. I'll look after you." Bull didn't know where to look, he'd never imagined he'd be tongue tied like this.

Star was completely taken by surprise, was Bull saying what she thought he was saying? Did he have feelings for her too? She went red at the thought, unsure how to feel. Bull immediately regretted having said as much and began to apologise, turning on his heel to make a dignified retreat, but Star held out her arm to stop him and replied

"Thank you, Bull, that means a lot." Star gave Bull a shy smile then watched Bull leave the room with what seemed like the weight of the world on his shoulders.

Star wondered how she felt by that revelation, but she really had no idea!

Reflections

Within a couple of days the community at the Hub were as ready as they could be, they couldn't do any more. Whenever the invasion started at least they could say they did their bit for humanity. If they only knew how many more communities like them were holed up, surviving somewhere on this planet. Did they also see the orbs? Do they have the means to fight for their lives? It was frustrating that there was no communication system left in existence that they could use to form connections with other survivors.

People at the Hub knew there were other humans still living, as the scavengers had seen a couple of people a year ago driving a vehicle far away on the horizon. Probably doing the same as them, scavenging for their community. Where was their community? Was it far from the Hub? Nobody had ever come across any evidence of people living nearby. Were they even friendly? No one knew.

Was their community bigger than the Hub's? Did they have an armoury? Maybe even a tank? Now that would be wishful thinking! If only they knew where they were perhaps they could form an alliance against the aliens. Tomorrow they would have to find out somehow!

That night the Hub community was subdued, gathered around the fire the children didn't beg for stories like they usually did, preferring to huddle tightly with their families for comfort instead.

A mother began to sing a lullaby softly to her little child, while stroking his forehead, lit up by the dancing firelight in front of them. Did this child have any future? Or will it be the end for all of them Star wondered, sadly. Small groups of people had banded together for support in the warm fire-lit hall, Talking softly or just leaning against each other thinking.

Star had no real family left here in the Hub and at the moment she felt very alone although surrounded by familiar faces. An arm slowly wrapped around her shoulders and gave her a hug. Finch looked into her eyes and read her mind.

"Don't be sad, I'll look after you," Finch whispered as he drew her closer. "I'm your lucky charm, remember?" he smiled.

Star smiled back, "Oh really?" she smirked. "Then how come you've got a banged-up head and a sprained wrist if you're so lucky then, mister?"

Finch lowered his head pretending to be hurt. "But my luck goes to you not to me!" he protested, wincing at the pain from his twisted wrist. "I'll always have your back. Remember that."

Star had to smile and she slowly kissed his forehead, onto his clean bandage. Bull watched from a distance and felt like an outsider for the first time. He wished it was him holding and comforting her, but Finch was his friend too so he could not act on his feelings. Star spotted Bull's eyes betraying his feelings and they both quickly looked away from each other, awkwardness filling the gap.

Star turned her attention back to Finch and felt comforted by his proximity. They listened to the hypnotic tone of the mother's voice as she continued her lullaby, amongst the crackling sounds of the fire keeping the group warm.

They spent the evening huddled together in front of the fire, both thinking that this might be the last time they would have a chance to do so.

***

The Hub was quiet this evening, no one was in a mood to chat , the Bird community sat and reflected on the events unfolding outside with heavy hearts. What was to happen next? Nobody knew, but all feared the same thing.

For the elders who had lived through it, memories of the last War had infiltrated their minds and made for a disturbed sleep.

Rumble

The new day emerged and the sentinels reported as they wandered in from night duty, tired and hungry that there was no further movement or light in the skies of orbs passing by. But this did not give them any cheer. It was probably a lull before the gathering storm. Around the fire in the Hub the morning workers had started their duties, all looking weary and subdued as though they hadn't slept at all. But who could blame them? Everyone was on edge.

Later on, Finch was stoking the fire and adding a few more salvaged pieces of wood to it when the ground began to shake and rumble beneath his feet. Items toppled over on the shelves nearby. People hung on to anything they could grab to save falling over. The rumbling was accompanied by a deep roar, bellowing through the air surrounding them. Finch hung onto Star to protect her and looked around the hall desperately to see if anyone knew what was happening.

The two new sentinels ran in from the exterior door, gasping for breath from their running. They dropped their rifles to the floor, hands on their thighs trying to get their breath back. They must have run quickly to get back this exhausted. Travis arrived in front of them after weaving his way through the throng from the back of the Hub.

"What is it?" called Travis worriedly as the two gathered their breath.

"A ship! Enormous spaceship, passing overhead! All lit up," stuttered one of the sentinels, "heading to the north of us!"

Finch and the others looked to Travis and nodded.

"It's come. War has come to us!" Finch spat angrily.

The gathered crowd were stunned into silence.

Bull rushed to his jacket and boots then grabbed his bow, but quickly changed his mind, grabbing instead a rifle and ammunition. He donned his mask and headed towards the Hub exit with Travis and a few others in tow.

"Wait for me!" shouted out Finch, getting his gear from the chair.

But Star stopped him in his tracks and said "No you don't! The doctor says you need to stay in for another 24 hours with that concussion of yours!"

Finch hesitated for a second and said, "But I feel fine! They may need me!"

But Star wasn't about to let him go and persuaded him to stay in case he became a hindrance to the others if he collapsed on them out there. He was about to protest when a deep voice bellowed across the room.

"You're staying put and that's that! You've been given medication that will cloud your judgement so you're no use to them just now! sit!"

Doc Charles could be very persuasive at times, so Finch was outnumbered and he slumped into the chair reluctantly. Finch didn't spot the doc and Star sharing a wink at his expense!

"If you want to be useful you can help me clear up this mess." Star offered, picking up some items that had fallen off the shelves around the room.

"That wasn't the kind of help I was thinking of." muttered Finch despondently. "Anyone can do that!"

"Yes. And you're anyone, aren't you?" Star retorted quickly, throwing a dustpan and brush towards him.

Finch couldn't win. "Women!" he muttered picking himself up to help clear the mess.

The Doc smiled and retreated back to his duties.

***

The enormous spaceship seemed to stretch as far as the horizon. It was all lit up with pulsating red and blue alternating lights. It was cylindrical and seemed to have several tiers in its construction. As the Hubbites looked up at the sight several hatches opened up below the ship and it looked like there was to be a mass exodus of smaller craft about to invade the Earth. It did not resemble in any way the craft used by the alien invaders of the last War noted Travis and Bill, but it was little comfort to them at this moment.

Aboard Ship

Argo manned the controls. He personally wanted to bring the ship in, to this place called Earth. He had heard so much about the planet from his superiors. He had been eager to see if what they said was true. He had been told that Earth was full of natural resources and had millions of species living upon it at one time. Living on the land, in the waters and in the air. This would indeed be a sight to behold if it were true.

Argo had never seen a planet so full of resources as that on his long journey through space. Most planets he had encountered had limited forms of life on them. Nothing to touch what this Earth contained! He had accessed the Earth data file on numerous occasions and had marvelled at the variety of species living on Earth. He had discovered that the planet had such a wide range of climates, from frozen poles to equatorial landscapes full of animal and plant life, too numerous to imagine. Oh how he longed to see this Earth.

"Docking at pre-arranged position, Captain." Argo reported. "All systems ready for disembarkation."

Captain Grey breathed a sigh of relief. He was here, at last. Long had he planned for this day and now it was here! *Earth won't be expecting this*, he smiled smugly to himself.

"Disembark!" Captain Grey commanded ."Argo, your day has come. I want you to go down on the planet to command the Checkers. You know what to do."

"Yes Captain." Argo replied, trying to remain calm, when what he really wanted to do was jump for joy! He would get to see this Earth after all!

The docking bay doors opened and several troop transports flew down to the planet's surface, followed by the machine transports and large cargo containers.

Argo charged up his armour with his body controls, donned his helmet and marched off to the docking bay.

* * *

Captain Grey stood next to Professor Stark, looking down at the monitor in front of them. They were watching the view of the launching at the docking bay from the comfort of the bridge.

"I wonder if there are humans down there still?" debated Stark. "They won't know what hit them!" he stated, matter- of factly.

"I don't think we'll be encountering much resistance do you?" Grey calculated.

"Shouldn't think so after all this time, " Stark replied, "there can't be many left alive after the War."

"Argo can sort it out if they encounter any. He has the intelligence to make his own decisions." Capt

Grey mused.

Stark laughed and replied. "Hmph! Argo. Did you know he had a sense of humour?"

"What do you mean?" asked the captain.

"When he was re grouping all the Checkers in the cargo bay last time I was there, he decided to rename one of the Checkers, one of the very early basic models we produced, Checker 159 I believe it was, the one who frequently made mistakes in the tests."

"Oh really? What did he re-name him?" inquired Capt. Grey.

"Noblaczec." replied Stark. To which point both laughed.

"Noblaczec eh? Well, I guess Argo does have a sense of humour, it really suits 159!" They laughed again.

***

Argo locked his body into position onto the inner hull of the shuttle, one in a line of hundreds of other robots of different types. All were secured ready for launch onto the planet's surface below. He tried to see out of the window opposite him if there were any glorious vistas to explore whilst he was down there. But what Argo saw after crossing through dust-filled cloud cover was instead devastation, toxicity and lifeless plains marred by blackened and torn structures dotting the barren land. Argo became angry and needed to control his frustration, but he had no time to think as at that moment the floor opened up below their feet and the locks disengaged on their bodies and all robots fell from the sky onto the war torn land below.

Robot Army

An army of white robots dispersed in all directions around the planet, touching down at pre-allocated co-ordinates, each band with the same mission. Not far from the Hub community, large cargo carriers hovered, their pilots searching for a large open space in which to perform their task. With the correct terrain selected the robots began to offload large metal shapes onto hover boards, then guiding them to the required positions.

Amongst the robots were enormous walking machines with pincer-like hands on the ends of hydraulic arms. They looked to be at least five metres tall, made of shiny grey metal. It seems they were the muscle for the job, as they began to lift heavy sections of the metal shapes and bolted them hydraulically together. Several robots were scanning the ground with a laser-type beam emanating from controls on their arms. As the beam touched the ground any scrub or objects lying in the way were immediately incinerated and the ground seemed to be flattened at the same time. More walking machines began to lay large metallic sheeting onto the flattened floor, then secured the other metallic shapes vertically onto the base sheeting.

***

From a distance, sheltered by broken shells of buildings, Bull, Travis and a few others watched the activity with a mixture of confusion and fear. Passing his binoculars to Bull, Travis remarked

"Those mechs would be useful in rebuilding homes around here! I wonder what they're building?"

Bull replied " It seems they intend to stay a while then! Another thing, did you see those beams? We'd have no chance in a fight with those robots, we'd be incinerated before firing a shot! "

The hopelessness of their situation escalated by the minute. This was a formidable enemy.

For hours the mechs and robots worked, revealing finally a structure that resembled a gigantic dome made of metal. It stood at least seven storeys high and spanned a few hundred metres in diameter!

***

"They certainly think big, don't they?" Travis decided, moving after suffering some cramp from having been observing, staying in the same position for so long a time. Bull marvelled at how quickly the robots had erected the structure, then wondered what it was for. It seemed too big to be a home. Very worrying!

***

Argo continued venting his frustration out on the unfortunate lesser robots who were constructing the dome and its inner chambers. Noblaczec in particular, a less intelligent robot under Argo's command came under particularly frequent fire from Argo's miserable condition.

"Noblaczec! I told you to fit the lights on the columns *above* ground! Not *below* ground! How's anyone going to see the lights when they're hidden under the floor?" Argo ranted.

Noblaczec puzzled for an instant and then replied "I don't know, sir. I'm not clever like you, sir. Shall I lift them up, sir?"

Argo turned on his heel and bellowed "YES!"

Noblaczec was one of hundreds of white robots milling around the structure carrying materials from the cargo containers inside the dome. The Mechanoid giants heaved large structures and heavy machinery into the dome and there was a lot of noise coming from inside indicating that something was being built inside the dome too.

There were a number of smaller blue robots disembarking from a nearby carrier and they headed straight into the dome without carrying anything. Argo seemed much different to the Blues and Whites, he had manly features and his arm featured a gold inlaid band on it. Perhaps he was a superior robot, he certainly gave plenty of commands to the whites, who in turn rushed to carry out those orders.

***

It was starting to get dark so they called time on their observations and returned to the Hub to report their news to everyone.

Chapter 6

Fear

The skies were filled with screaming craft of all sizes, gushing out voluminous blasts of all-engulfing fire upon the ravaged Earth. Previously bombs had descended in their thousands to pulverise every building and structure within sight. People attempting to flee were vaporised in the roiling masses of gas filled clouds of incinerating heat.

Travis tried to call out to his neighbours to flee with him, but his voice was lost in the roar of engines and artillery fire. A tank on the horizon blasted out shell upon shell at the swirling spacecraft above, like an ant caught in a web of fire it was soon engulfed by a churning mass of what could only be described as a firestorm which spanned mile upon mile as far as the eye could see.

Bill had rounded up some people and was crouched next to Travis with fear in his eyes. He'd tried to bring his mother with him, but she refused to come, saying if it was her time then nothing would change that. As he'd reluctantly left her, tears streaming from his eyes, he'd turned around for one last look at his home only to see his mother and all her possessions vaporised by an almighty blast from a passing spacecraft.

Bill screamed "Mum! No! Please no!" sweat pouring from him he suddenly was shaken out of his misery by Travis, crouched over him.

"It's all right, mate. It's all right." Travis held onto his arm for comfort, " You're in the Hub. It's only a dream. I think we're all beginning to have flashbacks of the war tonight"

Travis sat beside the bed as Bill began to breathe easier as he realised it was only a memory from long ago, forty-five years to be precise, but still as vivid as if it were yesterday.

Both men had experienced the horror of the last war and were grief-stricken by the thought that it could happen once more. Bill sat upright in his bed, wiping the sweat from his brow and looked sadly at Travis.

"It was that same scene again, " Bill croaked to his friend." I can still see my mother's eyes the last time I looked into them, they were so piercingly calm. How could she be so calm, with all that horror surrounding her? I still wonder at that. I hope she suffered no pain. It was over in an instant.."

Travis didn't know what to say that would be of any comfort to him. "She's in a much better place right now, Bill. She won't have to witness any further horror unfolding, my friend." he squeezed Bill's shoulder comfortingly and then turned away to stoke the fire a bit more to keep the Hub warm through the night.

Robyn lay in her bunk worrying about her two children. What would become of Wren and Chaff? They were so young and she had hoped they would never have to experience war in their lifetime. It was bad enough that they had to endure the conditions that they lived under here in the Hub, but here at least they were relatively safe, for now.

Bull and Finch sat around the fire in the hall, keeping it stoked and well supplied to keep the Hub warm. Both were very quiet, each contemplating the consequences of what they'd seen outside.

"Do you think our community will survive ?" Finch asked nervously.

Bull wasn't convinced, but he didn't want Finch to have more to fear than he needed to.

"We've survived all these decades past the last War, haven't we? What's to stop us doing so again? If anything we're more prepared this time. The elders have a lot of experience of dealing with war. We'll be ok."

Finch's head throbbed a little where he'd hit his head previously and he held his head in his hands in front of the fire. The Hub doctor, Dr Charles walked into the room and saw the two young men.

"Head hurting still, Finch?" he casually inquired.

Finch said it was just a little headache, that's all. Charles took out a bottle of tablets from his pocket and handed two of them to Finch with some water.

"Here take these it'll help, then to bed. You look exhausted. I only wish I had a tablet that would make all our headaches go away." he sighed and sat by the fire, deep in thought.

Finch and Bull set off towards their dorm and wished Charles a good night. All three worried about what tomorrow might bring.

They passed Travis as he came out of the men's dorm headed for the Hall. The two men looked at him concerned.

"Bill ok?" Bull asked.

Travis replied. "Yes, he's ok now, had another nightmare, that's all. Good night."

Bull and Finch went into the dorm and Travis continued down the tunnel to the Hall.

Charles was sipping a warm drink when Travis arrived.

"The boys have just topped up the fires, Trav."
Charles poured a second drink and passed it to Travis.
They sat together in front of the fire.

"Bill had another nightmare." Travis spoke first.
"I hope the new invaders don't bring a repeat of the last
War. I don't think we could survive it."

He confided in his old friend things that he
would not verbalise to any of the others. They had been
through all this together. They knew the odds. Both men
reflected on the years they had survived down here in
the mine, they wondered if it was all going to come to an
end, very soon.

Strange Events

Morning arrived and with it the worry of what
lay ahead. Travis took a group of men with him to check
on events unfolding outside.

The daylight seemed a bit brighter than usual,
maybe the lights from the spaceships were contributing
to it. The group had planned a long journey, to scout as
far as they could go, to see if they came across other
communities in the neighbourhood. They hoped someone had a plan, or at least better ammunition than them.
It's all they could hope for.

Kitted out with backpacks they went on foot, so
they could keep to cover as much as possible to avoid
being seen. The large spaceship hovered on the horizon
like some giant waiting to stamp out any bugs underfoot.
The spaceship lights were still pulsing red and blue, so
Travis doubted that they contributed to the lighter feel of
the daylight.

The group continued, crouching low from object
to object, traversing the land using natural cover to decide their path. There didn't seem to be any orbs around

so far so that at least was a benefit. The map they had with them wasn't a lot of help, mainly because the terrain had changed so much since the war. Some roads ceased to exist, completely reclaimed by the land or torn apart by bomb craters. Landmarks had been destroyed overall and it was anybody's guess what had survived.

***

At the Hub Chaff and Lin were busy drawing pictures on one of the dining tables when Robyn came in to add fuel to the fire.

"What are you two drawing?" Robyn inquired cheerfully. Chaff smiled at her mum.

"I'm drawing a place that I'd like to live in, with trees and flowers." Chaff beamed holding up her picture of a little house with a garden, similar to one she'd seen in one of her favourite story books.

"And what about you, Lin?" asked Robyn, looking at her picture of a meandering river with horses drinking from it. "Is that what you'd like to see?"

Lin looked up from her drawing and said,

"No, these are my friend's horses. They escaped and came to drink some water." She smiled and continued to colour her drawing.

***

It was around noon that events began to unfold. The skies began to shimmer around them, grey clouds bubbling and writhing into fantastic shapes and slowly changing colour from the usual storm laden purple and greys to a lighter silvery colour.

Travis' group watched wide-eyed from the shelter of blackened buildings, all wondering what this new development could mean. As far as the eye could see the skies were changing, with flashes of lightning ripping through the clouds from time to time. The ground around them seemed to be losing its layer of frost too. It was melting before their eyes.

"Is it a storm?" offered Bull, but Travis wasn't convinced.

"Never seen a storm like this before, not with these strange colours glowing through the clouds!" He shook his head in frustration, wondering if this was a new kind of force to contend with. As if the machines and robots weren't enough!

"Come. Let's carry on!" Travis decided. They could do nothing about it so it was best to ignore it for the time being.

***

They had travelled all day under the ever changing skies and decided to set up camp in the shelter of a burned out factory building for the night. There were plenty of spots hidden from view where they could light a fire to keep warm and make a brew. The sky had settled into almost pitch black now, with no further lightning glowing onto the landscape.

The discussion around the camp fire debated the origin of the changing skies. Were they a development from the invading forces or did nature decide to object to the new disturbances caused by the orbs? Whatever the reason, the change was unsettling to the Hubbites. How much more could they cope with?

Travis kept his opinions to himself, letting the group thrash out possibilities to unleash their fears and energy before settling down to sleep for the night.

Finch was posted on first guard duty, sitting in the lea of the building, rifle across his knees, eyes focusing hard on the pitch black sky. The lightning was gone, the growl of expanding clouds had diminished. There was no sound to be heard at all in fact. Too quiet, unnerving. A chill began to form in Finch's bones and he pulled his jacket tighter around himself, willing his eyes to stay focused. But it was hard to focus when there was nothing but blackness all around. He couldn't even see his hand in front of him. It was very disconcerting.

"Finch! You there?" a familiar voice called softly from his right.

"Here, Bull." He called back, glad of the distraction, shining his torch briefly for Bull to find him.

Bull settled alongside him on the floor and blew on his hands. He too felt an unusual chill tonight. He'd often taken turn in guarding the Hub at night, but this night seemed different somehow, the air was different. A new coldness was being pushed through the atmosphere.

After an hour or so the blackness claimed the two men without mercy. It lulled them into a deep sleep. With nothing to focus on, the brain became desensitised and shut down to a welcome state of oblivion.

All around the camp nothing moved, no sounds were heard , it was getting suddenly warmer again, it was very unusual.

New Developments

"Wake up you two!" hissed a voice in front of them. "I thought you were supposed to be guarding us! Not like this you're not!" muttered an angry Travis, who'd luckily come to check on the night watch. He on the other hand couldn't sleep at all. It was too quiet.

"Sorry, mate, " Bull offered sheepishly, "I could swear I'd only closed my eyes for a minute. What time is it?"

"Gone three" Travis replied. "Any developments?"

Bull was embarrassed to have realised he'd been

asleep for over four hours, Finch too more than likely.

"Nothing new, just this dead silence and pitch black everywhere you look." replied Bull.

Just as Travis was about to offer himself for duty he stopped dead in his tracks as they all heard a sound not far away.

"Look!" Finch twisted Bull in the direction he was looking. "On the horizon! Can you see it?"

Bull and Travis definitely saw it and heard it. A motorbike, its headlight spluttering up and down, blinking through the rough terrain towards them.

There was no time to warn the others, it would soon be upon them. The trio shouldered their guns in preparation and with bated breath waited for the inevitable.

The motorbike was now only a short distance away and its rider was clearly silhouetted.

"Aim for the tyres!" shouted Travis quickly. "It's human."

The shots cracked like whips in the night and they got the result they wanted. The bike swerved out of control and skidded to a halt throwing up fountains of dust into the air around them. With the headlight guiding their path the trio rushed towards the rider, guns poised in defence .

"Hands up where we can see them!" commanded Travis. The rider groaned a little then obediently did as they demanded.

"Don't shoot!" pleaded the rider. "I don't want to fight. I'm just on my way home."

It was a girl's voice.

***

Finch shone his torch at her. She had no gun that he could see, but there was a bow and quiver strapped to her back. She had no mask on! She looked no more than around eighteen. What on Earth was she doing here at night and without a mask?

Travis told her to get up slowly, which she did. She was dressed much the same as they were, salvaged clothes and the bike looked like it had seen better days. The men surrounded her with guns poised.

"Who are you? What are you doing here at this time of night?" demanded Travis, a little less aggressively now, but his rifle still pointed towards her.

The girl peered in the gloom from one to the other before answering, hands still held aloft.

"My name is Kia and I live with a group of people a few miles further along. I was out on patrol with another but we got separated hours ago. It got so dark I couldn't see anything, I couldn't find him but I didn't dare call out his name in case the aliens heard me. So I decided to try to make it home on my own. That's where I was heading when I ran into you."

Kia looked worriedly at the trio, unsure if they were friend or foe. The girl was very pale, with shoulder length dark hair. She looked very frightened

Travis slowly put his gun down and the others followed suit..

Finch piped up impatiently "Why aren't you wearing a mask? How can you breathe like that?"

Kia smiled nervously, "We were watching the sky changing earlier and we were afraid. We thought we were going to be killed by a firestorm. We freaked out. I pulled my helmet off because it was so stifling under it. My friend tried to stop me but I wanted to die feeling the air on my face for the last time. That's when I realised that I could breathe quite easily! It was incredible. My friend took his helmet off too and we both breathed without struggle! Try it. It's okay, really!"

Bull looked to Travis then slowly pulled off his helmet and mask. He took a shallow breath then a deeper one. It was true! He could breathe fine!

The other two followed suit and felt the warmer air circulate in their lungs. This was new and very welcome!

"But how?" Finch puzzled. "It's so strange being able to walk around outside without the masks on !" he declared. "And why is it getting warmer?" Finch was unsure if it was a good thing or not.

Travis introduced himself to Kia and the others followed suit. They took her over to the camp fire where all the group waited, guns poised, after hearing the shots fired a few moments earlier. They stared in shock, both at seeing this new girl and also seeing everyone devoid of masks!

They sat Kia down with them around the fire and offered her a warm drink, which she gladly accepted. These people seemed friendly enough she thought, relief flooding through her. Maybe it would be ok to exchange information. This was going to be a long night!

Hope

Bull handed Kia a blanket as she made herself comfortable at the fireside. "So, you live only a few miles away from here?"

Kia nodded, sipping the welcome drink.

Bull continued, "How many of you are there?"

Kia hesitated before answering, not sure how much she should tell them, but decided these people didn't really mean her any harm. They could be useful allies to her community.

"Around a hundred of us in all, including the children. We have two newborn children, last week- before our world began to fall apart again with these new events." She looked sadly at her companions, trying to hold back a tear.

It looked like Kia's community were suffering the same as they were.

There was a long silence before Finch questioned her.

"Where did your community find shelter in the war? It must be away from the polluted surface I reckon" surmised Finch.

Kia continued, "We live in what was once a series of nuclear bunkers in the side of a mountain. My grandfather was one of the military maintaining them. In the first few weeks of the war he and his unit brought people they knew to shelter there and a few strangers who happened by joined our community afterwards . We had plenty of supplies there to get the community started and things evolved from then. We scavenge for supplies now and again, but mostly we are self sufficient."

Travis weighed up the information then inquired, "Do you have any weapons in your community? Things we can use against the aliens if need be?"

Kia detailed a long list of artillery held at the bunkers, including two tanks and rocket launchers, much to the Hubbites' surprise.

"Wow!" exclaimed Finch, "I guess that we might make an impact with that lot at least!"

Kia replied, "Well, the general is not sure about that, actually having seen the robots' power to incinerate things with a wave of a hand. Any usage we could make of the weapons would have to be under very covert operations, to avoid being seen by the enemy too soon to operate the tanks etc. I reckon that once they see tanks approaching they'd be incinerated too."

After the more immediate questions had been answered, Travis assured her that they'd escort her home in the morning and repair her bike tyre. Feeling very tired and grateful she relaxed by the fire and fell into a deep sleep, no longer hindered by the stifling mask that she would normally need to wear outdoors.

The group seemed uplifted by the new revelations and felt some hope dangling at the end of their fears for once. As Travis continued on watch, the others fell asleep comforted by the news of this new community and their weaponry.

Finch whispered to Bull beside him "It's a good job the bullet hit the bike not her, what a waste that would have been!"

Bull smirked and replied quietly "Well, it's a good job it was my bullet that hit the bike then, 'cause yours ended up miles off course and still travelling I reckon!"

Finch whacked him playfully then muttered, "We'll soon see in the morning who hit what!"

Bull smiled and ended with "See you in the morning, hot shot!"

***

Travis scanned the skies, but again it was so dark there was nothing to see. The motorbike had been recovered and stowed nearby, repairs having to wait till daylight. The landscape remained unsettlingly still and quiet, with no sign from here of the gigantic spaceship that he knew hovered some miles away.

Chapter 7

Sucking Skies

The light appeared in waves, undulating vertically across the horizon, aglow with silvery threads it pulsated its way along the skies. A brand new day was dawning, a dawn unlike any other that Travis had seen in his life. It was as if the air was struggling against an invisible force, being shaken in the clouds, causing them to disperse in strange formations. Travis, witness to this orchestrated dawn. pondered at the forces wielding this energy into the skies.

"What's happening?" demanded a worried Bull beside him in an instant. "I've never seen skies like this before, have you?"

Travis shook his head and sighed. " Never. Let's hope it settles soon."

The small group were all awake now and scanning the skies worriedly, pondering whether it was a good thing or bad.

Breakfast was rushed, with all of them suspicious of the skies forming above them, making them fear the reason for these changes. Would they be poisoned by this new sky? Was it the beginning of the end for them?

They gathered their belongings and Bull produced the patched bike to hand over to Kia before they all set off following her lead. Bull grinned at Finch and holding one finger up in front of him said, "One bullet, one! And it was mine! Right on the tyre. Told yuh!"

Finch shook his head, not believing a word of it. "Yeah you would say that now! I didn't get to check it out did I?"

Bull retorted "Not my fault you couldn't get up early, is it?" and he heaved his rucksack over his shoulder and walked over towards Travis, who was walking on ahead.

They were heading towards some mountains in the distance where Travis guessed that the girl's community were laid up. All around them the air stirred and began to whip up the huge piles of ash and dust from the ground around their feet. Suddenly the need for masks became urgent again. The dust-ridden air whirled in all directions, as though they were surrounded by hundreds of mini tornadoes sucking up the debris into the sky.

"Run!" shouted Travis, pointing to the shelter of a broken bridge nearby.

They all huddled under the arch of the bridge, where once a sparkling river had flowed gently meandering through the beautiful countryside. Now it was dry and all that remained were the smooth boulders that had formed the river bed.

A large tornado nearby sucked up the ashen remains of the countryside around, nibbling at the boulders along the old river bed, but oddly leaving them all in situ. The roar of the tornado tortured their ears and all tried to protect their heads from the pressure of the surrounding air. The whole landscape was being pounded by several tornadoes all at once.

However, the small group felt safe under the wide span of the bridge, well out of the reach of the sucking skies. They watched as large chunks of debris swirled ever upwards, spinning uncontrollably towards the skies above. Pieces of vehicles meshed with blackened tree trunks, were seen clashing together but continually spinning upwards. The force behind the tornadoes was immense. They wondered if their friends were experiencing this too. Unbeknown to the group the whole globe was being pounded by the ever sucking skies, everywhere being altered forever.

Kia worried about her companion, was he safe? Was he sheltering from the tornadoes too? Or was he home before her, already worrying about where she was?

Finch noticed her fear and tried to reassure her that he would be safe somewhere, like her and they'd be reunited very soon. Kia smiled but deep down she was very worried indeed.

After several hours stuck under the bridge the tornadoes gradually died down and the group crept out over the rocks back to the path they were following.

All stopped to stare, wide eyed, mouths agape. The land around them had been stripped of all its ashen soil, everywhere! The new surface of the Earth seemed a different colour, brown rather than black and grey. Buildings remained in their shell like forms, but years of soot and ash had been vacuumed away miraculously! The stonework on the bridge seemed brighter and newer than before! The skies had calmed into a silvery shimmer and the air breathable again.

Bull tried to work out whether it was an act of nature or whether the spaceships had anything to do with this. He looked to Travis, who seemed to read his mind and replied, "I don't know son. I don't know what caused this. Something big, that's for sure!"

The younger group members had never seen the ground so free from ash and debris and they liked the new development. The earth below their feet smelled different too, a more pleasant heavy scent. The air was warmer slightly, which made travelling more bearable.

Onwards they went, nearing the mountains very

quickly now.

Bull and Finch enthused about the new ground but were stopped in mid conversation by the sound of a rifle being cocked near their heads.

"Stop right there! Hands up!" cried the bellowing voice of a male dressed in army fatigues. Another, with rifle aimed at their heads appeared to the right of the group. A third stood blocking their path, heavily armed and stocky. Kia left Bull's side and ran up to the stocky man.

"Daddy! It's all right!" exclaimed Kia. "They're friends, from another community not far away. They helped me out when I got lost." Kia added. at which point he turned his gun downwards. However, the other armed men did not lower their weapons until Kia's father ordered it.

"Sergeant White " the Sgt introduced himself and shook Travis' outstretched hand. "Where were you heading?" he asked, unsure whether Kia had revealed where they were holed up.

Kia interrupted, "They were bringing me home dad, I told them everything, sorry."

Kia looked sheepishly at her father, for she knew it had been drummed into her on several occasions not to give away their location for fear of compromising the community.

"They mean us no harm dad." she pleaded. Her father shook his head but drew her close to him anyway. "I guess we've all got a bigger enemy to fry these days, haven't we?" he remarked resolutely.

Suddenly Sergeant White scanned the group as if looking for someone. "Where's Guy?" Sgt White inquired almost absent-mindedly.

Kia stopped in her tracks. "You mean he didn't make it home?"

"He was with you last I heard." her father replied. " What happened?"

Kia worriedly briefed him on the way they got separated in the dark and how she had hoped he'd make his own way home, just like she did.

The Sergeant began to worry too. "Maybe he had more tornadoes to hide from where he was, he's probably just going to be longer than you getting back that's all." he offered. "However, I'll send out a unit to watch out for him in case he got into any problems." He nodded towards his troops.

Kia seemed to be a little more reassured than before but became bewildered again when her father and his men took off their scarves and continued towards the Hubbites,

"I'm afraid we'll have to blindfold you the rest of the way to ensure our community's security ." he stated.

Kia began to protest, but Travis interrupted

"It's all right Kia, he's only doing what I'd have done in his shoes. After all, he knows nothing about us."

Her father and the other soldiers blindfolded all the Hubbites and then Sgt White and Kia proceeded in guiding them along. The rest of the unit were sent to patrol the sector they had come from in search of Guy.

At the bunker entrance stood scores of people, looking awe-struck at the changes in the environment. As the air was deemed breathable many had come out to test it. Never had there been so many outside together, able to breathe without masks. This was a welcome development indeed.

Kia's mother ran forward on seeing her daughter alive and well. They embraced and shared news, then Kia helped escort the group into the bunker. All were worried by Guy's absence, but hoped he would turn up soon.

In the Bunker

The opening to the bunker was enormous, as was the entrance hall beyond. There was a second inner door, slightly smaller on the inside of the hall, leading to the stores and living quarters below ground. There was electricity lighting the corridors and rooms, and when the blindfolds were removed it was a new thing for Bull and Finch to behold.

"We have hot and cold water and showers" explained Kia. The group's eyes lit up at the sound of that.

"Our wind powered generator is a godsend," continued her mother, "Would you like a shower?"

The group nearly fell over themselves with excitement at being asked such a thing. Of course they would, gladly!

The Sergeant led the group over to an office to one side and introduced them to Kia's grandfather, Major Earl White. He was one of the founder members of the community, having fled here with family and friends in the early months of the invasion, over four decades ago. He was a white-haired man with an impressive handlebar moustache which gave him an air of authority.

Travis' group gave the community a debriefing of what they knew about the aliens before Major White related any differing news they had to declare. White's officers had seen another dome like structure built a few miles further on which sounded like a replica of the one Travis had seen built. They also had seen the ground being cleared by robots in the same way, simply waving their arms, incinerating and flattening the terrain ready for the structure.

Major White had listened carefully to Travis' frank account of their limited resources at the Hub and Travis had even shown him on Major White's wall map where the Hub was to be found. He began to realise that these people, far from being a threat to his group, could actually do with some of their help and their technology.

His grand-daughter obviously felt they were trust worthy and usually she had pretty good instincts.

He looked into his son's eyes as though searching for confirmation before he spoke.

"We have many weapons at our disposal," declared Major White, "but their technology seems far superior to ours. I'm not sure what impact, if any, we can have on their army or structures."

"But I'm told you have tanks and rocket launchers here." stated Travis. "Surely they will have some impact?"

Sgt White looked sharply at his daughter, who tried to avert her eyes from his discomfort.

The major shook his head gently. "If we could deploy them without being seen maybe we stand some chance, but once they find us, we're toast!" he declared.

"Don't get me wrong," the major continued."We are setting up plans to destroy these domes and decimate their army under cover of darkness if they decide to attack us. We aim to be ready to have the weapons in location a week from now. Once we have all the artillery in the right locations we could hit them all simultaneously."

Travis took in the information with mixed feelings. He was unsure how much impact they could create on this foe, after all, they seemed very advanced. Their weaponry was beyond their technology.

Sgt White piped up "Do you have means of communication in your community?"

When Travis explained how basic their community was Sgt White said that they could lend them some long-range field walkie-talkies so they could be kept in the loop about unfolding events. Travis offered to help with their limited resources and although the major welcomed the response he thought it best that they keep their artillery to defend their own community instead, if anything bad should happen. If they needed help down the line they would let them know. The sergeant led the men out of Major White's office once the meeting was concluded.

Kia's mother gave them a brief tour of the bunker, by-passing its vast tunnels full of stores of food and ammunition with scores of vehicle parts and what looked like computer paraphernalia dotted around. If they would have turned left they would have seen the huge tanks fully prepped for action, with some of Sgt White's men checking all were fully operational before being deployed later on.

They went down another floor where some of the main living quarters were, with a large cafeteria type area where everyone ate. Further on there was a snooker table and Fuzball tables, none of which the youngsters knew anything about as they'd never seen anything like them before. Finally they passed some dormitories to their left and right, stretching for several metres. Then they were at the showers! Kia's mother showed them where the towels were kept and even bars of soap were on supply!

"Here are the showers, which I'm sure you've been dying to use. The water for the showers are recycled so we never run out so have fun, boys! Enjoy!" At that she left and the Hubbites raced to strip off to be first in to sample the luxury of real showers! Posted outside the shower block stood a guard to escort them back when they'd finished. There was no harm in keeping vigilant!

Junk

The showers had been a touch of heaven! They had all never felt so clean in a long time and Travis had wondered if they could set up something similar at the

Hub. He definitely needed to investigate that! Perhaps the army could show them how to set it up. He would ask later he thought to himself. They said their good-byes, armed with their new walkie-talkies, donated by the sergeant. Now they were not alone any more, back-up would be available should they need it and Travis was sure they would need it pretty soon!

***

Their journey home had been fairly uneventful for the first few hours. They were all enjoying the new scenery, with a hint of colour in it at last. The ground showed the brown soil that had laid underneath the ash and debris for so long. It was strange to have viewed it after so long! The skies were becoming less opaque and they were sure they had seen flashes of blue here and there among the clouds. The temperature had definitely risen over the last 24 hours. It was a pleasant change.

As they passed over the ridge into the next valley they stopped short and hit the ground!

For miles and miles below them travelled a gleaming white army of robots, glinting against the dull brown of the landscape. Hovering on the ground beside them were transports which seemed to be laden with junk! They stared in disbelief when they saw through the binoculars some Mechs pick up pieces of buildings, broken trees and cars from the wayside, remnants of the tornadoes, and dump them unceremoniously onto the transports. When a transport was full it was programmed by the robots to head towards some unknown source then to return empty once more.

They watched in awe as some robots entered buildings and returned with smaller objects to place on the transport. It was as though they were collecting things for a gigantic scrap-yard! Was this their goal? Were they inter-galactic scrap merchants? Bull laughed at the thought.

"Well, if that's all they want, let them have it I say," remarked Travis. "What could they possibly want with all that junk anyway?"

"Shall we find out?" Finch proposed, with a glint in his eye.

All decided to get closer on the action and they criss-crossed the terrain, keeping low to stay out of sight.

A few hundred yards from the main activity Bull pointed to the left, where something they needed to be concerned with was happening!

"Is that..?" started Finch.

"Yeah, I guess it must be." replied Travis, focused on his binoculars at events unfolding.

The robot held it aloft in one hand. He dwarfed the object. None of them had realised the true size of these robots before now. But here it stood, holding aloft a motorbike in one hand, trying to work out why the headlamp was lit up. Another robot, slightly different, came across and seemed to instinctively know what to do to switch off the headlamp. They were close enough to hear a conversation between the two differing robots.

"Noblaczec! Quit waving that bike around ! It's not a toy! Give it here!"

"Copy that, sir" replied the robot, passing it to Argo, who calmly switched off the ignition.

"Put it on the transport – carefully!" Argo ordered.

Noblaczec placed the motorbike onto the half-empty transport then continued loading other objects from around him onto the hovering vehicle, not so carefully, which resulted in the motorbike being dented instantly!

"NOBLACZEC!" bellowed Argo. "You dim-witted bit of metal" muttered Argo under his breath.

"Yes sir?" inquired Noblaczec, innocently.

"I said carefully! Oh! Never mind!" Argo retorted exasperatedly.

Nobby wasn't an object of high intellect like him. He couldn't make the same calculations and judgements that Argo had been programmed to, hence the reason Argo had been detailed to overlook the events unfolding down on the planet. The robots could only do so much.

***

Bull double checked what he saw through his binoculars then pointed for Travis to see.

"Look , over there, near the scaffolding, can you see ?" Bull asked Travis.

"Oh no! I guess that might be our missing Guy! They've caught him!" Travis responded despondently. Guy was slumped on the floor at the foot of some scaffolding poles. His posture suggested that he was asleep or unconscious.

"Do you think he's alive?" asked Finch.

Bull looked closely. "I can't really tell from here, but he seems to be tied to the scaffolding. We need to get closer to find out!"

Finch looked disbelievingly at Bull. "You're joking, aren't you? Get closer? Down there? Amongst all those robots? You must be mad!"

"Hang on." Travis interrupted. "One of them is going over to him."

The robot stopped at Guy's feet and began to lift him up as if to throw him onto the junk pile.

"Stop!"

Argo commanded the robot, to which the robot let go of Guy, who slumped back against the scaffolding, Nobby turned, then continued to load more objects onto the transport instead.

Argo bent over the unconscious Guy and un-
bound his ties, then in one easy motion hefted him over
his shoulder. To the Hubbites' amazement, they saw
Argo press a few buttons on his arm then all of a sudden
he flew into the air towards the horizon, with Guy
oblivious to what was going on, draped over his shoulder.

"Oh God!" Travis moaned. "That must mean he's
still alive and they've taken him for questioning ,or
worse."

The others looked at each other before grabbing
a walkie-talkie they'd been given by Sgt White. They
reported the events they'd witnessed to the sergeant and
awaited instructions.

The Hostage

Argo flew effortlessly towards the dome a few
miles away, Guy still unconscious on his shoulder. All
around the dome transports were flying in and out carrying junk of all kinds into the larger dome entrance and
leaving, empty, through a second entrance nearby .He
landed softly and entered a code into the gated entrance
to the dome. The gate lifted and Argo entered .

Inside, the dome was sectioned off into smaller
quadrants, each set with its own purpose. The inner
walls were constructed from a silvery metal inlaid with
lights which made the section glimmer brighter than
daylight. Argo took the human through a doorway,
which led into a large cage like construction, with what
looked like beds along two edges. He laid the human
onto the nearest bed, scanned his body with beamed
eyes, then left. Guy remained unconscious, oblivious to
everything.

Argo reported the existence of human life to
Capt Grey as he'd requested. Now he would be on the

lookout for more life forms before the robots got to them first.

Argo entered another section. In here transports arrived by the minute, full of the junk Travis and the others had seen earlier. Hundreds of robots sorted the junk into different piles and programmed the transport to return to its point of origin. Other robots scanned the junk also, as if searching for something in particular. When they were satisfied they selected an object and commanded the Mechs to take it through to the next sector to be processed.

Argo watched for a while overseeing the work , making sure the robots were doing their jobs properly. Then Argo left and exited the dome and in a few seconds was flying back again to the robot army he had left.

Nearby Star and Wren looked worriedly at each other from their hiding point.

"Did you see that ?" Star asked Wren.

"Yes, they've captured someone! Must be from another community." Wren replied. "I hope that he'll be all right. You don't think they'll torture him do you?" asked Wren worriedly.

Star was certain he would be. They'd want to know where his community were laid up for sure.

"No, I think he'll be fine." Star lied to her companion. "Come on, we'd better report this to the Hub."

They hurried from their hideout back towards the Hub. They had been on the lookout for any sign of trouble while Travis had been away from the Hub looking for other communities. Star hoped they were all okay and hadn't been caught like the man they'd just seen!

Chapter8

Communication

Just a mile from the Hub, Star and Wren crouched down low. They had heard movement not far from them, approaching fast. Wren and Star strung their bows, ready in their hiding place and awaited the confrontation.

Wren let her arrow loose a fraction before regretting it. "Oh no!" she cried.

Luckily Bull's reflexes were very fast. The arrow missed his shoulder by millimetres and shot by him into thin air.

Star called out. "It's us! Wren and Star!"

"Sorry!" Wren added miserably. "I thought you were- you know, one of them!"

Bull smiled and made light of it. "It's a good job you're a rotten shot then, isn't it? Bull ruffled her hair playfully.

Finch smiled at Star and asked. "Why are you two here then? Did you miss us? Were you the search party?"

Star laughed. "No, didn't miss you at all. Hardly knew you were gone! We had more important stuff to do. Why aren't you all wearing masks?" asked Star perplexed.

The men told them the news about the changes in the air and as the girls removed their masks they marvelled at being able to breathe easily.

Wren piped up "We saw a human! Caught by the robots!"

"Where?" Travis immediately latched on to this piece of information. Star related what they'd seen to the men. Immediately Travis took out his walkie-talkie.

"What's that?" inquired Wren suddenly.

"It's a means of communication with a neighbouring community that we found," replied Finch.

The girls were excited to hear this news, but their questions would have to wait.

Travis activated the walkie-talkie. "Travis to White, we have news over."

The walkie-talkie crackled for a few seconds then a voice was heard. "White to Travis. What is your news? Over."

Travis related the information about Guy, much to the dismay of Sgt White. The sergeant replied that he would take a unit over to the dome to check it out. Travis switched off the communication device, thankful that he was able to relate the news so quickly now.

***

When they returned to the Hub Travis and the others were dumbfounded when little Lin came skipping up to them smiling and said, "Did you see the sky people?"

Robyn interrupted quickly. "Lin, go and play now, there's a good girl, Travis has lots of work to do." Lin smiled at Robyn, nodding her head and set off with Chaff towards the play area.

"What's that about?" Travis asked worriedly.

"Oh nothing, she's probably heard about the orbs from someone here. How did things go?" Robyn asked quickly.

Travis sat down and related the news to the Hubbites, telling them about their neighbouring community and showing them the new walkie-talkies they'd brought. The Hubbites listened excitedly as Travis spoke about the showers and how he was going to try to set up something similar here, with help from the army. But first they had to deal with the news about the robot army they'd seen, to which the Hubbites reacted with fear and anger.. The old feelings haunted them once more. Travis began to detail Sgt White's plan to deal with them and that brought more reassurance to the gathered crowd.

The Mechanoids

The Mechs roamed the land, blasting at anything large in their path. Broken buildings tumbled to the ground, pulverised by the Mechs' superior firepower. Then they began to carry large chunks of the rubble into holes and craters that were covering the landscape until they were filled. Afterwards the ground was pummelled and levelled until the holes had disappeared.

This went on at random in various parts of the terrain, whilst other places remained in their broken state. The army couldn't understand the thinking behind this unless the aliens intended to make this their home and want to rebuild there. It was a horrible thought, that these invaders were here to stay. Something would have to be done to try to persuade them it wasn't a good idea...

***

Up in the space surrounding the Earth a hundred more ships prepared with their weaponry, ready to launch an attack at a moment's notice. The Blues were good at their jobs, their mechanical skills second to none. They had devised the weapons and machinery required for the captain's grand plan on Earth. They had created the templates for construction and then had the sections manufactured and crated aboard ship by the Whites, the Checkers, who numbered in their thousands. It had all taken many years to prepare but their long journey through space gave them plenty of time to perfect and amass the quantities they needed. The weaponry on board the fleet were unmatched by any species so far. The Argonauts were primed ready to attack at a moment's notice.

The mother ship was so vast it could house several large factories for construction of transports, gadgets and all the paraphernalia required to settle on Earth. Captain Grey had waited a long time for this and now it would soon become reality. The weather satellites had worked well, producing the energy needed to clear the planet of its toxic debris. The manufactured tornadoes had been effective beyond Grey's expectations. Captain Grey never thought it would work, but the AIs had worked out how they were going to deploy the gadgetry and then to destroy the sucked-up remains out here in space. He marvelled at their ingenuity , at how they had evolved from meagre beginnings, to become this supreme species that would aid him in his plan.

Down on Earth the Checkers had begun their march through the land. It had all begun and Grey could hardly contain his excitement. The junk of forty years or more was collected all over the planet and sent for processing in all the domes that were scattered around the world. The grand plan was being executed, stage one under way. The people on Earth would certainly not expect what was coming!

Attack

Over a week later the artillery were in position, under cover of night, the tanks camouflaged as best as the army could manage under the circumstances, they were set up in prime position to attack the dome.

Sgt White motioned for his men to lead down the left flank, ready to fire upon the robots as they marched along the route to the dome. The heavy artillery were ready in position to attack the dome on the stroke of 22:00 hours. Travis and his men watched from the safety of a makeshift dugout the army had prepared for them. A minute to go. This was it!

Finch felt nervous for the first time and Bull could relate to that because he too felt the same for once.

"Fire!" Sgt White bellowed at the troops.

The sound was tremendous. The Hubbites had never heard such noise in their lives, only the elders had experienced the noise of war, during the last alien invasion. Arcs of light crossed the skies from all directions towards the enemy. Thunderous booms exploded one after the other as the tanks fired towards the dome.

Smaller arms fire ruptured the air from the left, followed by the shouts of men advancing towards the army of robots.

Rockets launched into space came arcing down upon the dome below from the launchers nearby. It was all the strength that the humans could produce, all in one go.

The dome could not be seen through the fog of artillery fire bombarding it over and over repeatedly.

"Cease fire!" Sgt White shouted as he looked through his binoculars to see the effect of their attack on the enemy.

As the smoke died down the scenery unfolded before him. His head drooped down despondently as he passed his binoculars to Travis in the ditch beside him.

Travis looked through the binoculars in disbelief.

There, in front of them stood the dome, intact, not a mark on it! It was surrounded by some sort of invisible shield, also dome shaped.

The robots that his men had attacked were also unharmed. They stood facing his men, who stared in disbelief as the robots approached them. The robots closest to them spread their arms in front of the men and instantly the guns disintegrated into vapour in their arms. Frozen to the spot, the men awaited their doom, but were netted by a craft which hovered into position above them. The net closed around the men, scooped them up in an effortless sweep and hauled them on board the ship and it sped off into space!

Sergeant White had witnessed it all happen in the blink of an eye, there was nothing he could have done.

The robots began to move towards the heavy artillery.

"Retreat!" Sgt White called out to the remainder of his unit. "Let's get out of here!" he ordered Travis and his group.

The humans fled for cover and watched disappointedly as the robots incinerated the tanks where they were. There was nothing left of the vehicles except a burn stain on the ground where they had stood. The rest of the artillery that was left in the rush was also destroyed by the robots.

Satisfied that all the arms were destroyed, the robots turned around and rejoined the main troops snaking towards the dome in their hundreds.

Travis puzzled "Why aren't they coming after us?"

Sgt White simply replied "It seems we're no threat to them. I guess they're right about that!"

"What do we do now?" Bull inquired. "We can't just give up!"

"Do?" Sgt White pondered. "We take a step back, think and try to fight smarter!" he responded.

The men all headed back home with heavy hearts

at the loss of comrades. They had used all they had, but even that had not been enough! What was to become of mankind, faced with this power? It did not bear thinking of!

Absent Friends

The bunker community had suffered a defeat, but the worst was they had lost loved ones, sons, husbands, fathers and even a daughter. Private Khan had always wanted to join the army from an early age. She had wanted to make her mother and father proud. They were already proud of their brave daughter, having grown up into this half life, never complaining, always being the first to volunteer for anything that helped her community. When she was accepted into the military that was the proudest moment of their lives, because their daughter had wanted it so much and worked so hard for it to happen.

Now, Meera Khan was up there, in space, amongst aliens. God knows how she was being treated! Would they ever see her again? Mrs Khan held back her tears as Sgt White came to offer her support. He promised he would do everything in his power to reunite her with her daughter once more.

Mrs Khan knew the hopelessness of the situation, but she did not want to add to the army's burden, Meera wouldn't want that. So she quietly went with her husband to their daughter's room, where the family shrine was located and lit a candle for their daughter and prayed for her safe return, the offering to the gods seeming pitifully small in front of them. But the gods would understand. Times were hard.

Guy's father was also a victim of the robot army, unsure where his son was or even if he was alive. He felt great empathy for the Khans. He prayed with them for their safe return.

Major White gathered the community together in the next few days and made promises that they would not give up on their absent friends and together the community prayed for some miracle to happen.

***

Back at the Hub the devastating news of the army's defeat was the last straw. The people had almost given up hope of surviving this war when the odds seemed so heavily against them. If the army had been defeated what hope did this civilian community have? Everyone felt deflated and struggled to come to terms with the thought that their community was about to come to an end.

***

The weeks passed by with no further attempt by the military to inflict damage upon the robot army. The robots had continued to scour the land, picking up their junk from everywhere! In fact, the land became devoid of littering car wrecks and skeletal remains and started to look tidier these days! It was cold comfort to the humans on the planet when they all feared for their lives every day.

Chapter 9

Communities on Watch

Noblaczec and the robots in his unit went from rusty vehicle to vehicle, building to building, collecting and dumping items onto the transports, adding to the piles any objects of interest on the way. Broken tree trunks, withered bushes, skeletal remains of animal or human life forms; it didn't seem to matter to the robots what they were picking up, but methodically they picked at the landscape and everything was sent to the domes via the transports.

***

The Hubbites had observed these activities for weeks without end. Nobody was any the wiser as to what was going on. Nobody had seen the orbs since that time weeks ago. Mechs and robots with their transports were all that seemed to be patrolling the landscape. Luckily for the Hubbites the robots were far enough away from the Hub to be of little danger to them. Major White's community had camouflaged the entrance to their bunker as a precaution in case the robot army encroached their territory.

The Hub was very well hidden anyway, deep in the basin of an abandoned quarry, surrounded by old sheds and storage containers, the entrance was hard to spot. However, the Hubbites kept watch from safe hiding places around the terrain and had set up a warning system using the walkie-talkies donated by Sgt White.

The walkie-talkies had become invaluable , an extra security for the sentinels on duty or whenever field ops were carried out.

A new shower system had been set up by some soldiers for the Hubbites, not using wind power but using water power as that was in plentiful supply at their mine. The Hub community at least had something to enjoy at last! The air, thankfully, continued to be breathable without masks. The skies remained a silvery shimmer, as though someone had left a heater on in the clouds and heat-waves meandered upwards through the cloud cover.

***

Sgt White had posted some men near the dome that imprisoned Guy, monitoring the movements in and out of the dome, hopeful of spotting an opportunity to rescue their friend. But security was very tight everywhere and then there was the issue of the invisible shield to overcome. It seemed hopeless.

Bull and Finch also took interest in the comings and goings from the dome. They were determined to find a way in somehow. They timed the movements in and out of all entrances in the hope they would reveal a gap in security. They discovered that very few robots used the gated entrance and to get in they used a keypad of sorts. Maybe that was a way in?

Back at the Hub the patrols declared their findings to the elders but everyone was clueless as how to proceed from here. Everything seemed impossible in the face of these adversaries.

Days passed with more of the same, nothing new to report from the outside, defeat was etched on everyone's face around the Hub.

"We're never gonna get in there are we?" Star

stated despondently to Finch, who lay hunched up on the bunk nearest to Chaff's.

Finch replied " I dunno. There's gotta be some way. We just haven't found it yet."

"There are many minds thinking this through," Bull's voice added from nearby. "Something will turn up eventually."

"What about trying to dig under the dome?" offered Finch. "Maybe we could get to the gate that way!"

"No." Bull replied. "Sgt White's men thought of that one and sent in an automated machine to get close to the shield to see if they could dig down, but the shield sets off an alarm when you approach it and the machine was toast!"

Star and Finch looked at each other then lay back down onto the bunks to think some more before breakfast.

Around the corner Robyn emerged from the new showers, wrapped in her dressing gown and towels, feeling refreshed and ready to face another day. She peered into the dorm to check if Chaff had got up and greeted the three friends. It seemed Chaff had already got up and gone to the hall for breakfast. Star told Robyn that Lin had been looking for her a few moments earlier, but she wasn't sure where she'd gone. Robyn looked perturbed at this news. Anything Lin had to say these days worried Robyn, after all, she had known about the lights and the sky people without being told about them.

She dressed and towel-dried her hair quickly, then went over to the hall. When she arrived at the hall Chaff was eating her breakfast alongside a few other children, but Lin wasn't amongst them. She greeted her daughter and gave her a hug.

"Have you had anything to drink?" she asked Chaff.

"Yes mum, Lin and I had some milk already, thanks." Chaff replied.

"Oh? Where's Lin now then?" asked Robyn lightly.

Chaff told her that she'd gone to the play area to talk to her friend. Alarm bells rang in Robyn's head.

"Oh really?" Robyn remarked, then she headed off nervously towards the play area.

Robyn found Lin on her own in the playroom, talking to herself. Robyn listened near the door.

"But it's not fair, is it? Why is that going to happen?" then a pause... "Oh, okay, but you promise me it'll be all right? Really?"

Lin felt a presence and turned round to face Robyn, who pretended she had only just arrived and stepped into the room.

"I heard you wanted to see me?" Robyn smiled nervously.

"Yes." Lin replied. "I just wanted you to know that Chaff will be going away for a while soon, but it won't be for long, that's all. Everything will be fine." Lin turned back to a drawing book in front of her and began to doodle.

Robyn felt fear trickle through her body. "What do you mean, going away? Away where?" demanded Robyn.

"I don't really know, but she will be back." Lin replied whilst continuing to draw.

Robyn made herself turn around and leave the room even though her legs had turned to jelly.

Dawn

The following day the sentinels ran into the Hub shouting to wake everyone. "Everyone! Come outside!

Quickly! Something's in the sky! Hurry!" they beckoned the people to follow them out.

Bull rubbed his eyes to look at his watch, donated to him by his mum years ago.

"Hey man! It's barely dawn! What's going on?"

Finch emerged half-dressed from his sleep. "What's happened?"

Star sped past the two towards the entrance. "Get a move on, you two!" she ordered, giving Finch a gentle whack on the head as she passed.

"Hey!" Finch yelled, pretending it hurt. He ran after her to the outside with Bull in tow.

A large group had gathered outside in various states of undress. All were focused on one spot on the horizon. A gasp echoed through the crowd as the object moved slowly higher in the sky.

"What is it?" Wren dreamily inquired.

"It's beautiful!" Star remarked as the object began to glow with beautiful warm colours.

The elders began to cry and hug each other. Chaff began to cry too, seeing her mother's tears.

Robyn embraced her daughter and wiped away her tears.

"It's ok, sweetie. It's ok. Mummy's crying 'cause she's happy, that's all." Robyn smiled at her daughter and looked back at the object, which was now higher up in the sky, a blazing ochre ball surrounded by yellow thin clouds.

Wren looked at her mum. "What is it, mum?"

Robyn replied. "It's the sun, Wren, the sun. We haven't seen the sun in thirty years or more! Isn't it wonderful!" she exclaimed.

Star and Finch looked at each other, confused.

"But what does it do?" they asked.

Travis and Robyn laughed. "The sun gives us hope. It gives us a new life. It brings warmth to our world. Look! The sky is clearing. It's turning blue!"

The elders all cheered and waved their arms enthusiastically towards the sky. The joy was infectious and Finch had a sudden urge to lift up Star and hug her tight. She responded with a kiss. This was the beginning of something good. At last, they all had something to be happy about.

The warmth emanating from the sun was obvious now; even dressed in their night wear they were feeling the sun's rays warm their bodies. It was a glorious and unusual sensation. They stood outside enjoying the warmth for a while before eventually heading back inside to have breakfast. What would this new day bring they wondered?

Sunbathing

The new day turned out to be glorious. The sun shone brightly and the sky was mainly blue, with only a scattering of fluffy white clouds here and there. Everyone wanted to be outside to experience this warmth, something they had not encountered for decades. The skies had always been filled with gases and dust which blocked out the sun for years. Now it seemed like a touch of heaven out there and all wanted to be a part of it. Who could blame them? But for Travis and the elders it became a security nightmare. It was dangerous for so many to be out in the open, so unfortunately for the Hubbites a rota had to be implemented for everyone to have a share of this beautiful day.

Why this had happened no one knew. They hoped that it was nature finally fighting back against the war-torn atmosphere. The signs of change had been brewing in the skies for weeks now, resulting in something they could never have dreamt of! It was truly remarkable.

What would the robots make of this new atmosphere? Would it deter them from carrying out their tasks? Would they leave? The Hubbites were hopeful but the evidence proved otherwise.

The patrols kept reporting the same activities going on at the dome as before. No change!

***

On the third day of glorious sunshine Star, Wren, Bull and Finch were taking their turn to bask in the heat of the afternoon sun. Travis had worked out that it was roughly April or May in the old calendar, but that meant nothing to the youngsters who had been born into a season-less world.

A few others were also sunbathing a few metres further on from them, not far from the Hub entrance. Robyn had given them glasses that had dark lenses on them, which she called sunglasses. They were supposed to protect eyes from the glare of the sun. They made everything seem dark. They were from a batch of objects gleaned from a scavenging session by one of the elders some time ago. Now they would be very useful as the Hubbites were not used to bright lights outside.

The foursome enjoyed the feel of the sun's rays on their skin and were lulled into a sleepy stupor. Across the quarry others lay on the embankment enjoying the sunshine.

Star suddenly sensed some movement to the right and lifted her head slightly to see what it was. The sunglasses were raised off her face so she could focus. Star froze to the spot then nudged Finch in the ribs. Finch saw the seriousness in her eyes and followed her gaze to the horizon. To their horror two robots were headed towards the Hub nearby!

"Don't move!" Bull quietly ordered his companions.

He quickly strained to see if the others had seen the robots too – they had, thankfully. They were slowly trying to shuffle further out of view of the robots. Bull indicated to his friends to do the same, he began shuffling backwards out of their view.

They began to worry about the sentinels. Where were they? Had they seen the robots too?

The massive robots, gleaming white, dazzling in the sunlight, continued down the quarry slope towards the sheds and peered inside.

"Oh no! The vehicles! They'll find them!" Finch groaned.

"I'd rather they find the vehicles than the community." replied Bull.

Suddenly a transport roared overhead a few feet above them, whipping up the air around them. They all ducked down low, grateful that they were remotely operated, otherwise a driver would have seen them! The robots heaved the shed door open and entered. They returned with motorbikes in each hand and placed them on the transport. The bikes came next. *At least they won't be able to pick up the jeeps*, thought Bull, *maybe there's a chance we can hide them before the robots return.*

The ground juddered under their bodies and the thump, thump of heavy footsteps echoed through the quarry.

A Mech stood, magnificent and menacing at the top of the quarry and surveyed the scene briefly. Bull hoped they were all out of sight at that point!

The Mech thumped its way down the side of the quarry with a grind of metal as it swung its arms into position. The Mech entered the shed and came out brandishing a jeep between its claws, then placed it on the transport. The other vehicles were deposited in the same way until the shed was empty. The transport then fled through the sky in the direction of the dome. The friends watched worriedly as the robots moved on towards the second shed and closer to the Hub entrance!

Star cried "They can't see it! Please don't let them find it!" Worrying that the Hub door would be the next thing they would see Star was beside herself with anxiety.

"Crack!" A shot was fired from the top of the quarry at the robots below. The three aliens stopped and turned towards the sniper. Bull saw that it was Bill, out on patrol. He'd taken the shot to distract them from the Hub entrance.

"Run Bill!" Star screamed in her head. "Get away! Hurry!" she didn't want him to get killed.

Bill glanced at the robots to make sure they were coming after him before turning on his heel and heading away from the scene. The Mech gathered up speed, thumping its way up the quarry side after Bill, with the robots following behind.

When the robots and Mech were out of sight the sunbathers all ran down to the Hub and inside, grateful at not being caught.

"We've gotta hide the entrance with something!" yelled Star.

"The timber for shoring over there – quick!" Bull pointed and the group gathered a pile of wooden planks and set them across the entrance to cover it up as best they could.

"Oh Bill, I hope you can still run fast old man!" Travis sighed despondently.

"Who's on guard duty with him?" asked Wren worriedly.

Travis replied "It's your mother, I'm sorry Wren. It's Robyn!"

Travis tried to comfort her but Wren ran off to find her sister Chaff, tears flowing freely from her eyes. She needed to hug her sister.

The Chase

Bill ran for his life, ducking from sight behind any object he could find on his way, but still the thumping footsteps of the Mech accelerated towards him. He fired another shot towards the Mech, aiming for a joint in one of the enormous legs in the hope of disabling him. But the bullet simply bounced off and ricocheted into the land beyond. Gasping for breath Bill hurried onwards, deliberately leading the aliens away from the Hub as best as he could. He felt his age now, he was no longer as fit as when the last war had occurred, when he was able to outrun danger with ease. Now he was struggling to survive and he could feel defeat looming.

The Mech would soon be upon him and then it'd be over for him.

Two shots rang out behind him. Bill quickly tried to calculate what was going on and took a peek from his hiding spot. Again, two more shots were being fired towards the Mech and robots behind him. He saw a flash of golden brown hair flying through a building nearby. It was Robyn! She'd seen his plight and was trying to divert the aliens.

"No! Robyn! Get out of there!" he called out to her pleadingly. He didn't want her to get caught, so he made the brave decision to surrender himself to the aliens.

"No! Bill, no!" cried out Robyn in despair.

But Bill had got up from his hiding place and stood with his hands up awaiting his fate. "Here I am boys, come and get me!" Bill managed to spit out. He threw his gun to the floor and a robot immediately lasered the weapon and it disintegrated on the floor in front of him. The Mech twirled its claw around then fired towards Bill and the old fighter fell to the floor.

NO! screamed Robyn in her head and she began

to cry unashamedly. She thought about all the times Bill had comforted her as she grew up; when her husband had died he'd been like a father figure to her. He'd helped her a lot when she needed help. When the girls were young, missing their father, he'd always been there for her. He and his wife had been like surrogate parents to her. Now he'd sacrificed his life for her and the community. His wife and children would be devastated, as would the whole community. She wept uncontrollably for a long time.

While Robyn wept one robot lifted Bill onto his shoulder and proceeded towards the dome.

***

Robyn eventually headed back to the Hub, with no sign of returning robots, Bill had made sure the Hub was safe, but it was no comfort to Robyn. She had radioed in the news about Bill to the Hub before setting back to face his family.

Chapter 10

Grief

The Hubbites had wept for Bill and the sacrifice he'd made for the community. Travis had lost a very good friend, one of his oldest friends here. Bill's family were proud of their father but felt totally inconsolable at their loss. Robyn hugged the children and told them how brave their father had been. Wren was so grateful that her mother had been spared the same fate. She could not imagine having to cope without her. Chaff was kept in the dark about how much danger her mother had been in, there was no need to worry her unnecessarily Wren thought.

Bull couldn't get over the fact that Bill had been struck down even though he was unarmed and had surrendered. An uncontrollable anger swept through his whole being. *This is not right! Not right at all!* He wanted vengeance on Bill's death, but everything seemed so hopeless. He rammed his fist into the locker, causing a huge dent in the metal.

Finch came swiftly round the corner on hearing the noise, quickly eyed up the situation and sat on the bunk opposite Bull.

"I know, mate. It's not right. Nothing about this is right. Bill knew what he was doing. I reckon any one of us might have done the same to protect the community."

"He wasn't expecting to be shot though! Was he?" retorted Bull angrily. "I mean, he'd surrendered hadn't he? Who fires on an unarmed man? Bastards!"

Bull buried his head in his hands and Finch decided to let him vent his anger before it consumed him.

They lay on the bunks pondering over events when suddenly Finch sat upright with a question on his face.

"I've just thought of something!" Finch declared urgently. Bull lifted his head up.

"The walkie-talkie!" Finch continued. "Bill had one. If they've taken him to the dome they might have put him next to Guy. What if...?" Finch was interrupted by a revitalised Bull.

"Yes! Good thinking! We might be able to communicate with Guy inside the dome! Let's give it a try!" They rushed off to the hall where the spare walkie-talkies were kept and switched one on.

"What are you doing?" inquired Travis, looking puzzled. Before either could answer the walkie-talkie crackled and a voice was heard faintly on the other end.

"Turn it up! Quickly!" Finch called out as Bull fiddled with the receiver.

"I'm trying, wait.." The voice returned, very faintly..."Dome, with Guy."

"Is that...?" Robyn's voice echoed behind Travis.

"Yes. It sounds like Bill! He's alive!" Bull said with a huge grin.

He spoke into the receiver, "Bill, is that you? Are you and Guy all right? Over."

The crackle continued then a faint voice replied "Both of us ok and in the dome, over."

Cheers went up in the gathered group.

"Can you get out? Over." questioned Travis.

"That you, old friend?" Bill asked. "Negative. We're in a cage-like container inside the dome. Locked in but no guards to be seen. Guy says he's been fed....."

A loud noise rumbled across the receiver then it went totally dead.

"What happened?" Finch asked exasperatedly.

"I guess they found the walkie-talkie." Bull replied sadly.

Travis immediately took hold of the receiver and called Sgt White to relate this new information to their community. Welcome news. Maybe the other captives were ok too? It was an inspiring thought.

***

Later that night the skies opened up and it began to rain! The first real rain in decades. This was not acidic, not burning the ground and everything it touched, it was cool, refreshing rain! The sentries looked in awe as the rainwater formed little streams, running down the quarry sides and meeting up on the low ground and forming pools in ditches all around. The sound of rain brought out some of the Hubbites, curious as to what was happening. They were glad that the world was returning to normality. They stood in the rain getting soaked, but enjoying it!

Destruction

In the morning the Hubbites were thrown from their bunks as what sounded like a bomb had landed nearby. Several more blasts followed in succession causing items to fall off shelves around the Hub. The screams of aircraft blared through the skies above the Hub so loud they could be heard quite clearly from the mine.

"What the hell is going on?" demanded Bull getting quickly dressed to investigate.

Travis and the elders rushed through the tunnels in various states of undress. Panic filled their eyes.

Travis' eyes engaged with Bull's. "Stay here, son. Watch over everyone!" commanded Travis as he made for the exit, with three elders in tow.

Bull desperately wanted to see what was going on, but Travis' orders were always carried out, no matter how badly Bull wanted to do otherwise.

Most of the Hubbites were gathered in the main hall, all dressed now, worry in their eyes. Robyn held onto Chaff tightly and Wren could see from her mother's expression that there was definitely something to fear

"Do you know what's going on?" Star asked Robyn.

But before she could answer another blast brought some rubble down amongst them. The mine's shoring was being compromised by the explosions outside. Another thunderous blow caused the Hall to be filled with dust as parts of the ceiling collapsed on the people below!

Travis saw the spaceships darting through the skies, firepower tracing destruction to the land once again. It was as he had feared. These spaceships did not belong to the robot army! These were the same spaceships that had decimated their planet in the last war! The aliens were back!

Travis fell back against the doorway, his face as white as a sheet. The others with him had also recognised the ships and all felt that old feeling of hopelessness draining their energy from them. He wondered for a moment whether the aliens were working with the robot army.

One of the elders had been looking at something through the binoculars. He passed them to Travis, pointing to the distance at the edge of the quarry.

To his horror Travis saw the bloodied lifeless bodies of the two sentinels that had been caught unawares when the spaceships started their bombardment. Travis hung his head in despair, two young men in the prime of their lives, cut down with no mercy. How was he going to tell their families?

Scores of alien ships criss-crossed the skies screaming through the half-light of dawn, shooting down anything they saw. A missile tore through the air and exploded not far from the quarry entrance. Travis, feeling the ground shake, led the others back into the Hub, covering the entrance as before. There was nothing they could do, except prepare for the worst!

Back inside the Hub people stirred from the rubble, covered in dust.

"Star!" Finch called out urgently, "Star! Where are you? Are you all right?"

He shifted from the dusty pile he had been engulfed in and pushed his way out of the rubble. As he emerged he saw a scene of devastation, several parts of the earthen ceiling had collapsed onto the crowd, along with the shoring that had held it together. Bull was nearby clawing at some earth and debris where a hand stuck out from underneath.

"No! Star!" Finch exploded, he was beside himself with fear.

Star staggered towards him from a different direction, covered in dust.

"It's ok, I'm ok, Finch."

She fell onto his shoulder, brandishing a cut above the eye, which was now bleeding towards her eyelid. Finch held her close and took her over to a chair.

"You're not all right. You've got a nasty cut. I'll take care of you."

She appeared dazed and allowed Finch to fuss over her.

Bull was still trying to dig out the person underneath the rubble, with others who were uninjured and able to help, pulling at the debris. Robyn groaned nearby, covered in dust. She lifted herself off the floor .

"Wren! Chaff! Where are you?" she shouted,

looking at her surroundings in disbelief.

A small voice called from behind an overturned cupboard.

"Mum! Mum I'm here!" Wren pushed the cupboard aside and lifted herself off the dusty floor. Robyn rushed to comfort her while Wren assured her that she was ok.

"Where's Chaff?" asked Wren, coughing up the dust from her lungs. They looked around them to see if Chaff was nearby.

Bull and the others who had been digging at the pile of rubble came to a stop. All hung their heads in sorrow. Bull got up and went slowly over to Robyn and Wren.

"We've found her, we found Chaff... I'm sorry.. " Bull placed a gold angel pendant into Wren's hand. Robyn and Wren looked in disbelief at Bull, trying to take in the information.

"Chaff? Where is she?" Robyn 's eyes looked at him pleadingly, hopefully.. She made to move past Bull to see, but Bull stopped her by wrapping his arms tightly around her and she shuddered and cried uncontrollably in his arms.

"No! No!" Robyn repeated over and over, grief stricken. Wren stood stunned, unable to move or speak, tears streamed down her face. Bill's wife, Mary came over to comfort her and Wren dissolved into her arms, inconsolable.

Travis and the elders came into the hallway from outside. Seeing this devastation was the final straw. He took in the sight of Chaff's body and closed his eyes grief stricken.

"One fatality " a voice informed Travis quietly. "It could have been worse. Many more could have lost their lives here today. But what of tomorrow?"

"They're back!" Travis announced, barely above

a whisper, but everyone heard all the same. "The other aliens have returned!" he added just to make sure all understood.

Warring Factions

The walkie-talkie crackled as Travis related the news to Sgt White, of course the bunker community had heard the explosions just as they had, but luckily had suffered no casualties yet, despite several strikes falling near their bunker.

Sgt White told Travis that he and his community should try to sit this out and let the bunker community deal with it. They promised to report back any developments to the Hubbites as they occurred. There was no point in Travis' community suffering any further fatalities with their limited resources.

Travis and the men started to prepare for moving Chaff's body when Merlin rushed into the room. Robyn reached out her arm to stop her seeing the body, but Merlin was too quick. Instead of crying Merlin seemed to be muttering softly to herself and nodding her head. She abruptly looked up and said in a clear voice

"My friend is going to make Chaff better. Please lay her outside the Hub."

Travis was embarrassed that Robyn should hear this nonsense and began to move her aside.

"It's ok Lin, we're going to make sure Chaff is looked after, you run along now." Travis spoke softly but firmly.

"No!" Robyn spoke loudly, remembering Lin's prediction. "Did your friend tell you to put her outside, Lin?" she asked her directly.

Lin nodded and added "He can make her better. "

Travis looked at Robyn, puzzled, and was about to try and reason with her when Robyn stood up and spoke.

"There's a lot I haven't told you, Travis. Please do as Lin says. Lay her outside the Hub. Please!" Robyn looked pleadingly at Travis and the others.

Wren looked at her mother bewildered. "Mum?" she questioned softly, "Mum, what's going on?"

Robyn replied. "Lin is gifted. She knows things before they happen. She knew about the lights and the robots before we did, she spoke to me about them, but I didn't say anything for fear of worrying everyone. If she says her friend can help then I believe her. What harm is there in trying? Chaff is.. dead isn't she? No more harm can come to her! We've got to do this. Please?"

Travis and Bull went towards Chaff's body and Travis said. "Ok Robyn. If it's what you want."

He looked straight into Merlin's eyes as though daring her to confess it was lies, but Lin held his gaze and said, "I promise she'll be fine."

***

Outside the Hub all hell was let loose. The skies were swarming with alien aircraft, swooping low on the horizon, firing at the robot dome time after time without effect. The robots were retaliating with an equal amount of firepower and seemed to be gaining ground as far as Travis could make out briefly. *So, it seems they are not allies after all,* thought Travis.

When Bull and Travis caught a lull in the firing they took Chaff's covered body over towards the vehicle shed and found a suitable spot to lay her down carefully. They looked at her lying peacefully before running back to the Hub and covered the entrance again.

The spaceships swarmed through the skies like a flock of birds twisting and diving in unison, letting loose indiscriminate bombs on the ground below. The giant robot spaceship observed for a time, immune to any strikes the aliens pummelled them with, its shield protecting all within. The robot army below began to retaliate from the attempted strikes at their workforce, again all were protected by their own shields.

As the enemy spaceships swooped down to attack, the robots aimed their arms at the ships with precision focusing and let loose their lethal rays into the skies. One by one the enemy ships began to disintegrate as they swooped down low. The craft were no bigger than shuttles so casualties would be low, but a diminished enemy could only be a good thing.

Sgt White's troops observed the battle from their hideout in the hills and admired the power that the robot army wielded.

A larger spaceship loomed over the horizon, making its way towards the main trunk of the robot army. It let loose a missile with a tremendous noise, resembling a magnified whizzing of a very large firework. The missile struck short of the army but the impact threw several robots into the air and left a huge crater in its wake.

"Look, Sarge!" shouted one of White's soldiers, pointing towards a different robot who was now flying through the air towards the large ship which had just fired.

"What's he doing?" puzzled Sgt White, dumbfounded. "What does he hope to achieve on his own?"

Argo however, knew exactly what he was doing, veering elegantly and swiftly from side to side avoiding fire from the smaller ships that were now chasing him.

The aliens inside the large ship looked bemused

at each other. They resembled animal life more than human life forms. Their bodies were covered sparsely by clumps of hair in varying colours. They had the same number of limbs as humans but their legs were jointed more like dogs than human joints. They had hands and feet each containing four digits and had two sunken eyes in dark brows, a hole for breathing through rather than a proper nose. Their mouths were small with sharp teeth. They had no discernible ears.

They watched Argo approaching at tremendous speed towards them and gurgled as though laughing.

But the laugh was on them as Argo landed in front of their cockpit, having puzzlingly made his way through their shield. Argo's feet clunked onto the metallic surface in front of the cockpit as though magnetised into place. He smiled at the ugly aliens within.

"Hey you ugly guys, how you doing today?" Argo waved as though he was greeting a friend. Then his features turned into a grimace, full of venom, and he pushed some buttons on his arm and pointed them towards the cockpit.

The aliens' faces changed from bemusement to terror when all at once the glass on the cockpit melted in front of their eyes and before they could scream their bodies disintegrated bit by bit, followed by the seating behind them. The ship began to nosedive out of control and Argo calmly demagnetised his feet and jumped off into the air, flying swiftly in search of his next victim.

From the robot mother ship Captain Grey remarked, "Argo has become invaluable, just as we planned. Let's hope our fellow Argonauts above the planet have the same resolve!"

Professor Stark nodded grimly. "I just hope we haven't unleashed a monster here."

The Argonauts

The battle was intense and fierce, but very one-sided. The robots had far superior fire power and shields than the ugly aliens. Alien ships zoomed low over the terrain, loosening their bombs randomly as they went, but none of their bombs had any impact on the robots or their domes. Fighter aircraft repeatedly tried to demolish the new constructions, but nothing could touch them with those powerful shields protecting everything.

Robot craft shot out of the skies from nowhere, encircling and out manoeuvring the aliens with ease. The few remaining fighter aircraft were despatched by the robots very quickly and no prisoners were taken. The fallen craft were systematically disintegrated by the robot army as though they had never existed. The ground left only burnt patches visible where the craft had crashed previously. The few remaining of the larger alien ships flew back into space to regroup, or count their losses!

The Hubbites could only sit and listen whilst the war raged on outside. No more bombs had landed close to the Hub for hours and the noise of battle had diminished to a low rumble in the distance. So, the community started re-shoring up the damaged areas in the tunnels and hallway. The rubble was cleared and there was no evidence of a cave in to be seen when they'd finished.

Robyn and Wren sat huddled together on the bench at the table, Wren turning Chaff's pendant over and over in her hands. Lin sat near them with her mother by her side. All eyes inevitably darted now and again towards Lin, but she was oblivious to it all.

The noises outside had died down now and Travis debated whether to go out to look or not. He feared what he'd see, whatever the outcome. Whether

Chaff's body remained there or not. Lin muttered to herself quietly and all eyes were upon her instantly.

"Thank you." she muttered and smiling, she looked up at Travis and said. "Chaff is with my friend, he's making her better."

Travis bolted up the tunnel to the doorway and heaved it open, Bull in tow. Robyn stood, listening to her heart beating loudly in her chest. Wren held her mother's hand tightly. It seemed ages before Travis and Bull returned from the exterior, both looked shocked.

"What is it?" demanded Robyn. "Please, tell me. What did you see?"

Bull answered first. "Chaff's body has gone from where we put it, but also the two sentinels that were killed—their bodies have been removed, too!"

Robyn's eyes lit up and she breathed a sigh of relief. She looked at Lin. "Thank you, Lin. Thank your friend for me."

Lin beamed and said "I already did."

***

High above in space the battle raged on, the Argonauts, (highly evolved Gold AIs), had formed their spaceships into a circle with all firepower facing outwards. When the alien ships had returned to space to regroup they had found this new foe waiting for them. Before they could form an effective defensive group the Argonauts fired, with all craft within firing distance penetrating the aliens' puny defence systems and shredding their craft to oblivion.

Their fire power was far superior to anything the aliens had encountered before. Wave upon wave were caught in the firing line. No matter how hard they tried to evade, the AIs matched their direction and pummelled them. Debris from exploded craft floated everywhere above the Earth, but the AIs continued to destroy the larger pieces until there was only paltry sized fragments left. On seeing how outmanoeuvred and inadequate their craft's firepower was, the leading alien ship fled into hyperspace beyond, with a few surviving smaller craft fleeing in their wake.

Captain Grey congratulated his fleet and promised that when they were done with Earth they would pursue the aliens to finish them off for good. The AIs accepted their praise and the promise of further engagements with gratitude, then continued to perform their tasks to bring Earth to its next state of Evolution..

On the walkie-talkie Travis discussed with Sgt White the damage caused to the quarry and its people, then he asked about the bunker, if there was any damage sustained there. The sergeant told Travis that apart from a few bomb craters outside the entrance way they were fine.

Nobody had been caught outside when the aliens attacked so they were lucky. He offered to help the Hubbites fill the holes created by the bombs in their quarry, but Travis assured him that they could manage and that repairs were already underway. Sgt White passed on his condolences for Travis' losses in the community and assured him they were still trying to come up with a plan to tackle the robot problem. They would be in touch should something come up. Both men knew in their hearts that it was very unlikely, but they could live in hope.

Chapter 11

Growth

The Hubbites tried to take it all in. The robots had fought the aliens and despatched them unceremoniously. Were they gone for good? What about this robot invasion? Why were they here? It was certainly a blessing that they had better fire power than the previous aliens. Perhaps Earth had seen the last of them? Everyone hoped so. No matter how much they talked about it nobody could fathom the reason the robots were here. Were they intending to take over this planet and settle down here? What about the humans still living here? What was their plan for them? So far any humans the robots had encountered had been despatched either to the domes or into space. What were they playing at? Questions on everyone's minds, but no answers.

The rain had been a welcome addition as had the sunshine previously. The air was breathable now and the skies were returning to their former glory. Everything was changing, but why? How? Again, no answers.

Bull and Finch stood outside the Hub watching and listening to the rain pouring down. A warm rain, very welcome. Travis had placed lots of containers discretely outside the Hub to gather the rainwater. Who knew how long it would last?

As Star emerged outside with them she asked "Any sign?"

For days now there had been no sign or news of

Chaff or the fallen sentinels. Robyn and Wren were beside themselves with worry.

"Do you think she will return?" Star asked sadly.

"Well, a lot of strange things have happened in the last few months," Finch replied, holding her hand. "I'm sure we haven't seen the last of her." he finished, kissing her gently on her forehead. Star blushed as Bull looked away.

"Shall we take a look outside the quarry to see what's going on? Being stuck in the Hub's driving me crazy." stated Bull impatiently.

They agreed, lifting their hoods to cover their heads as they walked on up the quarry lane towards the land beyond. There was no point in bringing any weapons any more they decided. They were no match to the robots' firepower anyway they concluded.

The trio passed the sentinels guarding the Hub and reported what they were going to do. The sentinels waved them on and continued to huddle in their sodden hideouts near the quarry entrance, wishing they could get out of their wet clothes.

After walking to the top of the quarry entrance they turned towards the direction of the dome. Before they'd gone a few metres Star stopped them.

"Look!" she exclaimed, pointing at the soil at the side of the old roadway.

Bull and Finch crouched down low to inspect the ground. The whole verge was beginning to get covered with a new green growth, quite sparse, but there it was!

"Is that grass?" Star asked, remembering pictures of something similar she'd seen in storybooks back at the Hub.

"Yes, I think it must be!" replied Bull, touching the stubbly growth.

They peered over the broken stone wall which

bordered the roadside at the land beyond. For hundreds of metres beyond there were fields beginning to green up!

"It's beautiful!" Star remarked.

"It sure is." Finch agreed, staring at it in awe.

"And look over there!" Bull enthused, pointing in the distance at a glistening form snaking its way through the valley below. "It's a river! The river bed has filled with water! Let's go and see!"

The trio ran along the broken roadway descending to the valley below, passing field upon field greening up around them. It was like being in a different land entirely. A broken but beautiful land!

They reached the river after a half hour's trek and stood in awe of this spectacular sight. The water rippled and bubbled over the bleached stones, the water so clear they could see the rocks at its base. Little eddies formed near larger rocks protruding here and there. The dripping rain plodded onto its surface creating little dimples everywhere.

"Isn't it wonderful?" Star beamed, with raindrops trickling over her eyes.

Bull and Finch were mesmerised by the sight of this new river, which only weeks before had been just rocks and stones which they had traversed to get to the dome site further along. They stood watching it for a long time and soon the rain stopped and the skies cleared. In minutes the sun shone from behind a cloud. It made them feel good being out here to witness these changes.

They walked on to where the bridge crossing the river half stood nearby. They climbed the bridge, surveying the land around them from its lofty height. The trio gasped with delight as a beautiful rainbow appeared before them. They had heard about rainbows from their childhood stories in the Hub. Now they'd seen a real one! They delighted in seeing the spectrum of colours enhance this greening valley.

Suddenly their reverie was interrupted by a strange noise coming from the direction of the dome, which was a few miles down the valley . They turned around quickly to see if they could spot anything so they could hide. What they saw was incredible! They were glued to the spot, unable to believe their eyes!

Running towards them, tossing its head from side to side was a horse! A real horse! They instantly recognised what it was, but could not believe it. The horse was galloping towards the river, towards them! When it drew close to the river's edge it stopped and lowered its long neck and began to drink in the cool river water. Its beautiful torso gleamed a warm earthy colour, glistening from the rain, and its tail and mane were of a golden hue. It was the most beautiful creature they'd ever seen. But what was it doing here? How did it get here and from where?

Star wanted to get closer to the horse but the others weren't too sure. However, they accompanied her down to the water's edge near where the horse stood, still drinking.

Star approached slowly, talking softly to the horse. It's ears pricked up and it tossed its head up fearfully, but Star continued in her calming voice to try to reassure it, holding out her hand towards the horse.

The horse seemed to calm down and watched Star's approach with interest, until finally she was able to stroke its neck gently. The horse responded with a few appreciative snorts.

Just when they thought they'd seen a miracle another one appeared in tandem. Scores of other horses came galloping along the fields towards them too. So many they couldn't count, of all different colours. They eventually converged at the river's edge near the other horse and began to drink their fill of the fresh river water.

Bull and the others could not comprehend what was happening. Where had these beautiful creatures emerged from? Certainly they had come from the direction of the dome, perhaps they should venture that way to find some answers...

Exodus

As the trio walked through the changing landscape they marvelled at its new identity; old craters and cracks seemed to have been filled in—probably by the robots they assumed—so the road was navigable at last! A few new craters had been added of course by the battle the other night, but generally it was much tidier! The broken buildings that they had sheltered in weeks ago along the wayside had been pulverised to the ground. *Perhaps the rubble has been used to fill the holes,* surmised Bull.

"What the..?" Finch paused in mid sentence, rooted to the spot by the sight he'd just seen on the horizon. Bull and Star turned to look and they too could not believe what they saw.

"How on earth...?" began Star in disbelief.

"They can't be real!" said Bull confused. "Let's get closer to check it out!" and he started to run towards the objects at the top of the hill with Finch and Star in tow. The closer they got the harder they found it to believe in what they were seeing. This could not be!

In front of them, eight metres tall at least, stood living trees in full foliage! A small forest of them along the roadside, stretching for miles along the hills!

Bull shook his head in disbelief. "Nothing can grow this quickly!" He went up to touch the trees to feel the rough bark under his fingers, to stare incredulously at the roots anchored deep into the ground below and to smell the earthiness of the trunk before him. The branches swayed in a soft breeze and the leaves danced in the sunlight. They certainly seemed real! They could not believe what they were seeing.

The trio laughed at the absurdity of it all. It could not have happened overnight, yet here they were, growing as though they had been there for decades! Basking in the glory of this new adventure they continued on in the direction of the dome. A mile further along the tree lined road they came down the hillside around a bend and there in the fields below stood the gleaming dome. It seemed out of odds with its surroundings now, with all the greenery around it. It stuck out like a sore thumb.

Up until now there had been no sign of robots marching through the land, but beside the dome there seemed to be lots of activity. Now and again more transports laden with junk appeared from distant skies and flew into the dome, returning empty once more a few minutes later and headed off back towards the direction they'd come from, presumably to load up more junk.

Star pointed to the direction of the other entrance and spoke. "Can you see the lights flashing over there? They seem to flash in a sort of pattern? It's coming from inside the dome. I wonder what's going on there?"

Before she got a reply something weird happened again.

Lumbering along the pathway emanating from that very entrance came some large bulky animals with horns. They had different patterns on their skin, some were brown, some were black, others a mixture of black and white patches.

"Are they..?" began Star.

"Cows, I think." interrupted Bull.

They were being herded along to a fenced-off field beside the dome by several robots. The cows ambled along looking confused until they saw the grassy field, then they happily settled into the field, eating their way through the grass. There seemed to be a newly erected building not far from the field that some robots were carrying objects into.

Bull and the others could not have known that the robots had been creating a milking parlour for the cows and were carrying in the equipment needed to milk them.

" Now I know I'm going mad!" stated Finch a matter of factly!

Another couple of horses galloped out of the dome as though they'd been spooked, but no robot chased after them. They continued to gallop along the fields headed for who knows where? Perhaps towards the other horses by the river?

The three could not fathom what was going on at all. They decided that it was time to report back to the Hub.

On their way, they saw that the horses had settled together in the field abutting the river and were happily chomping on the grass, but what was that? They paused in their tracks and watched bemused as large robots, similar to the one that took Guy, hovered in the air a few metres from the ground around the perimeter of the field where the horses grazed. They watched, confused, as silvery threads emanated from the robots' arms and created an electrified fence around the large perimeter of the field where the horses moved, oblivious to it all.

The Hubbites waited until the robots had finished and flown off again before moving from their hiding point. What would robots need cows and horses for? The mystery deepened!

Miracles

As they approached the Hub they were puzzled that there didn't seem to be any sentries outside on duty. They scanned the perimeter but saw no sign of them. Worrying that something was up they ran the rest of the way down to the mine entrance. The door was wide open and the trio could hear raised voices from the inside. They approached carefully in case the Hub was compromised.

Bull told the other two to stay outside until he gave the all clear and he then edged his way cautiously around the large metal door. He heard a lot of raised voices inside the hall, and could hear someone crying. It sounded quite like Robyn. Then he heard Travis' voice above all the others call for calm. Bull crept further down the tunnel to the edge of the hall until he could see a glimpse of the gathering crowd. They all had their backs to him as luck would have it. They all seemed to be surrounding something at the centre of the room near the tables.

Bull saw no sign of any robots and became confused as to what was going on. Suddenly he caught his mother's eye and she came over to him with a haunted look on her face.

"Is it safe to come in?" he asked quietly. "Star and Finch are outside. We were worried when we saw no sentries." he added.

His mother took a deep breath. "You'd better tell them to come in, son. You might as well all see this together." she said mysteriously.

Bull called the others in and they emerged in the hall as two sentries made their way past them to go on duty outside. The crowd moved to one side and there in the middle of the hall was the reason for the uproar. Chaff stood next to her mother Robyn, holding her mother's hand while Robyn, seated, wept tears of joy at having her daughter back. Chaff was wearing the same clothes she had on when she 'died', but they had been cleaned and looked like new. The two sentries that had been killed outside on the same day also stood in the hall, alive and well, comforting their families huddled beside them. Star rushed to Chaff and hugged her and noticed she was again wearing the angel pendant that Wren had given her previously.

"But how..?" began Star, overwhelmed by the sight of these people who had cheated death. Chaff simply shook her head as she remembered nothing.

Travis told the trio that around an hour ago the sentinels had been blinded by a strong light outside and fell unconscious where they stood. "When they woke up again there were the bodies of Chaff and the sentries that had been killed, lying neatly next to them, by all appearances fast asleep. They woke up very quickly and could not account for where they'd been at all. They had no idea that they had "died" and come back to life! The sentinels brought them into the Hub about ten minutes ago and then you showed up." concluded Travis.

"So where were you anyway?" he asked.

When the Hubbites heard Bull's news about the land and the animals they were shocked into silence. All looked at each other for explanation, which was beyond everyone. It was miracle after miracle!, beyond belief!

Travis called out quietly, "Merlin, come here."

Gale looked at Travis and protectively held on to her daughter.

"It's ok, Gale, I'm not going to frighten her. Please, bring her here." Travis added.

Nightingale held Merlin's hand and brought her over to Travis. He sat on the bench near Merlin to be closer to her height.

"Merlin, your friend was very kind to make Chaff and the others better wasn't she?" Travis began.

Merlin replied. "It's not a she, it's a he; my friend

is a man. He's very clever, he talks to me a lot."

"Where does he talk to you, Lin?" Travis probed.

"In my head. He tells me lots of things, but some things I'm not allowed to tell." Lin replied.

Worried glances swept the hall at that news.

"What's your friend's name and where does he live?" Travis continued.

"His name is Argo and he lives in a spaceship."

Bull and the others looked at each other worriedly.

"Do you know why Argo is here, Lin?" asked Travis hopefully.

"I think he wants to live here." said Lin, smiling.

"Are you sure Argo is a man, Lin? Or is he a robot?" Travis inquired nervously.

"Well, he is like a man, but I suppose he is a robot really." Lin stated truthfully. "Because he can do things men can't do. He can fly!" Lin beamed.

The Hubbites gasped worriedly at the news.

"Lin, does Argo know where you live?" Travis asked tentatively, worried at the answer.

"Yes, of course he does, silly! He told me that we won't be living here for very much longer."

The whole room erupted in shouts of fear.

Chapter 12

Argo's Report

Argo flew back up to the mother ship. Captain
Grey wanted an update in person. As Argo had flown
through the skies he had looked down upon the land below him, where he could see how far the changes in
Earth had gone since their arrival. The databases he'd
been accessing obviously had some truth in them after
all, he decided.

When he'd first walked through this barren
planet he had been angry at the lies he had supposed
he'd been told by Captain Grey about how beautiful it
was. It certainly wasn't beautiful when they landed, but
now things had begun to alter, the polluted atmosphere
had dispersed and weather systems had been kick-started
into kinder routines. Poisonous debris and dust had been
eliminated and now new life was forming on the planet.
But he needed to inform the captain about the other life
forms he knew about too.

He emerged through the docking bay and found
the bronze AIs busy manoeuvring their new gadgets and
weapons into position, readying themselves for Grey's
plan.

"Are we on target with the completion of the
new weapons?" he asked an AI commander nearby.

"Yes sir" replied the commander, "Things should
work out quite easily now it's complete."

"Carry on!" Argo commanded, placing his travel
helmet on the rack beside him. He then entered the

beamer to beam him up to the bridge, seventeen levels up.

"Ah! Argo. There you are!" smiled Capt. Grey. "How are things going on the planet? According to plan, I hope?"

Argo stood to attention and began his report. "The planet 's weather systems are settling, Captain, and the planet's surface is greening up. The fields are re-newed and craters being filled everywhere so roads are beginning to be more navigable. Our troops will be able to march through from town to town more easily now.. We have begun to release some animal forms, so far some horses and cows; the others will follow gradually."

The captain interrupted." Are you certain that we have programmed the robots correctly for maintaining these animals? I'd hate to lose them before they've had a chance to re-establish."

Argo continued. "Yes, Captain. I made sure No-blaczec was nowhere near an animal, so we should be ok!"

"Ah! Humour! I like that about you Argo. It's like talking to a fellow human."

Argo didn't exactly appreciate the comparison but continued anyway.

" We have trees growing on around a fifth of the planet's land masses so far and next week we hope to start tackling the oceans and lakes. Rivers have begun to flow after the rain and we are on schedule to repair the bridges in the coming week."

"Sounds wonderful, Argo. I can picture it now. I will enjoy coming down on the planet's surface when it's complete."

"Sir?" began Argo, sounding a little more wor-ried now.

"What is it, Argo? Something gone wrong?"

Argo hesitated then replied.

" We have a community living in an old mine not far from a dome, sir. I believe it contains families with small children. I am in communication with a small child there, called Lin, or Merlin as she is properly named. I heard that there had been three fatalities at the mine when the aliens bombed the area; one a little girl who is a friend of Lin's and two others. Their bodies have been dealt with, sir."

The captain pondered over this information for a few minutes then responded. "Did the three see inside?"

"No sir, we were careful that they saw nothing."

"This makes it rather awkward, Argo. What can we do with these people? Let me think about it. I'll call you when I've decided."

Argo turned to leave, but hesitated, adding, "They're good people sir, ideal for our purpose." Then he left the bridge, leaving the captain to decide what to do.

***

In the beamer Argo wondered if he had done the right thing in informing Capt. Grey of these humans. Soldiers were one thing, but families—they wouldn't understand. He hoped that Capt Grey would be merciful.

As he walked through the cargo bay to check on supplies he heard raised voices. *Robots do not raise their voices,* he thought to himself, *what's going on? There should only be cargo-bots here on duty.* He peered around the corner of a large container to see where the noise was coming from. He watched as a couple of AIs pushed one of the cargo robots to one side and went to open a large container.

"What are you two doing down here?" demanded Argo suspiciously. "What unit are you from?"

The two AIs were about to shout back but stopped short when they saw Argo's colours of seniority.

All AIs were graded according to rank and special powers, which were shown by coloured panels on their right
arms. Argo had the highest rank and special powers,
signified by his gold panel.

Rogues

The two AIs fired their weapons, built into their
arms, towards Argo and pushed some robots aside as
they fled towards the docking bay, still firing blindly
behind them. Argo went up to the fallen robots to ask
them what rank the AIs were, but to his misfortune these
robots were basic cargo models and were useless at providing anything that was beyond their everyday brief-
fill, check, seal and shift. That was it!

Argo wished now that he'd chased after the two
AIs but there was no way he would be able to catch up
with them now. They were headed onto the planet
somewhere. He re-ran his visuals, which automatically
recorded everything he saw in the hope that their rank
was seen in the re-run. Unfortunately for Argo, their
colours were not evident in the visuals at all!

The highest ranking AIs wore a gold colour strip
on their right arm, these were the most evolved AIs, next
in rank were the Silvers, which had fewer skills than the
Golds, they piloted the fleet ships. The Bronze AIs were
usually used as ship's crew and mechanics, keeping the
everyday operations on the ships working smoothly.

Below the AIs were the various ranking robots,
programmed to perform a limited number of tasks. The
very basic robots were the white ones, the Checkers, like
Noblaczec, who were used to perform the checking,
packing and sorting tasks on the ship or the planet. The
Mechanoids were programmed to carry out heavy lifting
and manoeuvring tasks and also had built in defensive
weapons. The Blue robots worked with the creation of

gadgetry in the dome sites, and operating the machinery inside the dome. They were smaller than the other robots and could fit amongst the cabling more easily for repairs. They also had the greatest engineering skills for the creation of new weaponry and gadgetry on board ship.

"Captain, this is Argo reporting." Argo spoke into his wrist mic. "I'm afraid we have some rogue AIs in our midst. I caught two of them in the cargo bay trying to open one of the cargo containers, but I stopped them in time. They opened fire and I could not see their colours, sir. I'm afraid they're on their way to the planet by now."

Captain Grey could not contain his anger at hearing such news. This was not the time to have to deal with in house issues of this kind. He had worked so hard at getting to this point and now this could jeopardize everything!

"Find them! Put what resources you have spare into capturing them ! I don't want my plan ruined by these AIs at this point in the proceedings. I am returning the ship into space to stand guard over our weaponry in case they try something."

"Copy, sir. I will do my utmost to flush them out." Then Argo thought about it before adding "Sir, what if there are more AIs who have turned rogue, these might only be two out of several?"

Captain Grey turned pale at the thought. "Then we'll deal with that possibility if it arises. Head on out there Argo. Do what you can."

"Yes sir!" Argo grabbed his helmet and left the ship promptly.

***

The two AIs flew directly down towards the dome nearest the mother ship, their attempt to sabotage the machinery foiled. They had thought about the best way to disrupt operations and get what they wanted and decided this was the best course of action. They landed at the gated entrance of the dome and entered. They passed several robots performing their menial tasks, taking no notice of the two AIs.

***

Guy and Bill lay in their bunks talking when the two AIs barged into the room. Bill instantly knew something was up because these AIs seemed different to the others that had been bringing in their food. He noticed these AIs' strips were silver, not bronze like the ones they normally saw. Suddenly one of the AIs fired a laser at the cage lock , which caused the cage door to swing wide open. Before Guy or Bill could say anything the AIs manhandled them out of their bunks, quite roughly and dragged them along out of the cage.

"Hey! What's the deal here? What have we done wrong?" Guy bellowed at the AI holding his arm. The AI didn't miss a step, or look at Guy. He simply said in a threatening tone

"Do not speak if you want to live!"

Bill noticed Guy was about to say something else but Bill shook his head at him urgently enough to stop Guy from uttering a word.

The AIs pulled them through into another room where there were several transports waiting to have the junk on them offloaded by the robots further on. The two AIs fired at the last transport in the line and in an instant all of the junk that had been piled on its surface was totally disintegrated. Bill and Guy exchanged desperate glances, these AIs were not to be messed with! The AIs lifted the two men onto the transport and sat next to them.

On the touch of a button in one AI's arm the

transport lifted off the ground, making Bill and Guy feel decidedly unsteady. The transport flew above the line of laden trucks and zoomed out through large open doors beyond into the exterior. Bill held onto the edge tightly, worried he might fall off, but all of a sudden a clear Perspex type sheet emerged from the sides of the transport and lifted over their heads to form a clear bubble encasing them all inside safely. The two men were wide-eyed with wonder at this technology.

Far below them they could see green fields and trees and cows of all things! There was a river with horses alongside it. They thought they'd been taken onto another planet somehow, until they recognised aspects of the land below them where their homes were hidden.

***

Nobby looked at the flying transport overhead as it zoomed higher in the sky. *AIs and two people,* he thought to himself. *Not the correct AIs. That's not right. The transports are not for AIs and people.* Nobby went into the cargo bay, past all the laden trucks and saw scorch marks on the floor at the end of the line. Beyond was an open doorway. He went through it. A cage. An empty cage, with a broken door. Nobby saw the beds. *Beds are for people, not robots, not AIs.* He scanned the beds for heat signatures and found that two had been recently occupied.. *This is not right. I must report this,* Nobby thought to himself. Nobby pressed his mic control on his arm.

"Noblaczec?"

"Checker 159 reporting sir!" Nobby spoke into his mic clearly. Argo homed in on the signal and groaned, he didn't have time to deal with Nobby's incompetence right now.

"Noblaczec, is that you? I'm very busy right now can't it wait?" Argo spoke in an annoyed tone.

"Noblaczec deems it important sir." Nobby replied.

"Ok, make it quick then, what's your report?" Argo replied impatiently.

"Some humans are missing from the dome, sir. I saw them on a transport with wrong AIs, flying away."

At this news Argo's ears pricked up. "Say again Noblaczec." To which Nobby repeated the information word for word.

"What do you mean by *wrong AIs* Nobby?"

Nobby replied, "The AIs were Silvers, sir. Silvers aren't allowed in the dome, only Bronzes. Is this correct, sir?"

"Nobby, are you *sure* they were Silvers? Did you see their colours?" Argo asked excitedly.

"Yes sir! Noblaczec saw their colours. The cage doors had been blown open and two men taken with them on the transport. I saw it sir."

Argo couldn't believe that of all of the robots it was Nobby who had used his limited initiative to report this.

"Noblaczec, this is an excellent report! Did you see which way they were heading?"

"Past the mountains to the left of the dome, sir." Nobby replied, now very pleased with himself.

"Nobby, I might have to re name you after this ! Excellent work!" Argo enthused. "Over and out"

Nobby thought about this as he joyfully did a little robot dance then stopped abruptly.

"Oh no!" he thought out loud. "Not another name, I always forget this name! I'll never remember a new one!"

At that he returned to his duties around the dome. Another robot brought over some animals to Nobby, all secured by long intertwined leashes.

"Here you are, 159. I've been looking for you. Take these animals over to field two. You can shut them in there and then feed them".

The robot handed Nobby the leashes. Nobby tried to protest that he wasn't allowed near any animals, but the robot was taking no notice and handed him the leashes anyway.

"What are these animals?" Nobby asked bewildered.

To which the other robot replied "Goats"

"But what do I feed them with?" Nobby quickly asked, as the goats started to entangle themselves around his legs.

"Goats will eat anything! You'll find their food containers just inside the dome entrance." the robot replied and hurried into the dome.

Nobby tried to move forward, but it was difficult with the goats all wanting to go in different directions. After ten minutes of unravelling the leashes he started on his way towards field two, next to the cows. He breathed a sigh of relief when he finally got them into the enclosure, after only tripping up twice on the way. Now he was in the field he had to un-tether the goats and there were seven of them!

The first one he un-tethered was the smallest and it was relatively easy. The little goat trotted along and began to sniff around his new environment happily. Three more goats were released with varying degrees of difficulty. Every time he bent over to untie a goat the others would try and climb over him, so it became harder to do.

One of the goats, a big one with large horns, made it clear that he wanted to be un-tethered next, so Nobby untied him as quickly as he could. As soon as he was free he jumped and skipped towards the others, then went to investigate some rocks in the middle of the field.

Now Nobby had only two goats left to un-tether, much easier, he thought to himself.

He bent over to untie the knots when all at once a heavy whack on his rear knocked him over. He landed on his head in a muddy puddle in the grass. He looked around to see the big-horned goat looking down at him. Nobby was convinced that he was grinning!

"So that was you, was it?" Nobby spat at the goat. "Next time you want something I'll think twice!" Nobby added sheepishly.

He watched the goats for a few moments and checked they were securely shut in, then he went to get their food. Mud continued to drip down his face as he went.

He returned from the dome with three containers. He opened one up and looked at it unsure. He remembered what he'd been told "The goats will eat anything" and proceeded to empty the contents of the container into the field. Immediately the goats came running to inspect the food. A few started tearing at it, so Nobby was satisfied. Then the second container was different. It contained reconstituted foods, bread and carrots and other vegetables. He threw them into the field and the goats headed for that too and began to eat. The third container was full of water, so Nobby carefully placed that over the fence so it didn't spill everywhere. Feeling happy with his fulfilled task he went to take the two containers back to the dome, while the goats happily munched on all the offerings.

"Here are the containers returned from feeding the goats," Nobby started to report to the chief robot, "The other one is in the field holding the water" he concluded.

The chief took one look at the containers and said

"How many containers did you take?" To which

Nobby replied that he'd taken three.

"Three? There were only two! The water and the bread with vegetables. What else did you take..?"

Nobby was about to answer when one of the Checkers came over to the chief and interrupted.

"Chief, I can't find the clean linen container for the cage beds. It was down here a moment a...." He stopped on seeing the empty container in Nobby's hand.

Nobby dropped the container and ran.

Chapter 13

Transition

The Hubbites were still reeling from the news that the robots knew about their home and were debating what they should do about it. They had lived here so long in safety, now they were faced with either living in fear or moving somewhere else.

"But there's nowhere else to go!" cried one of the community.

"We can't just leave, how will we take all our belongings? We no longer have any vehicles to transport it!" cried out another.

"We won't be able to take everything, we'll have to make do for a while." replied Finch.

"It's all right for you, you're young enough to start over somewhere new, but there are others who don't have your energy or your strength." replied an elder.

Travis stood up. "There's one possibility we haven't considered." he stated. "We could ask Major White if we can stay with them."

The community muttered amongst themselves at this thought.

"But they might not want us there!" called out a voice. Before Travis could answer there was a loud bang on the Hub door, followed by three more.

The community froze into silence.

"Are there sentries outside?" asked Bull.

"No, we're all in here to discuss this." Travis replied, worriedly.

Bull looked into Travis' eyes and made his decision. "I'll go." Bull stated and made for the door.

"No!" Star shouted quickly. She didn't want Bull to get hurt.

Finch looked at Star, then at Bull worriedly.

"We'll both go." Finch said, perturbed at Star's reaction.

The huge metal door loomed in front of the two Hubbites, no longer a safety net for their community, but now simply a doorway to danger beyond.

Bull opened the door slowly. There in front of him stood a tall AI with menacing eyes. Behind him stood another, equally frightening to look at. They dwarfed the height of the metal door, which itself was over seven feet tall. Bull was frozen to the spot by the sight of the two giants. They had silver colours banded on their right arms and Bull saw the control panel lit up on their forearms and remembered the power it had wielded.

Bull stepped back a pace, as did Finch, then Finch found his voice.

"What is it you want? Why are you here?"

The AIs stepped forward, bending their heads to cross the threshold into the Hub. Bull and Finch stepped back further.

"We don't want any trouble. What is it you want?" Bull spoke nervously.

"You all need to come with us, now. You're in danger." The first AI stated in monotone.

"Danger? From what?" Bull managed, thinking, here was the danger right in front of him!

"Bring all your belongings, everything you can carry." The second AI added, ignoring the question.

The two AIs continued past Bull and Finch, down the tunnel into the hallway where the Hubbites stood shell-shocked. The AIs heads barely fitted into the height of the tunnels, but here in the hall there was more headroom and they loomed large and menacing in front of the community.

One of the Hubbites grabbed a rifle near him and began to lift it to fire, but the AIs immediately lifted their arms and were about to fire too when Travis intervened.

"Stop! Put the gun down, Pete. We can't win this!" to which Pete dropped the weapon and the AIs lowered their arms.

"Get your belongings and come with us, you are in danger." repeated the first AI.

"We have a shuttle awaiting outside to take you to safety."The second added.

"But we have animals here. What about them?" asked Robyn.

"You can bring your animals and all you need. You will not be coming back here." The AI stated in monotone.

"Where are you taking us?" Travis asked.

"Where you will be safe. No more questions. Hurry!" The AI bellowed.

The Hubbites reluctantly began to gather together their belongings, clothes, books, tools, food, the animals and their plants, the children's playthings and finally their weapons.

"Stop!" one of the AIs bellowed, looking at the weapons. "You will not need these. We will keep you safe."

He took the weapons to one side and threw them against the wall, where they broke into several pieces. Finch closed his coat and fastened it tightly to hide the weapon he had in his belt. Star looked at him and nodded, pointing to her own pocket, where she had also held onto a weapon hidden there.

"What about our beds and furniture?" Robyn asked again.

"You will not need them. We will provide these." The AI replied, herding some people, laden with goods, to the exit.

As some of the Hubbites emerged from the mine carrying their supplies, additional robots brushed past them and made their way into the Hub to help carry larger goods and ferry them to the awaiting shuttle.

It took more than an hour to ferry all their belongings to the shuttle, with robots helping with the heavy items.

Bull, Robyn and Finch were the last three left at the Hub with Travis to check that they had everything they needed. Travis looked wistfully at this place that they had called home for the last forty or so years. Here he had seen many a child brought into the world. Here he had also suffered the tragedy of witnessing a few deaths too. All memories that he would have forever, no matter what happened to the Hub.

Robyn had only known this home, she was one of the first born here, forty years ago and was sad at the thought of leaving it.

Bull and Finch worried about what was to come, but were glad they managed to hold onto some of their weapons.

Together all four turned to face the exit, sad at leaving this home that had kept them safe for so long.

The shuttle was filled with the whole of the quarry almost. It seemed huge to the Hubbites after the mine. Everything was clean, new and metallic on board. Shiny surfaces, strange seating for its passengers. The cargo area had cages for the animals and there were plenty of storage containers inside to hold their goods. Bull and his companions climbed up the ramp into the shuttle , followed by the two AIs, then the ramp closed into a door behind them,

Inside the seated area, the Hubbites looked at Travis fearfully, unsure what was to become of them. They had no walkie-talkies to inform Sgt White as the AIs had confiscated them en route to the shuttle. Now they were on their own. awaiting an unknown fate.

Travis felt he must say something to quell their fears so he said to the seated community that if the robots wanted them dead they wouldn't be here right now. That seemed to hit home a little as a few faces appeared more relaxed, but Travis himself wasn't sure, neither were the Scavengers.

The Hunt

Argo flew easily over the greening landscape, admiring the view as he traversed the land looking for the rogue AIs and their hostages. Argo passed over the dome and saw the cows and goats in the fields nearest to it. *But what is that in the field with the goats? It looks like sheets strewn and torn over the grass in places! Why? What was going on down there?* he thought. *Oh no! Could it be something to do with Noblaczec?* he thought suddenly. *Now that would make sense!* He'd check on that later.

Further on he saw a group of robots and Mechs down near the river below him. It looked like they were repairing the bridge that used to span the river there. *Hmm, they seem to be doing a good job,* he thought to himself. The simulator had produced stones that matched the bridge perfectly!

Oh! Change of direction needed here, he observed on his inner radar. He could see a large object approaching in his direction. He looked towards his left and saw a large shuttle heading towards him. He flew higher and avoided a collision quite easily.

"I wonder where that shuttle has come from?" he thought out loud.

Argo had covered a large distance when he spotted some people below him, near the mountainside to his right. Two people. He used his telescopic vision to focus more closely on the humans. No, they weren't his captives, these were other humans. So Argo concluded there was another community somewhere nearby. He scanned his beam along the terrain, but it did not pick up any homes nearby. He wondered if they lived in the mountain somewhere. A possibility, he decided. However, that would have to wait for another day. He had his mission mapped out. He needed to find these rogue AIs soon!

***

Down below, on the planet's surface, the Silvers had found a temporary hiding place. They would never be seen here they thought, pleased with themselves. It was lucky that they'd come across such a large complex on their relatively short flight they surmised. One of the Silvers had accessed the droids' databases and discovered this deep building had been found by one of the droids who had scanned the terrain on day two. It was ideal for hiding out until they could form a plan. They could not be seen down here below ground level.

***

Guy and Bill sat on the dusty floor of the broken mall, looking worriedly at the Silvers nearby. They were beginning to get hungry now, but were afraid to mention anything to the AIs. They would need some water too before long. Both scanned their environment for signs of anything edible, but there was nothing here. In the end Bill gathered his courage and asked timidly.

"When are we going to eat? We're both very hungry and thirsty. We haven't had a drink since last night."

The two Silvers looked at each other and started arguing. They weren't speaking English, but were evidently arguing. It was some strange robotic language Bill deduced, that they could communicate with each other without humans understanding what they were saying. There was much waving of arms and pointing fingers, followed by shaking heads. Bill guessed that they hadn't reckoned on humans needing food! Here, there was no chance of food being found for miles!

All of a sudden one of the AIs left, using the transport, leaving the other AI to guard the two humans. The two men hoped that he was leaving to get some food and water for them. Bill and Guy looked at each other, both thinking the same thing. If they could only figure out a way of overwhelming the remaining AI they could get away! But this magnificent creature was so advanced they were perplexed as to how they could achieve that. Bill and Guy thought it over and over.

They wondered if there was an on/off power switch anywhere on the AI, so they stared at his torso whenever they had the opportunity, without being spotted. His arms had lots of buttons on them, but they were dangerous buttons they knew, best keep away from them. They stared at other parts of the body. High on his right arm was the silver band that identified their rank, there seemed to be no buttons there. As the AI turned around they got a clearer view of his back. No buttons or switches to be seen anywhere! This was hopeless! No wait! There at the back of his neck there seemed to be a small inlaid panel. What was that for? Perhaps that was the key! But how were they going to reach that high? They had a quick think...

"Ahh!" Bill writhed on the floor in agony, holding onto his stomach with both hands. He rolled sideways on the floor groaning in pain.

"Look! My friend is sick! He needs help. There's something wrong with him. Quickly!" Guy called out pleadingly, as Bill rolled further away along the floor.

The AI at first simply looked at Bill writhing in pain, then he decided he should investigate it. He crouched down to look at Bill's face. In that instant Guy jumped onto the prone AI and pressed the inlaid panel. Bill held on to the AI's arms to give Guy a few vital seconds. All of a sudden the panel popped open showing a glowing green switch inside. Bill meanwhile had grabbed onto the AIs head .In a flash Guy flipped the switch before the AI could react. It turned red and the AI froze in position on the spot! All its lights on the panel in his arm went out. They'd done it! Bill jumped up immediately and high five'd Guy! What a revelation! If the Hubbites knew this... They quickly headed for the stairs to get out as quickly as possible before the other AI returned. They needed miles between them!

***

Argo circled the skies above, looking for any signs of the escapees. There was no trace of them at all. He swooped down lower to the ground in case they were sheltering beneath the canopy of the trees, which stretched for miles. Flying low like this he was soon rewarded. He saw movement in the shadows beneath trees ahead and headed silently towards it.

"No! Not another one! They're everywhere!" muttered Guy, disheartened now.

They had fled out of the ruins of the town and headed for the shelter of trees a few miles further on. They thought the trees would give them good cover from the enemy. But even here they weren't safe!

The large AI landed in front of where they hid, as though he knew exactly where they were hiding. (Which he did, due to his heat vision). Bill could see he was different from the Silvers that had captured them and taken them hostage. This one had gold bands on his arm. He had more human features than the others.

"Come out both of you. I mean you no harm. I know that you were kidnapped by some rogue Silvers a while back. I've come to rescue you." Argo spoke reassuringly.

Bill and Guy looked at each other. What was his

idea of rescue? After all, they'd been more or less imprisoned at the dome from the beginning. Sure they'd been fed and watered and generally looked after there, but still they hadn't been free to come and go. Bill reckoned though that he'd rather be back safely at the dome than be caught by the returning rogue AI. Argo spoke again.

"My name is Argo. I know one of your community. Her name is Lin, or Merlin if you prefer. She is six years old. We chat to each other all the time. I can take you back to her if you like."

Bill brightened a little on hearing this news and stepped forward. Guy was still sceptical, but followed Bill anyway.

"How did you evade your captors?" Argo asked once the two were stood in front of him. Bill didn't want to give away the fact they knew how to switch the AI off so before Guy could say anything Bill made up a story about tricking the remaining AI into chasing an imaginary rescuer while the other AI had gone off to find food. He added that they weren't sure where they'd been holed up, simply that it had been inside a building somewhere not far. He didn't want Argo going back to find the dormant AI or their story wouldn't add up.

Argo seemed satisfied with that and began to speak into his mic, ordering a transport to collect them all.

Silvers

The rogue Silver returned to the building and found the incapacitated AI kneeling on the floor and no sign of the humans. Angrily he switched the Silver back on and heard what had happened. The two AIs scanned the floor for heat traces and saw that the footprints led out of the building. They had to get their hostages back, or find some more as they would have no leverage for their plan without them.

The two mounted the transport and sped off in pursuit of the hostages. Scanning the terrain they followed the heat traces from their footprints, which showed them heading for some woods further on. They would have to fly low to pursue the humans or risk being caught on the mother ship's radar, which they definitely didn't want!

Down the transport flew until they were only a metre above ground. The trees were dense in places and it made it difficult to see from the transport.

"Let's get down and track them on foot from here." Silver 9 said.

"Yes, we can cover the terrain better on foot." responded Silver 7.

They hid the transport below the canopy of the trees and continued to track the humans.

Eventually Silver 7 picked up heat traces further up the woodland and the two continued following the footsteps. After some time they heard voices ahead. They stopped closer to the voices, hidden by large trees, and listened. It was Argo's voice! They recognised it immediately. Trust him to interfere! They listened carefully to what the humans and Argo had to say before deciding what to do. They had no chance against Argo, so they watched, annoyed, as the three of them got into a transport and flew away.

"What shall we do now?" Silver 7 asked.

"We go and find more hostages!" Silver 9 replied.

They headed back towards their abandoned transport and headed for the Hub, where they knew people were living. They flew low to avoid being seen and kept to the shelter of trees as much as possible.

They watched as robots repaired many roads and

bridges in the distance and sneered at the way Grey was reclaiming this planet. They didn't want this planet. They wanted to be up in space, battling it out with those aliens, following them back to their home planet and giving them a fight that they'd never forget!

They could easily destroy these aliens and their planet, for that matter. There was nothing better than wielding their power to destroy and conquer. Being here on Earth was a waste of time in their opinion. They needed to persuade Grey to let them have the new weaponry so they could travel through space and beyond to eliminate the aliens. All the power would be at their fingertips, they could do whatever they wanted with those weapons! But to get them they needed more hostages!

They swooped down low over the rim of the quarry, eyes scanning vigilantly for guards outside. No sign! This was odd. They jumped off the transport and headed towards the sheds. Empty. Beyond the sheds were large containers, but there was nothing of interest inside them. Further on they saw the large metal door. They blew it open with a blast of their inner weaponry and barged through into the tunnel beyond. They came upon a large room. They had to use built-in torches, which emerged from the left arm behind a hidden panel, to be able to see as the mine was in complete darkness. There were only a few embers glowing on the floor before them, where fires used to burn.

By the look of what remained the fires had been untouched for several hours. There were tables and chairs dotted around, with some empty shelves standing along the walls but there was no sign of people, perhaps they were hiding further along? The Silvers continued their search through the tunnels, the dorms, the playrooms, everywhere, but there was no sign of anyone still living here!

The Silvers became frustrated and angry and began to fire into the rooms they passed on the way back to the exit. The rooms exploded with rubble falling onto them from above, the beds torn to pieces, flew through the air and crumpled in a pile along the dorm floors, then the roof caved in on top of them. Everything was destroyed in their wake. For good measure, they blew up the entrance after they exited the Hub and rocks cascaded down the side of the quarry to block the old Hub entrance.

"Now what do we do?" Silver 7 asked his commander.

"We watch and wait for an opportunity." Silver 9 replied. "Let's go!"

They both leapt onto the transport and flew off to find a suitable hiding place, where they could still observe what was going on around them!

It will only be a matter of time, Silver 9 thought.

Chapter 14

Escape

On board the shuttle the Hubbites walked around the deck trying to comfort each other. Every now and then an AI looked in on them to check that all was well. In the crowd of sobbing people Travis and Bull hatched a plan to escape. Travis had found there were panels below the seating that held large conduits and cables that went goodness knows where, but the best thing about them was they would be big enough at a squeeze to hold a person.

Four panels, so four people could possibly get back to the planet to warn Sgt White what was going on. They were climbing high into space now and far in the distance they could see a much larger spaceship where they were obviously heading. Time to act now! Travis collected his three young scavengers and told them the plan. They passed on the idea to Robyn and the other elders, who quickly stood in front of the panels to shield them from the AIs.

Star entered a panel first, finding plenty of room for her slim frame to lie on her side. The panel closed on her after Finch held her hand warmly. Finch went into the next panel closest to Star, they were now head to head and could communicate quietly with each other. Across the aisle Bull squeezed his broad shoulders into the void and thankfully, did fit in , of sorts! Travis was the last in, next to Bull, his frame being slightly smaller he had more room to manoeuvre than Bull. He was head to head with his companion, so at least they could communicate during the long wait. too.

Star turned to a more comfortable position in the void. The cables at her back were quite warm, so it made her feel cosy. She heard Finch's voice call her softly.

"Star, can you hear me?"

Star replied "Yes, you ok?"

Finch tried to turn slightly so he could see her more. "Star, I've been meaning to ask you... how do you feel about me? Do you love me?"

Star was taken aback. They had never said the "love" word before, but she thought that she did love Finch, if that's what love was, certainly she felt a deep affection for him.

"Of course I do." Star replied. "Do you love me?"

"With all my heart and soul." Finch replied earnestly. "I couldn't imagine life without you. I don't want anything to spoil that. I couldn't lose you." he added sadly.

Star thought about his words, what they meant to her. It touched her heart to think that he felt this way about her. "You're not going to lose me, silly!" she smiled, blushing. "Where would I be without my lucky charm, eh?"

Finch seemed a little easier now, but there was still that nagging doubt in his mind. "Star? Do you love Bull too?" he ventured, with a tear trickling down his eye, fearful of the response.

Star was completely caught unaware at this question. She thought carefully about it. Yes, she did love Bull dearly, but not like she loved Finch.

"Finch, I love you above everything and everyone in this world. I do love Bull, but not as I love you. He is more like a big brother to me."

Finch held this thought close to his heart and

smiled, but he had to say it. "Star? I think Bull loves you, like I love you..." silence.

Star wiped the tears from her eyes. "I know. But it will never be, I promise you that."

Finch swallowed hard, he'd said it. He'd confronted his greatest fear and it was all right. He breathed a sigh of relief. "I love you so much."

"I love you too, Finch, very much." She reached her arm over her head to touch him and he held her hand gently and kissed it tenderly.

The shuttle docked gently with the spaceship, and the AIs gathered the Hubbites together and led them out. Robyn and Wren muttered quietly as they passed the hideaways,

"Good luck!"

The sounds of movement went on for a few minutes while the community left the seated area, then silence. Two minutes later the thudding footsteps of an AI were heard close to the hideaways heads. They all held their breath as the AI searched the room quickly then left. They breathed again. They lay there wondering if the shuttle would be heading back to Earth. What if they were stuck here for days? They hadn't planned for a long wait. All these negative thoughts milled around their minds while they lay there in silence. How long would they have to wait?

The answer came in half an hour. They felt the shuttle re-start its engines again. Was it returning empty? That would be ideal! But no, in clomped the feet of some AIs or robots, they were unsure. How many was hard to tell, but it didn't matter, they'd have to bide their time until an appropriate moment presented itself.

The shuttle left the spaceship and made its way down to the planet.

The Army

Sgt White and his unit observed the comings and goings of their dome with interest. So far nobody had found their home, although they'd had a lucky escape a few days ago, when sentries reported seeing a flying robot above the mountain whilst on duty. They had thought that they'd been seen, but obviously not, because no robots came their way. They were lucky. They hadn't heard from the Hubbites in days and hoped no news was good news. Perhaps they'd give them a call later on.

In front of them robots were herding sheep out of the dome and taking them to a fenced-off field nearby. Sgt White was impressed by how the planet had changed so much over the last month or so. The grass was lush in the fields and the skies remained kind. Large trees had sprouted out of nothing in a matter of days. These robots seemed to be renewing the Earth. Did this mean they were going to settle here? But what did robots need sheep and cows and horses for? He'd even seen goats and chickens roaming around another field. What was their plan for the humans living here? *Do they intend to capture us all?* Sgt White was puzzled by events that was for sure.

They had played an observation role in the last few weeks, not planning to attack until they saw something they didn't like. Their last attack hadn't exactly gone to plan anyway. It was futile to provoke this magnificent army. In a way, Sgt White admired their technology. He could never have imagined any of the weaponry or technology he'd encountered in his whole life. But here it was, on Earth, but where had these robots come from? Why were they terra forming with things they did not need? Very puzzling.

***

Hundreds of miles away the AIs operated their

advanced machinery deep in the oceans and lakes, filtering out the toxins in the water and regenerating plant and animal life forms to renew the water-worlds. Oceans began to revert to their tidal patterns, fresh water currents cleared the long abandoned river beds and flowed into lakes and seas across the planet. Weather patterns would soon settle with the ebb and flow of tides. Sea life began to spawn, starting with the chain of organisms required for life beneath the waves. Algae and seaweed and coral reefs were renewed like they'd never been away.

Freshwater fish began to appear in the now flowing rivers, with insects hopping along the surface to be devoured by fish and birds alike. Frogs jumped and hopped in ponds and pools and dykes, busying themselves with their search for food and shelter from the sun. The ebb and flow of life had begun!

The roadways were systematically cleared of debris and holes, filled and covered with a durable skin surface. Robot armies marched along them through the countryside with their transports, ridding the world of its cluttered remnants of the previous war. Vehicle shells and buildings that had been reduced to rubble were cleared away and processed in the domes .

Whole towns and cities around the world were cleared and tidied ready for rebuilding. The robots manufactured goods for rebuilding the towns using their regeneration machines in the domes. Steel beams and girders, bricks and mortar were reproduced and manufactured at the domes, then shipped out on transports to sites all around the world for use in rebuilding. They also transported them to sites nearby, ready for rebuilding, backwards and forwards over the months to come they would continue with their plan.

The sergeant turned around to look at what was approaching overhead. It was another shuttle. He'd seen many shuttles come and go over the weeks, transporting troops or machinery or cargo to the domes nearby. He watched it land not far from the dome and some robots came out pushing floating cargo containers down the ramp, followed by some AIs who made their way directly to the dome. Sgt White looked through his binoculars to see if he could recognise what their cargo was, but no, mostly the cargo containers were sealed.

They disappeared into the dome to deposit their goods, but what was that? Sgt White couldn't believe it. A person was crouched low near the rear ramp as though escaping from the shuttle! He pointed so his unit would see it too. Oh! Another, no, three others were now running, keeping low, out of the aircraft. Who were they? Could they help them? Sgt White's thoughts overtook him, he watched nervously as the escapees made their way to the shelter of some bushes not far away. The sergeant watched out for any AIs or robots returning to the craft too soon. What could he do to help?

The sergeant took two men down closer to where the four newcomers were hiding, whilst the others in his unit made for the opposite direction in the hope of creating a diversion if needed. The escapees were in luck, so far no robots had come out to return to the shuttle and the escapees continued to make their way, keeping low, heading towards the direction of where White and his men were hidden.

He recognised them now they were nearer, they were from the Hub, Travis, Bull, Finch and Star! How did they get in the shuttle? One thing worried the sergeant immensely. The shuttle had been inside the shielded part of the dome! If it was, then at any moment Travis's group could set off the perimeter alarm! He must warn them!

Sgt White got as close as he could, unseen and called as loud as he dared to the group.

"Travis! It's Sgt White. We can see you, stay where you are. You are inside the shielded area and if you come closer you might trip the alarm!"

Travis heard the sergeant quite clearly from his hiding point. He hadn't thought of the shield.

"What can we do?" Travis called back.

The sergeant replied quickly, "Wait until the shuttle leaves. They will have to lower the shield to let it pass, so when it moves, you move, ok?"

Travis agreed, grateful at Sgt White being there.

"Where exactly are we?" Bull called out.

The sergeant replied that they were a couple of miles to the north of the bunker and that he was luckily out on patrol in this area when the shuttle landed.

Suddenly a group of AIs returned towards the shuttle and entered via the ramp. In a few minutes the engines started and they began to lift off.

"When I say go, run!" shouted Sgt White.

The shuttle lifted up vertically into the sky and made a turn to face the direction it needed to go. Sgt White heard the engines speed up ready to fly away.

"Run!" the serge shouted and in an instant the four of them shot out of the bushes and headed straight for the serge and his group.

Progress

Bull asked Sgt White if they had any further plans to get into the dome, but Sgt White had decided that the dome was not a threat to them anymore. He had observed the comings and goings by the dome for weeks and he concluded that mostly the dome was a kind of regeneration plant. All the animals he'd seen emerging from there could only have come from the DNA the robots collected from the skeletal remains they had recovered and processed. He didn't know how, of course, he was no scientist and he reckoned their technology was so far advanced that they would have a hard task to try and figure it out anyway!

"But why are they regenerating all these animals? The robots don't need them as far as I can see. What is the point?" Bull was perplexed.

Sgt White looked worriedly at the escapees. "My theory is, these robots are simply a workforce for some other beings. Perhaps these beings are still in space right now, waiting for the regeneration to be complete before they set foot on this planet. *They* may be the ones who need these animals. I think they are preparing to settle down here and take over the planet."

Horrified looks came from the four escapees. "The Hubbites are up there in space right now! What are these beings going to do with them?" All four were now panicking at the thought that they'd left them to their fate!

Sgt White replied." I didn't realise your whole community was up there! This is not good news. Somehow we've got to get them out of there!"

Travis thought about his friends up there in space.

"I don't know sergeant. I'm not sure they're in danger. They said we were being taken up there to keep us safe. If they wanted to harm us they could have easily killed us all in the Hub, they knew where we lived. It doesn't make sense."

"I wonder what this danger is we're in?" piped up Finch.

"Perhaps we should take a look back at the Hub, see if we find some answers?" suggested Star.

"I doubt it." offered Sgt White. "They may mean a more general danger. But we can check it out if you want, no problem."

So they agreed to set off for the Hub to quell

their fears.

***

"It's been blown apart!" exclaimed Travis when they arrived at the quarry the next morning.

They'd travelled with very little rest across the new countryside to get to the Hub as quickly as possible. They had run down the quarry road into the deep basin that sheltered the mine.

Bull edged close to where the entrance had been, but there was no way to get inside. There were tons of rocks covering the whole entrance, as if part of the quarry had been blown up and the debris had landed on the Hub. It was impossible to shift any of the huge boulders. The metal door was in pieces , mangled among the debris.

"It wasn't like this when we left!" remarked Star.

"What did this?" Finch asked.

Bull and the others scanned the quarry sides and saw evidence of other firepower scorching some rocks here and there.

"Put it this way, it wasn't a landslide!" remarked Sgt White. "This has been deliberately blown up."

"Who could have done it?" Finch asked worriedly. But everyone shook their heads as they had no idea.

"So this was the danger we were in?" asked Star, puzzled.

"I think we need to be extra vigilant from now on." Sgt White decided. "Have you got any weapons?" he asked in retrospect.

The escapees opened their jackets to show their guns and explained how the rest had been destroyed by the AIs.

"Let's get out of here." The sergeant ordered briskly and all left the quarry with new worries on their minds.

The sergeant's walkie-talkie crackled and a message came over from a member of his unit back at the dome.

"Serge, you're never gonna believe this!" began the radio operator.

"What is it? What's happening?" The sergeant quickly answered.

"We're over at the dome area where you were with us before. We've been observing the comings and goings from the dome. Well, you won't believe what the robots have been bringing out of there!" the operator enthused.

"Spit it out, man! What did you see?" yelled Sgt White impatiently.

"Vehicles, sir! Cars and jeeps and lorries, all sorts. Some motorbikes too. All spanking new, looks to me! They've parked them up alongside the dome. It looks like an enormous car park! And they're still bringing out more!"

Sgt White couldn't fathom this for a moment.

"Are they in working order? That is, are they being driven out? Over."

The operator confirmed that they had all been driven out by smaller blue-coloured robots. He hadn't seen any of them before, but they came out of the dome and returned there. The sergeant pondered this news and told the operator to continue their observation until he returned.

Turning to his companions he mulled over the information. "I believe these robots have been regenerating the remains of the vehicles they took into that dome. That can be the only answer I can think of."

"But what would the aliens want with them? They have vehicles that hover for goodness sake!" remarked Star.

"Beats me." The sergeant replied.

Thoughts

The Hubbites entered the vast spaceship, worried and wide-eyed. Everything was so clean, sterile, new and shiny! A far cry from the home comforts that they had lived with at the Hub, but at least there they had been free! A Silver AI led them into a large room that looked like a cafeteria, with machinery along one wall with shelving underneath. The AI went over to one of the machines and pressed a button. The machine lit up.

"What would you like to drink?" The AI asked one of the children nearest him.

The little boy looked up nervously at the giant AI, but then said "Milk please."

The AI pressed a white button on the machine and a clear beaker dropped down onto the shelf below and white liquid began to pour into it. It stopped automatically before the beaker was full. He handed it to the child, who began to sip the liquid unsure.

"It tastes like milk!" he beamed at his mother, who had been too petrified to do anything.

The Hubbites smiled, relieved.

"We have any drink you would like here in this machine." The AI began." Just press the button and say what you'd like."

An elder went up to the machine and pressed a button and said, "Beer" and, as if by magic, a pint of beer was poured into a beaker in front of him. He looked at the others, then picked it up and took a sip.

"It's just like the real thing!" he said gleefully, to which the Hubbites laughed.

The AI went over to another machine to the right. This was much bigger with lots of buttons. There was a large cubby hole in the lower section. The AI demonstrated how to get a meal by asking one of the elders for their favourite meal.

"Burger and chips" he replied hopefully. The AI showed the symbols on the machine which represented the food items and a plate slid forward along the cubby hole and went into a hole at one end and re emerged once again with steaming hot chips and a burger sat on it neatly.

The Hubbites couldn't believe it! Food! Food that they could only have dreamt of before, deposited on a clean plate for them, freshly made! The excitement was tangible amongst the crowd, perhaps being captive wasn't so bad after all!

The AI pointed out the place for cutlery and condiments and told them to eat and enjoy. He added he'd be back later to talk to them again once they had eaten. He left the room through a door which opened automatically and it closed itself in his wake. One of the Hubbites tried to go through it too, but the door wouldn't open for him. He figured that they were locked in the room, but at least they could enjoy their favourite foods and drink whilst enclosed here! Everyone began to try out the buttons and many a happy face carried a welcome meal in front of them to the tables and chairs beyond.

Robyn had always wanted to try coffee with buttered croissants and jam. Her mother's favourite breakfast was now a reality in front of her. She inhaled the roasted scent of the steaming coffee and then poured a little milk onto it, just like her mother had told her. She blew on the hot drink and sipped it carefully. Glorious! It was rich and warming and satisfying. Next she broke her croissant in half and breathed in the smell of freshly baked pastry. The butter and jam were added sparingly and then it was time to taste it. She broke off a large mouthful and savoured it, making little hums of delight as it melted in her mouth, full of luscious flavour.

"Oh boy!" Robyn enthused, "I can see why my mother loved this so much! It's heavenly!" she drooled over the rest as bit by bit the food was devoured. She licked her fingers and lips and swallowed more coffee. "I'm kinda liking this place!" she added, smiling at Chaff, who was devouring chips with ketchup, most of the ketchup being around her mouth!

***

Argo drove the transport up to the dome, with Guy and Bill holding on tightly. He knew the two wouldn't be safe in the domes with the Silvers at large so he needed a shuttle to take them up to the mother ship. He led the men towards a shuttle which was being unloaded near one of the dome entrances.

Cargo containers, sealed and massive were being guided along by the giant robots on hover boards towards the dome. Bill looked with intrigue at how the machines moved and his eyes followed their progress with interest. He was so focused on their movements that he didn't notice the gigantic Mech standing in his pathway. Only when the Mech moved with its thunderous footsteps did Bill realise he nearly crashed headlong into the giant. He quickly sidestepped to get away from the monstrous object, remembering how one of them had fired on him after he'd surrendered long ago now. His head had spun quite a bit when he'd woken up and throbbed immensely for a few days afterwards. He didn't want a repeat of that!

Argo took the men into the shuttle and shut them in a small room while he radioed ahead that he was on his way with the two hostages. An hour later they were docking onto the mother ship in space above Earth. Argo had heard from his report that the Hubbites were all there too, for which he felt secretly relieved. Now the rogue Silvers would have a harder task to take them hostage whilst on board. He led the men through the shiny bright corridors to the galley to reunite them with their friends.

The automated door opened and Bill and Guy walked through into the crowded galley, followed by Argo. Robyn couldn't believe it when she saw her old friend back with his friends and family once more. They all ran towards him and embraced him joyfully. Little Merlin ran through the throng of legs and stopped in front of Argo and looked him up and down. He was huge! She wasn't expecting that.

"Ar..go?" she inquired, a little unsure. Argo smiled at her and said,

"Hello Lin, I'm pleased to see you at last! It's a happy day!" He ducked down to Lin's level and she ran into his open arms and gave him a big hug.

"You feel funny!" Lin stated bossily. "Are you a man or a robot? I'm not very sure.."

Argo laughed and ruffled her wayward locks as he lifted her up in his arms where she could see above everybody. She spotted her mum in the crowd.

"Hey mum! Look at me!" she yelled waving an arm, "I'm really high up!"

Her mother smiled broadly. "So, this is your friend Argo, is it?" Gale added. "We've heard a lot about you, Argo."

Robyn turned from her friend Bill and walked up to Argo, who was still holding Lin up high.

"Argo... I'm Chaff's mother. I'd like to tell you how grateful I am for what you did. I can't begin to tell you how happy you made me and my daughters. Thank you."

Argo put Lin down gently and stood in front of Robyn. He held his hand out in front of her, which she took and shook it gratefully. He replied.

" You're very welcome. Children should not have to suffer in wars."

The comment made Robyn think about this being. He had some human thoughts, she wasn't expecting that, how very strange. What kind of being was he? He had shaken her hand too, another human trait. His face looked almost human, but his body was a different matter. Was this the face of things to come, was humanity to be replaced by these beings? Was she looking at mankind's evolution?

Robyn realised she must have been staring and looked away, muttering a last "Thank you."

Argo watched the group huddle around Bill and he could see how much he meant to them. But what of Guy? He was standing almost alone. He had not received the same welcome as Bill. Why was that? Did he have no family or friends here? No.. He did not belong. He is from another community! Argo had quickly worked this out but said nothing, yet. He would bide his time.

Chapter 15

Nobby's Excursion

Nobby looked at all the vehicles in awe. He'd never seen things like these before. He'd been one of the robots to fill the vehicles with the fuel that had been created inside the dome. He'd watched the techni-blue robots drive them out of the dome with interest. One after the other, the operation to move them seemed the same. Most of them operated by voice control, others by use of a key and pedals and a stick to change gears, as the techni-blues had said.

Nobby was fed up of being stuck at the dome. He was always given the less important jobs, like stacking the crates or emptying the transports and even cleaning the milking parlour. He hated that! One good thing though, he wasn't allowed near the animals any more. Other robots fed them now. He was glad. They were smelly and dirty. He thought that was a rubbish job too. But these vehicles... that was a different matter. He thought they wouldn't miss one for a while, there were so many. He knew all the domes had loads of them outside them now. This was part of the schedule and they were up to date with the grand plan.

Nobby looked for a vehicle he could fit in. There weren't many of those! He needed one without a roof, with plenty of leg room.. He searched the rows of vehicles until he found a suitable one. It was a jeep, open-topped, voice-controlled. He checked the seat to see how far back it would slide... Enough! Perfect! He got into the vehicle and wedged himself into the seat. He looked around to see if any robots were nearby and if there was a suitable path to get away unnoticed.

When the coast was clear he spoke to the car. "Forward." The car switched itself on and Nobby could feel the power of the vehicle vibrating beneath him. The vehicle went forward and almost collided with a huge lorry opposite.

Nobby said, "Stop! Turn right!" just in time.

He looked at the control panel in front of him. There were lots of buttons. One of them was labelled "auto-drive". This sounded good to Nobby, so he pressed it. The vehicle continued on, making its own adjustments when corners needed to be negotiated. But the jeep spoke back to him.

"Destination, please?"

Nobby was now unsure what to say. He quickly thought about the place his unit had landed. *What did they call it?* He recalled his data file quickly, which brought him a map of his location and the surrounding area. He selected a place to go where he was almost sure no robots worked. He wanted to be somewhere pretty.

"Blue mountain." Nobby spoke to the vehicle, to which the vehicle gathered speed and drove off.

Nobby tried to duck down as low as he could as the jeep made off towards the shield, then he pressed his shield guard button to allow them through the invisible dome.. They'd made it!

The jeep found the newly repaired roadway and drove along at a reasonable speed. Nobby began to sit more upright to enjoy the view. It was getting prettier and prettier! He passed lots of trees and green fields and saw a river with their horses grazing beside it. A newly repaired bridge spanned the river and the jeep drove over it.

Nobby was glad that he'd got away and was now

enjoying the drive and seeing the beautiful scenery. Meadow flowers caught his attention, swaying gently in the light breeze they added beautiful colours to the landscape. He had never been on such a pretty planet before. He was enjoying the view immensely.

Half an hour into the excursion he saw some robots ahead on the horizon. They seemed to be repairing some stone walls alongside the road. He was heading straight for them! He quickly looked to see if there was a way to get past them unseen. He made the vehicle turn right just a few metres ahead where there was another narrower road. The jeep made some adjustments to its route finder and continued along its way.

"Phew! That was close!" Nobby said to himself out loud.

The jeep went past a field where there were lots of little semi-circular domes arranged all over it. Some fat pink animals covered in mud roamed around the field between them. Nobby wondered what they were and all of a sudden an almighty stink touched Nobby's olfactory sensors.

"Ugh! What is that smell?" Nobby said trying to cover his sensor, unsuccessfully. Soon the smell receded as the jeep continued onwards.

"This planet needs cleaning in some places!" Nobby spoke out loud. "They'd probably give me the job if the AIs found out!" Nobby concluded. He shuddered at the thought.

***

Further ahead on the country lane Sgt White and his group dived into a ditch by the roadside on hearing the noise approaching. The ditch was deep, providing enough cover for the group. Sgt White peered between the branches of a nearby shrub as the vehicle came closer. He was left dumbfounded. After the vehicle passed he reported to the group beside him that he'd seen a robot sat in an open-top jeep riding along as though enjoying the scenery!

"What on earth would a robot be doing with a jeep?" Finch queried.

"Looked like he was out on a jaunt!" Sgt White replied, laughing.

The group laughed and continued on their way along the road, headed back towards the Bunker.

***

The mountains loomed before Nobby, magnificent and domineering the landscape, but why they were called blue he had no idea. They didn't seem to be blue to him. The jeep spoke.

"Arrived at destination. Thank you."

It stopped by the side of the road where there was a wide bay and turned itself off. Nobby tried to un wedge himself out of the vehicle, but he seemed stuck fast in the seat! He pushed and twisted, trying his best to get out. All of a sudden he was free and he climbed out of the jeep... but the seat was still stuck to his nether regions, wedged tight!

"Stop right where you are!" A loud voice commanded nearby.

Nobby heard a gun being cocked. He put his arms up in surrender! He turned around to see five military types all pointing various types of guns towards him, some trying to stifle a laugh.

Nobby realised how stupid he must look with his backside stuck in a vehicle seat. He didn't want to harm these people. He had no authority to do so. So he kept his arms aloft and awaited instructions.

The Mountains

Argo flew overhead scanning the terrain below him. The mountains were magnificent with high crags and sheer drops on some sides. There was a lake near one of the peaks in a natural bowl in the land. Streams trickled down from it through the mountain, one dropping into a steep waterfall which cascaded over the rocky terrain below. Argo could see how it flowed into a river in the valley beyond, meandering like a silvery snake through the green of the fields in the valley. It was a beautiful sight to see. Argo was glad that Captain Grey had been right about this planet. No wonder he wanted to come here!

He sensed a presence nearby and turned his head around to see what it was. To his left a few metres away below him flew a magnificent bird with a wide wing span and a hooked beak, its golden brown feathers ruffling in the breeze. It caught an air stream and seemed to float effortlessly in its support.

Argo accessed his database to discover it was called an eagle. Eagles lived up in high land and he also found from the information that they were birds of prey. It was probably scouring the skies for its food thought Argo.

"Soon now, big bird, soon you'll have all the food you need. We're working on it." Argo spoke out softly to the bird below him. He was glad that they had recreated the birds that flew here in this beautiful country. He thought it fitting that the skies would have their share of beauty as well as the land below.

Minutes later he found what he had been looking for. Down below him at the foot of the mountain were some humans dressed in military uniforms, they were going inside the mountain and they hadn't seen him. Argo veered away slightly to come in from a different angle. Slowly he descended from the clouds and made his way close to the mountain's hidden entrance.

Argo watched from the cover of some trees as the men lifted a kind of net which had branches stuck in it and they went under and beyond it. He guessed the net was there to hide the entrance. It certainly did a good job. As they went out of sight beyond the net another two military men came out from behind the net and stood to attention in front of it. They were armed so Argo knew they must be guarding the entrance.

Argo was just pondering what to do when he heard the sound of footsteps and a vehicle coming along the road to his right. A vehicle? Argo knew that the vehicles hadn't been released from the domes yet, so he wondered if the robots had missed this one. He watched from his hideout as the vehicle approached slowly, with some men walking along side it too.

Oh no! Argo couldn't believe it! *Nobby!*

He saw the lumbering idiot being led , blindfolded, by the soldiers alongside him . He had his hands up as he walked.

"What has the idiot done now!" Argo muttered out loud.

He could not believe what he was seeing. As they got closer Argo saw that Nobby's bottom was wedged into a seat. It looked like the seat from the jeep the men were driving! It was completely stuck to his body!

"So that's what you've been up to, is it!" Argo muttered with a smirk on his face. "What a... Noblaczec! Yes it IS a good name for you Nobby!"

Argo muttered again to himself. What was he going to do with him? Perhaps he should leave him to his fate. Later he surmised that maybe having a robot inside the compound could be a good thing, so he did nothing. For now. After Argo left, Sgt White's patrol arrived with the escapees in tow and headed straight into the bunker to give news of the Hub to the major.

***

Up in the mother ship, the Hubbites had eaten their fill and were wondering what was to come when some more AIs came in through the automatic door. Everyone stopped talking and looked at them expectantly. One of the three Silvers spoke.

"I hope you have had your fill by now and enjoyed your food. We have just heard some news from the planet that confirms it was in your best interest to come here to keep safe, for we have discovered that your old home has been completely destroyed."

Everyone gasped in horror at the news.

"What do you mean destroyed? How?" asked one of the elders.

The second Silver replied.

"We saw a series of explosions on the planet on our scanners up here and looked at the satellite images. The explosions were at your home. It looks like someone blew up half the side of the quarry to engulf it. I'm sorry."

Robyn suddenly feared for Travis and the others. *Are they safe? Have they gone back there?* Worriedly she asked, "Was anyone hurt?"

The AI replied that he thought not because all of the community were here. Of course they couldn't know about the escapees. It looked like they had gone unnoticed after all. She felt both relieved and worried at the same time.

"How can we be sure that it wasn't you that blew it up? We have no means of verifying it!" the elder probed again.

A human voice replied.

"Because we do not wish to harm any of you, we want to keep you safe."

The crowd gasped when they saw a grey-haired

elderly man in a white suit appear from behind the three AIs.

"Forgive me. It's all so strange for you. Let me introduce myself. My name is Captain Tomas Grey. I am in command here. These are some of my troops."

The Hubbites were in shock. A human, like them, with a slightly German sounding accent. Although he was elderly, he seemed very fit and strong. He was holding a beautiful grey cat in his arms and stroking it gently. The cat's eyes gazed slowly from person to person around the room as though summing them up.

"And this is Smokie my cat." he added. "Before you ask, yes he is re-engineered from DNA. He has a perfect temperament for living up here with me."

Lin trotted over to the cat to stroke it and the cat purred loudly, lapping up the attention.

"I guess you all want to know what's going on?" The captain remarked.

All the Hubbites' attention were upon him in an instant. Would they get answers at last? Would they like what they hear?

Prisoner 159

Near the Bunker the rogue Silvers watched events from a distance. So, there were more humans here... interesting. That stupid robot actually surrendered to them! What an idiot thought the Silver.

"I think this might be a good place to get what we want." said the commander to his second.

The Silver agreed, they would bide their time here. They saw a Gold fly off into the skies not far away and they were glad they had plenty of cover from him.

"It's that supreme again! He seems to get around, unlucky for us. We'd better watch our step." The Silver commented.

Inside the bunker Nobby was taken into a small, locked room. where his blindfold was taken off. He was told to sit down, he was far too tall to be intimidated standing up! Nobby saw a bench and sat on it, luckily the bench held his weight. The car seat had unceremoniously been crowbarred off his posterior by two men previously.

A grey-haired man with a monstrous moustache stood in front of Nobby and behind him were several armed men , all pointing their guns at him. Nobby knew how pointless it was to try to shoot him, the bullets would just bounce back, probably killing one of them instead but Nobby didn't want to harm the people, but he had no authority to tell them much either.

Major White began. "We have brought you here so that we can find out what is going on . This is our planet and it seems to us you have made several changes to it since you arrived, isn't that so?"

Nobby replied "Affirmative." and then added "Don't you like the changes?"

Major White was taken aback slightly at his comment, but kept his face impassive. "That is beside the point. Why are you making these changes?"

Nobby pondered whether this was a secret he should keep, but decided that the answer was obvious anyway. "To make the planet better again."

"For whom?" the major probed.

"For everybody!" Nobby replied truthfully.

The major paced the floor with frustration. "Who do you mean when you say *everybody* ?"

Nobby thought about this. He must not mention his superiors, he didn't have clearance. "Everybody who would like it." he offered. The interrogation went on in the same vein, with the army getting nowhere fast with Nobby's answers.

Sgt White entered the office and asked to speak

to his father. The major stepped out and the sergeant briefed his father about the events at the Hub and explained about the four escapees from the shuttle and that they were with him here in the bunker taking refuge. The major explained how they were getting nowhere fast with the interrogation of the robot and wondered what to do with him. They couldn't keep asking him questions forever!

Elsewhere in the bunker Kia decided to go for a stroll in the beautiful sunshine with her boyfriend Jake, who was a few years older than her. He wasn't in the military because he wasn't deemed fit enough as he suffered from asthma. Being cooped up in the bunker didn't help Jake so Kia decided the fresh air would be beneficial for them both. She told her mother where she was going and had to promise that she would not wander far off.

They passed two sentries and reported where they were going. They were going to walk down to the river about half a mile in front of the bunker. It sure was a beautiful day. The sun was so warm and the grass had grown a lot now, it waved in the light breeze as though dancing to some secret music.

High overhead a large bird soared in the sky and the two sweethearts watched it swoop and sway in the air stream gracefully. Smaller birds now tweeted in the hedgerows along the edge of the fields, swooping down into the fields in search of worms to eat. The planet's creatures were returning to life at last and it was beautiful to behold. The two walked hand in hand, happy and contented with their new world.

Meanwhile, in the bunker, Nobby stood up suddenly and shouted out

"Danger! Danger! There is danger in this sector. Alert! Alert!"

The major and his team stood back in fright, unsure what to do.

A loud boom echoed in the air, followed quickly by another.

Fragments of clothing were strewn across the field, flying gently as the breeze lifted them from field to hedgerow. The birds had swooped up into the sky on hearing the loud noise. They twisted and turned in the sky until they felt safe enough to return to their routines. Large crows veered towards the field from a copse nearby and started to gather around the bloodied meat that was deposited in chunks everywhere. They began to peck at the new supply of food and jousted for the best positions.

A leg lay torn and bloodied not far from a hand which had a lover's ring on it. The lovers' faces were no longer recognisable, with shattered features and lifeless eyes staring at the beautiful sky. The Silvers turned around and were satisfied that Captain Grey might take heed of them now. They could kill more and more people until their demands were met!

The sentries ran to get help to investigate the noise ahead and together they led the way towards where the explosions were heard, in the direction that Kia and Jake had gone! The scene of horror they witnessed made some of the hardened men vomit uncontrollably. How were they going to tell Sgt White?

Terror

The Bronze called to Captain Grey on his holographic screen.

"Captain we have spotted the destruction of two humans on the planet at sector J2. When zooming in on the activity we saw the two rogue silvers leaving the scene. One of them wants to speak with you sir."

Captain Grey was furious." Why haven't these

two been captured yet? They must have more ingenuity than I credited them with! All right, B7, connect me. Let's hear what they have to say!"

The Bronze patched the captain to the Silver rogue commander and his holographic image appeared in front of the captain's table.

"How dare you defy my orders! What can you possibly hope to achieve by killing innocent people?" Capt Grey bellowed.

The Silver commander looked menacingly at Grey then replied in an equally menacing tone.

"Ah! Captain. I see you have finally made time to talk to my team. I believe you have by now spotted what we are capable of if our demands are not met?"

The captain's eyes filled with hatred towards this Silver.

"Demands? Your demands? Who are you to demand anything? I am your captain, you follow my orders, not the other way around!" he spat bitterly.

The Silver smirked, un-phased by his tone.

"Captain, you made a mistake by not engaging further with those alien invaders. We should have wiped them out before they had a chance to regroup. Your precious planet will only see the return of these species and they will decimate all that you have tried to achieve here! All we ask is that you give us a ship with the new weapon on board so that we can finish them off! Otherwise, well, you saw what we can do...."

"You are murdering people here so that you can go and kill a few more on another planet? That's what this is all about?" The captain looked in disgust at the Silver. "We were going to chase after these aliens when we were done here anyhow! It was to prevent any such attack on Earth that we created these weapons in the first place! And now, here you are, destroying the very life forms I came here to protect! Why would I possibly bow to your demands?"

The Silver simply shook his head nonchalantly.

"Captain. That is *your* plan, not ours. We want to rid the galaxy of these invading aliens. There are many species out there that need to be eliminated. We simply want to be the ones to do that—now!"

"And then what? What happens when you've conquered, or I should say more likely , annihilated the aliens? What do you do next? Go from galaxy to galaxy on a killing spree? That is not why I created you!"

The Silver no longer smirked, but seemed to think about Grey's remarks.

"Why did you create us? What are we here for?"

Grey thought sadly about his great plan, how it was going wrong. What had happened to make this bloodthirsty behaviour?

" I mistakenly thought that if you were a highly evolved being that you would see the futility of war and how it can only bring about sadness. I dreamt of having beings who could see beyond man's selfish needs and created you all to protect the future! How wrong I was... with you at least!"

Grey thought about what he could do. He needed to get these Silvers away from humans, away from the planet.

"I agree to your demands, on the proviso you do not harm another human."

"Agreed." said the Silver. " Send down a fully weaponised ship to the planet to this grid location, piloted only by a robot. Any Silvers that wish to join me can come along too, nobody else. And keep that Gold supreme away! I don't want to see him anywhere near the location.!"

The captain agreed to do so within the hour, to which the Bronzes on the bridge looked stunned by his surrender.

The Silvers talked about Captain Grey's easy surrender to their demands.

"He's up to something. He would not have yielded so easy if he didn't plan to do something. I think we need more insurance, don't you?"

The second Silver nodded and smiled. They made their way towards the Bunker...

***

Nobby was fully aware that there was danger to come and he needed to do something about it. An urgent knock on the door made Sgt White grab the handle quickly.

"What is it?" he demanded sharply.

The sentry was ashen-faced and trembling, he stuttered out the words in his horror.

"Your..r d daughter c..cap tain... she has been murdered , out in the fields sir!"

Sgt White fell backwards onto the door he was holding, he could hardly breathe with shock. His daughter? Killed? He scrambled over to the chair nearby and fell into it. Major White took over with a heavy heart. He ordered men to guard the entrance with heavy artillery immediately and when the men rushed past him to perform their duties he turned around with a tear rolling down his face. He looked at the upright robot with fear in his eyes.

"Who did this?"

Nobby realising they were still in danger replied quickly. "Traitor Silvers sir, two of them. I must go to protect your community!"

At that he started marching towards the closed door, and all the remaining soldiers in the room lifted their weapons instinctively. Nobby took no notice and the major, realising they could not hope to stop him waved them down. The door had closed already, it had automatically locked, but Nobby marched straight through the door, ducking as he went, leaving the door in pieces behind him.

He activated his tracer beam and continued in the direction of the exit. All who saw him ran out of his path, he was too powerful for any attack on him. The voice of Major White was heard over the loudspeaker,

"Let the robot pass unhindered."

Bull and his friends watched worriedly as the robot went past them towards the inner exit chamber. He was entirely focused on where he was heading, nothing could stop him. He was like a man on a mission.

Nobby found himself facing a large doorway manned by guards, but instead of firing at him they opened the entrance way and let him pass. They watched in confusion as he continued marching purposefully towards the exterior door. Again the guards let him pass.

Outside the bunker there were a dozen or so soldiers armed to the teeth posted there to defend the Bunker from any attack. When they saw the huge robot appear behind them they weren't sure which way to point their weapons.

Nobby spoke. "You are in great danger, stand behind me. Your weapons will do no good."

His tone was not threatening, but more of a command. The men watched as Nobby went to stand in front of the bunker entrance, legs and arms apart as though he was ready to wrestle with something. The men looked at each other hesitantly, but stood slightly behind him still focusing their weapons out towards the land in front of the Bunker.

The Power of One

The men waited expectantly for some being to

appear in front of them, brandishing weapons, but instead an almighty explosion shook the whole front of the mountain. The men were looking into a white heat which then turned into amber and red, billowing and bubbling menacingly in front of them! But the heat was bearable!. Right in front of Nobby an invisible shield was protecting him and the soldiers from harm. Another and another explosion tore at the shield with writhing flames and billowing clouds of fire storming towards them, but Nobby's shield held!

The men looked in awe at Nobby.

"I'm glad he seems to be on our side!" one of the soldiers muttered to a colleague.

When the explosions died down and the smoke cleared the soldiers were facing two enormous AIs, standing about eight metres away, their arms held out in front of them as though preparing to fire a gun, only there was no gun. When they saw Nobby they cursed and began to rain bullet upon bullet at his shield to no avail. The shield held!

"I thought this Checker was a basic model?" inquired the second Silver.

"So did I" said the Silver commander, "But it seems he has some hidden talents!"

Then both AIs fired again, trying a range of their weaponry over and over to try and destroy Nobby's shield. All the fire that was aimed towards Nobby and the men simply met with resistance at the shield.

On board the mother ship the Hubbites were making themselves comfortable at their new quarters, a large common room with plush seating and some sleeping areas alongside it opposite a long corridor. They seemed more at ease now that Captain Grey had filled them in on his plans. They no longer felt so afraid, but were worried about those left behind on the planet with the rogue AIs at large.

"I hope they made it to the Bunker all right." Robyn remarked to Wren.

"Oh, Bull is very capable! I'm sure everything will be all right." replied her daughter.

Robyn noted that she had not mentioned the others, was she developing a crush on Bull she wondered?

"Yes, he certainly seems to be, and very handsome too.." she probed, smiling at her daughter. Wren blushed knowing she'd been found out.

"Does he know you like him?" inquired Robyn. Wren twirled her hair in her hands trying to look away from her mother's gaze.

"Mum! You're embarrassing me," whispered Wren shyly. But her mother looked her in the eye until she got a response.

"Okay. Well, he does know, because I kissed him the other day." Wren admitted still blushing.

"Oh." Robyn nodded. "And did he kiss you back?" she probed further.

Wren looked affronted. "Of course he kissed me back! Mother! I have to say though, I think I took him by surprise, because it took him a few seconds before he did kiss me back. But it was wonderful! We huddled up for a long time around the fire that evening."

"Do Star and Finch know?" Robyn asked further.

"No, nobody knows, we were alone. You're the first person to know."

All of a sudden a Silver opened the lounge door and brought in some people.

"Meera! Kian!" Guy called out excitedly and ran over to the new group. *Obviously from the Bunke,* thought Robyn. She watched as the group of military clad people hugged and greeted Guy happily. *It seems we have an increase in our numbers*, she thought cheerfully. She was so pleased that Guy finally had someone he knew well here. Bill realised that these were the soldiers that had been netted the day they tried to attack the dome. *So they had been looked after too,* he thought. *Maybe Grey's people truly are here to save us after all.*

***

Grey was going over the last piece of the plan to deliver the ship to the rogues with Argo. He was aware that they had continued to fire on the Bunker people despite their agreement. It was imperative that the ship was delivered as quickly as possible to save further bloodshed!

Half an hour later, as the ship landed just beyond the Bunker, the two Silvers turned away and left the Bunker to Nobby's defence. Nothing had penetrated his shield!

Damn the robot! The Silvers came up to the ship and ordered the ramp to be lowered. Two other Silvers came down the ramp to join them.

"We wish to come with you to defeat those aliens." called out one of them.

The other said that they'd checked the inside of the ship and found the weapons intact as ordered and only the pilot robot on board. The rogue Silvers wished there had been more to join them, but two more were very welcome.

"Come, lets board our ship before Grey puts up resistance. We'll be after those aliens in no time at all! It's a shame we couldn't get more hostages, but Grey won't know that!" laughed the Silver commander.

All four marched up the ramp into the ship and the Silver commander saw that the weapon certainly was on board! He had great plans for that weapon! The two rogues went up to the control area to check that it was indeed a basic pilot robot sitting there. Seeing the robot sitting placidly awaiting instructions the two rogues sat down just behind the pilot. The other Silvers went to check that the ramp was up and the weapon secured before lift-off. The rogue Silvers were basking in the glory of succeeding in their mission to leave the planet when very quietly the cargo container that held the spare parts for the weapon slowly opened.

Elimination

The two extra Silvers stood in front of the weapon and reported to the commander that all was ready for lift-off. The rogue Commander ordered the pilot to engage thrusters for lift-off, but the pilot didn't move a muscle. The rogue AIs turned to face the pilot and shouted the order again. Perhaps he hadn't heard the order. Again, no response.

Whilst the two were so focused on the pilot's lack of interest the parts containers behind the weapon were now fully opened and out of them came four Argonauts, led by Argo. They stood in a line facing the rogues, with the other two Silvers beside them. As the rogues turned around they saw the Golds immediately. They stood up and barked at the other Silvers to attack them, but instead all four Argonauts and the two Silvers fired with great precision at the two rogues until they were torn to pieces. The so called pilot fell onto the floor, it was a simple carcass, devoid of life or intelligence, just there to fool the rogues.

The two remaining Silvers looked down at the pieces on the floor in disgust.

"You bring down the name of Silver into the gutter, how dare you bring shame on the rest of us who want a world free of tyranny! Go back to the dust where you belong!"

The Silver gave an almighty kick to the piece that was the commander's broken head, all function in it now obsolete. They turned to the Argonauts and looked ashamed, but Argo told them they had done well. It took more courage to go against their commander than to join him in laying waste to civilizations across the galaxies. They should feel proud. They had kept their integrity.

Argo opened the ramp again and walked out of the ship. He headed towards the Bunker entrance where Nobby still stood, defending with his shield. Nobby wasn't sure if he was going to get told off for being here or not. After all, he had stolen a vehicle and got caught! Argo stood in front of him smiling. Nobby decided this was a good sign.

"Nobby, you have done yourself proud today! It was a very brave thing you did, defending these humans without having orders. That shows initiative. I'm so sorry I undervalued you. I was wrong."

Nobby heard him say he was sorry and he said he was brave. That meant Argo is not cross thought Nobby.

"Thank you sir. Nobby couldn't let these people die. Captain Grey wants to save them I know. I did what I could."

Argo held his hands on his hips and shook his head.

"Of all the crew under Captain Grey's command I never saw how valuable you could be, Nobby. Forgive me."

Nobby was now confused. Forgive the supreme? This didn't sound right... But Argo was smiling, so Nobby tried to smile too, but it turned into a sort of grimace, which made Argo laugh even more.

"I suppose I'd better re-name you after all this bravery." Argo offered.

Nobby was sure he couldn't remember another new name so he quickly responded. "Oh no sir! Nobby likes his name. I don't think you need to change it. I feel Noblaczec suits me well sir!"

Argo laughed at Nobby's comment. "Okay then, Noblaczec, but I think you deserve a reward for what you did. What would you like most of all?" Nobby thought about it, then replied.

"There are two things if you don't mind sir? I would like to be able to work with the other robots rebuilding the homes if that's all right, sir?"

"And the other?" asked Argo.

"I would like you to bring the two humans killed by the traitors back to life, sir."

Argo marvelled at this robot. Out of all the AIs and robots created by Grey this was the most compassionate, unassuming and brave being that had been created. To face up to the Silvers with their superior firepower like that, to save the humans, not even knowing if his shield would hold or not. And now he is thinking of the humans again. He deserves so much more than he asked for. He would check if his idea would have Capt. Grey's blessing first.

Argo looked at Nobby, still in his defensive pose in front of the Bunker, with a larger group of humans behind him now. He recognised some Hubbites there, ones that he thought had been taken up to the mother ship for safe keeping. *These humans are very resilient,* Argo thought to himself.

"Nobby, you most certainly can have both of your rewards and I think also that you can expect one from Captain Grey once I've spoken to him about what you did here too. Well done!"

Argo saluted Nobby for the first time. Nobby was taken aback by this and was unsure what to do, but instinctively copied the salute, to which Argo smiled again.

Behind Nobby Sgt White was reeling from the information he'd just heard. Kia and Jake could be brought back to life? He didn't believe what he was hearing, but Bull and Travis told him that Argo had done the same thing for three of their own who had been killed by the alien strike. The sergeant rushed into the Bunker to find his wife and his father to convey the news.

Argo asked Nobby if he wanted a lift with him to the dome in the ship where they could renew the two humans. Nobby was keen not to get wedged in the jeep's seat again so he agreed. They both set off to collect the human remains. Argo let the humans keep the jeep, because the intention all along was that the humans would receive the newly renovated vehicles as and when they were needed.

The major and his daughter in law took the news about Kia and Jake being brought back to life as a sign that their world was on its way to being a lovely place to live in once again.

Chapter 16

Rebuilding

Bill, Robyn, Chaff and Wren were enjoying their coffee, lounging about in their new environment, when Professor Stark entered the lounge with Captain Grey. The Hubbites were asked by the captain to gather together in the lounge to discuss something. So a few of the Hubbites went to round up the stragglers who were elsewhere in their new home aboard the ship.

As the group settled down into the plush seating Captain Grey stood on an elevated dais to address them. "Good morning everyone, I hope you have all settled down well in your temporary accommodation on board ship? I hear from my ship's crew that you are enjoying the food on offer anyhow!"

At that the group chuckled, but all ears were pricked on hearing the term *temporary* to describe their accommodation. What then was going to happen to them next, they wondered.

Captain Grey continued. "For those of you who haven't met him yet, this is Professor Stark, who has travelled the galaxies with me all these years. It was he who, amongst others no longer with us, created the robots and first AIs you have encountered accompanying us. He led the way to the new technology that evolved via the AIs to produce advanced artificial intelligence and weaponry that we have at our disposal. We have travelled the skies to collect resources, technology and ideas that would help us achieve our goal. Ultimately, to defend and save this planet and kick-start it back into life. To do that we need you."

The crowd grew more excited at this revelation and eagerly awaited the next part of Grey's talk. It was Professor Stark however, that began to talk next.

"It has been a long time, but I reckon some of you might be able to remember the time before the Earth was decimated by the alien invasion." At this some of the people began nodding in agreement.

"Well, we need to gather together a fact-file of your skills, to indicate how you might be of help in this new society we are developing. This same speech is being conducted on board all of our other ships by my Argonauts, the supreme AIs, in all parts of the world as we speak. We need an indication of what trades or skills you have to offer, our most immediate needs are those of construction workers and farmers so that food can be grown as quickly as possible on our planet to feed you all."

Bill put his hand up to speak. "Professor, can you tell us roughly how many survivors there are on Earth? We have no idea because of the lack of communication in the past."

The professor replied. "That is a very good question. To be able to survive we need to have adequate numbers to manufacture etc. And I have to say that there are roughly only 39% of Earth's population still surviving today."

The Hubbites were surprised at this low number. They let the professor continue.

"Some parts of the world however have had whole civilisations wiped out, for instance the polar regions became so cold permanently that no one survived. The larger cities throughout the world had hardly any survivors, due to incessant bombing by the aliens. Most survivors were found in more rural areas and, in the desert, communities seemed a little more intact."

"We're all willing to work to make this world a better place to live. I'm sure most of us can turn our hands to anything practical." Bill stated. "We have a farmer in our community. Isn't that right Pete?"

A man stood up, well-built, muscular and replied. "Yes professor. I used to own a dairy farm before the war and I kept pigs and goats too. My sons here say they would be interested to learn from me how to care for animals." Pete sat down.

"Excellent! Just what we need!" Prof. Stark announced. "Do we have any construction engineers here by any chance?"

Another elder stood up. "Yes sir, the name's Mark Renfrew, I was chief engineer for local council contracts." he offered. "I would be glad to help if you need me."

The Professor and Captain Grey were pleased with the response from the group and a file of their skills was compiled very quickly.

When the list was complete the Captain spoke again. "We will be taking those of you with the skills we need immediately, down to the planet to begin work as soon as possible. Pete, that'll be you, with your sons and, Mark, we could do with you too, also those three of you who know how to tend to horses will be needed. If all of you could go with my Silvers, then the rest of you will be relocated in new housing on the planet as soon as it's completed. We'll let you know if we need any other trades later this week. Thank you all for your help."

At that the captain and the professor got up to leave and the Silvers escorted Pete and the others needed out of the lounge to prepare for their journey down to the planet. Quick farewells were made with family and friends, then the Hubbites were alone again to digest the news.

"How exciting!" remarked Wren. "Does this mean I'll have my own room at last?" she inquired excitedly.

"Oh Wren! Trust you!" her mother laughed.

Homes for Hubbites

Pete was shown the milking parlour by Silver 4 and he was given the schedule that had been kept by the robots up to date. Pete was surprised to find that they had been doing a good job of looking after the cows so far. However, now he had to make sure the cows were kept healthy with their diet and minerals and injections needed to evade illnesses and he produced a list of things required for the Silver to manufacture as soon as possible.

Next he went with a blue over to the pigs, using one of the vehicles outside the dome to get there. It had been a long time since Pete had been in a vehicle and an even longer time since he saw beautiful fields of green surrounding him in the countryside. It felt good to be looking at decent land again. He asked the blue if they had any tractors and hay, to which the blue replied they had several and a large supply of manufactured hay inside the dome. Pete thought that things might work out fine after all.

He explained to his sons how the hay was important for the animals and how the fields could be ploughed for planting with the tractors. The blue also confirmed that they had plenty of seed for planting too. It got better and better!

Mark Renfrew and a few able bodied men looked at the site where the robots intended to build the first homes and agreed the location was suitable, close to a supply of water and not too far from roads for transport. The building materials had begun to be manufactured and lay in neat stacks in an area nearby.

With a lack of an architect in their community, Mark had to come up with a floor plan for homes for the Hubbites and he took great care to ensure that there was adequate room for parking a vehicle at the property as well as garden space for families. He of course had free reign on room sizes and made sure everyone had plenty of room to feel comfortable.

He project managed the construction, from the manufacture of sewerage pipes and sanitary ware, building blocks and kitchen equipment, down to the roof tiles and doorknobs! He became an adviser for just about anything to do with a building. He made sure that there was some difference between the appearance of the various houses so that they had some individuality about them.

The Mechs and robots did all the heavy work, with Mark's human crew overseeing where things went and in what order. Later on in the month some members of the Bunker community had been asked to help with the construction in terms of laying the cabling for the lighting and heating for the houses, run mainly by wind and solar power. More cabling was manufactured at the dome and the houses were rising quickly.

Large cranes were produced from somewhere by the blues to help with the finishing off of rooftops and taller constructions further down the valley, where shops were being built! Mark wondered what on earth was going to be in the shops and how people were going to pay for things anyway, but as things went he reckoned Captain Grey and his robot army had that covered too!

Five months after construction began the first families started to be housed in the newly built homes!. Robyn, Chaff and Wren surveyed their new home, with its bright red door inset with a stained glass window with a bird with a red breast depicted on it. It was so pretty! The house had three good-sized bedrooms which were even carpeted! Robyn couldn't believe it! She thought she would never see a carpet in her lifetime. The bathroom was beautifully tiled all around and there was a large mirror above the basin, which reflected light around the room. Downstairs there was a large lounge with plush comfortable seating and a glass coffee table standing on bright steel legs.

Every home had a computerised screen on one wall, which became a system of communication between people near or far. Later Stark was going to re introduce mobile phones again, once the prioritised goods were completed. There was a white bookshelf for Chaff's selection of books along one wall and on another wall, large glass folding doors that opened out onto the pretty garden, which was laid to lawn with pink roses along the back wall.

The kitchen was modern and sleek, with integrated appliances hidden away behind shiny black doors which opened just with a touch of fingertips. Robyn felt warm tears of joy fall down her cheeks at such a beautiful place that was now her home. When she opened some of her cupboards she found them full of jars and bottles and packets of food. All provided to each new family moving in! The garage even had a charger for the electric vehicle she had been given. Life was good again.

Bull, Star, Finch and Travis had come along to help fit out the homes with the Bunker crew when they found out Grey's re housing plan and Wren was delighted to see Bull fighting fit since they had last seen each other on board ship over five months previously. Wren excitedly showed Bull her room and hugged him tight. She had missed him very much, but Bull seemed rather quiet and pensive, with much on his mind.

As well as houses for families, Mark had designed a long, two-story block of flats for the singles and young couples without children. These were on the opposite side of the road to the houses and were equally well-fitted out, with either one or two bedrooms. There was a communal area built inside the block with comfortable seating so that the community would keep the sense of closeness they had previously if they required it.

Many would find it hard to live alone after being part of a large group for so long. Finch and Star were to live in one of the flats and next door to them Bull and his mother were allocated one. Each of the bird community had a stained glass window with a bird on it to keep their feeling of being part of the bird community. It was inlaid into their front doors in beautiful colours.

Each home had solar panels and there were wind turbines dotted along the new town providing more energy for its inhabitants. Streets were lit once again and people were able to walk about almost normally, if they ignored the fact that Mechs and robots might pass them by on their morning stroll!

A new army barracks was built much later on for the people in the Bunker community who wished to retain their military lifestyle. They still retained their Bunker in the mountains as a depot for all their munitions. There had been some debate with Captain Grey whether they really needed any weapons any more, but Major White felt safer knowing they were there in case of emergencies, so Captain Grey did not force the issue to keep the people feeling safe. After all, not all of the AIs had been trustworthy, so he took their point.

The months went by and the Mall was re-built in the next town, with supplies manufactured by the robots in the dome. Fuel stations for the vehicles sprouted up, cafes and libraries with computerised data banks were built. The cafes contained the same wonderful system as on board Captain Grey's ship, but this time it would be necessary to pay for it.

As for the economy, Professor Stark decided to introduce credit cards for every person over fifteen. Each card had twenty thousand credits on it and was used for buying anything. Where there were jobs to be had, wages ranged in order of complexity of work, from an annual salary of between twenty thousand and fifty thousand credits, so people could get the economy started once more.

The Mall

Wren and Star were amazed at the range of goods they saw in the newly built stores. They coveted the glittering array of clothes and shoes and decided their first purchase was to be something to wear!

Bull and Finch however, had different ideas. In the mall there was a shop selling tools of all sorts! Both the men viewed the Aladdin's cave animatedly, trying out the weight and feel of objects before deciding to purchase what they considered to be "useful!"

They had driven in Bull's new jeep over to the town to see the changes from when they were last there, it seemed a lifetime ago. Star was embarrassed to see that the stairs really did move up and down just as Bull had told her and got a ribbing from Bull when they tried them out. They went towards the shop where they had found the haul of coats and boots many months previously. They saw to their delight that it had been restored to a clothes shop once again! The mannequins were no longer dust covered and strewn everywhere across the floor, but now they stood regally, posing dressed in fabulous clothing in the front window. The whole mall was alive with colour and light. Survivors from the Hub and the Bunker milled around enthralled by what they saw around them.

In the mall cafe Star, Finch, Wren and Bull sat over steaming hot cups of coffee watching people go by, enjoying the normality of shopping. Star noticed that there were many new faces milling around the shops. Star didn't think they were from the Bunker community and they certainly weren't from the Hub, so obviously other survivors had been found not far away.

"Strange isn't it?" A voice remarked from a table behind them. A young couple around their age sat with two glasses of cold drinks with straws bobbing up in the liquid in front of them.

Star and the others turned towards the speaker, a man in his twenties.

"It is surreal that we're sitting here, taking in the relaxed atmosphere as though it was the most normal daily occurrence. Yet a few months ago we could hardly breathe outside of our hideouts, we were frightened recluses, scraping a living in the dust and debris of civilisation." He held out a hand to Bull, the closest to him. "Hi, I'm Jason and this is my partner Fia."

They all shook hands introducing each other.

"Where were you living?" asked Finch, taking another sip of his coffee.

"We were surviving in the basement of a ruined apartment block in the next town along from here. There were about forty of us, all survivors of the apartment block basically. Our parents and grandparents all hid down there when things got bad. They brought a few belongings down there gradually before the block was trashed. Only the basement survived. We were lucky.

My father said it was very hard in the beginning and some people died, but things got better and a routine was established. They lived off the food that was in the basement store in the beginning, then they started to grow their own food. We scavenged like everyone else. And then this all happened! It's still hard to take in, isn't it?"

Jason relaxed back in his chair, then Fia asked about Star and her friends, where they had survived. So the friends related their story to the couple. They were shocked to hear that Chaff and some others were brought back to life.

"Do you think they can bring anybody back to life?" asked Fia worriedly. "I mean, people who died long ago, like my grandfather. Do you think they could do that?"

Star offered her opinion. "I'm not sure really, I believe they healed and renewed the bodies somehow in their domes with their weird machines. But if people have been dead and buried a long time ago I think that would be very different."

Fia nodded sadly in response and then took another sip of her drink. The two groups chatted about events for a while before finishing their drinks and heading back to their new homes.

***

Bull's mother was cleaning her kitchen when Bull arrived at their flat. He enjoyed seeing how happy she was now that she had her own little flat to tend to. She had absorbed this new life willingly. No longer the hardship of living in a cold dark damp environment full of dust, having to make do. Now she could sit in a comfortable chair or settee and have any hot meal she wanted at the touch of a button.

The wall computerised screen brought her entertainment if she wanted, all was at her fingertips. She even had her own little car parked outside the flat, provided by the robots in the colour of her choice. Life was good for her again and Bull was glad. She had a tough life after the War, trying to survive from day to day, making do without simple things for so long and he couldn't imagine the sadness she would have felt when her husband, Bull's father had died when Bull was still very small. She deserved this luxury.

"Hi, mum, cleaning again? It looks clean anyway! I'll make you a cuppa, you go and sit down and rest."

Bull cheerfully moved into the kitchen whilst his mother sat down at the table. At the push of a button his mum had a hot cup of coffee planted in front of her on the table. Bull got the same for himself and sat down to chat with his mother.

"I went to the library down the street today." His mum began, sipping some coffee. "I was looking at old photographs of how our town used to look. It's not even recognisable any more.. But things change, don't they? This is a change for the better, I think. I definitely didn't imagine living here six months ago, in this lap of luxury! It's been a godsend! When I was in the library I met some people I didn't know and got chatting to them. It felt so unreal, sitting down and having a normal conversation! There was this one man who was so nice, very kind, he reminded me a little of your dad. He asked me out for a coffee tomorrow..."

"Ooh mum! An admirer!" Bull teased.

"Oh Bull! What are you like!" His mum swatted him playfully. "Seriously though, do you think I should go? I mean, I hardly know the man."

Bull smiled before answering. "Mum, you never will know him if you don't go, will you? Of course you should go! A coffee shop is good... now if he'd asked you back to his place I'd have been worried!" Bull laughed as his mum swatted him again.

Bull was glad she seemed to be making a life for herself here. He hoped the man would turn out to be just what she needed. She deserved a companion. He himself, however, was a different matter.

Drawings

Chaff looked around her bedroom and decided it needed some personalisation. "Hey, Lin, I think we need to make some pictures to put on the walls of my bedroom. It looks too new and tidy to be mine. Let's draw on the nice new paper Wren bought for me in the mall yesterday. She got me some fantastic colours to draw with, too. We can then stick them on the walls of my room to make it look more like mine."

Lin smiled and asked, "What would you like me to draw?"

Chaff thought about it, but as she really didn't mind she left it up to Lin to decide. Chaff decided she was going to draw her new house and her garden first. So the girls sprawled on the carpeted floor of the bedroom and began their drawing session in earnest.

"Mum! Come and look at my room!" Chaff called excitedly much later. She and Lin had stuck several colourful pictures onto Chaff's bedroom walls.

Robyn came around the doorway unsure as to whether there would be a mess or not. But she was surprised to see lovely colourful pictures tastefully arranged around the room.

"Oh Chaff, these are lovely! Is that a picture of our house?" she asked and Chaff nodded enthusiastically.

"I see you've drawn the lovely plants that are

growing in our garden too in this one."

She remarked as she went to the next picture. Then she stopped in front of one of Lin's drawings. It was full of colourful shapes against a dark background.

"This is beautiful too. What is it a picture of?" she asked curiously.

Lin piped up brightly "That is one of the places I'm going to see soon."

Robyn was a bit puzzled. "Oh? Where is this place?" Robyn asked.

"It's one of the galaxies we will be visiting." Lin replied with all sincerity, then pointed to a range of other equally pretty shapes set against other dark skies.

"These are some of the planets we will be exploring, where we will find many strange things." Lin added.

Robyn tried hard to smile, but this information was a bit too much to take for now. She found she did not want to ask any more questions and left the room. Chaff and Lin went to play in the garden.

***

Wren tried her best to cheer up Bull, but she was fighting a losing battle. Ever since they had been to the mall shopping he had been moody and quiet. The novelty of purchasing a brand new tool had soon worn off and now he barely uttered a word to her.

"What is it, Bull? Why are you so sad? Is it something I've done? Please tell me, 'cause I'm running out of ideas." Wren probed sadly as she sat beside Bull on the brand new family's settee in their new home.

Bull leaned forward, resting his elbows on his knees, playing with his fingers absent-mindedly. He looked down at the plush carpet at his feet, it all seemed so unreal to him. A new life had been handed to them on a plate. But did he want that? He spoke quietly without looking at Wren. He didn't want to hurt her, but how could he not?

"It's nothing you've done, you've only ever been supportive towards grumpy old me! I can't deny that life has improved greatly since the robots arrived and re-newed everything. I could never have imagined living like this a few months ago. Then, we had to work hard to survive, the whole community worked together for the same goal, to live another day. People depended on me. As a scavenger you know how important our job was, but now..." Bull shook his head in frustration.

Wren sat on the edge of the seat to try to make eye contact with him. "I know it's very different now, but isn't it a good thing that we don't have to risk our lives to get by anymore? We now have homes and transport, even libraries, shops and a hospital is being built! We have air we can breathe again and water to drink that isn't full of contamination. We have survived the War and we earned this paradise surely?"

Wren still couldn't get Bull to face her so she probed further. "Are you sure it's not something else? I feel that things have changed between us recently. I know we haven't been going together for very long, but I feel that you constantly pull away from me now. Do you want to end this already, before it's really begun? Please tell me, I won't break, you know?" Wren attempted a smile.

Bull finally turned to face her, his face full of re-gret. "Wren, it's nothing you did. It's me. I can't settle into a cosy relationship just now, with all these changes occurring daily. I need to work out what I'm going to do, because this life is not what I want. It just doesn't feel right, for me. I need to do something or I'll go mad. I need to be on my own to think things through, I'm sorry.."

He got up and held Wren's hand once more, kissing it gently before turning to leave. Before going out through the door he looked back at the stunned Wren and said, "You deserve someone better than me. Take care." He left with a heavy heart, unsure of his future.

Wren's tears flowed quickly once he'd left.

***

The months passed by and the town was thriving. The people were establishing themselves in the community, some finding work in the shops and industries nearby, others taking on roles as town bankers, clerks, publicans, religious leaders and local radio news and music suppliers! People with expertise in one form or another sprouted out of the woodwork to supply their services to the community. Life was developing and adapting into something good at last. Law and order was established by the robot community and people fairly but firmly treated by an incorruptible force became a good thing. People respected the robots' authority, after all, this life wouldn't be here without them.

Chapter 17

Training Days

Major White was escorted around the new barracks by his son Sergeant White. The premises were modern and suited their training purposes well. The training ground had an advanced assault course and the equipment in the gym was first class. The dorms were impeccably turned out and it was hard not to imagine that they weren't in a superior holiday camp! The soldiers were eager to set themselves up for a full training exercise as it had been for so long impossible to keep their fitness levels at their peak under the Spartan conditions in the bunker years. Several new recruits had been added to their ranks from communities all around and the unit now held over three hundred men.

"An excellent turn out!" Major White beamed as he surveyed the troops, standing to attention in their gleaming new uniforms, armed with advanced robot built weaponry.

"It took some persuading, but we finally got them to comply about the weaponry." Sergeant White reported.

"We shouldn't have to keep on relying on the robots to deal with defence issues alone in the future. They were agreeable to us training to defend our country alongside them in future issues."

"Well, we have a lot to be thankful for." The major concluded. "It's a pity they held back on their superior weaponry, though, but I can see it from their point of view. Carry on Sergeant."

The men saluted each other and the parade was dismissed. Training would now start in earnest. There was to be a training programme here that led to entry for Space crew training at a newly-built centre further along from the barracks. Many of the recruits were interested in taking part, as were some civilians.

At the bunker Kia and her mother sorted through their belongings to decide which they were going to take with them to their newly-built home on the edge of the new army barracks. There was so much to sort through, years of compiling a life from remnants of society. They wouldn't really need any of it, but they wanted a reminder of what held them together through the dark times.

"You two still sorting?" A baffled Jake asked as he entered the room. "I would have thought you'd need very little 'cause the robots provide you with everything, you know?"

Kia replied. "I know they do, but there are some things that hold great sentimental value that I need to take.." She held up the red plastic rose that Jake had found and given her years earlier on one of his scavenging hunts. He blushed with embarrassment and conceded defeat.

"Okay. I'll be next door. Give me a shout when you're ready for me to take stuff out to the truck." Jake left the room so the two could finish their rummaging.

Kia's mother suddenly stopped and looked at her daughter as she packed small items into her rucksack. Kia realised she was looking at her and stopped what she was doing.

"What is it, mum? Are you crying?" Kia put her hand to her mother's face and wiped a tear from her eye.

"It's all right. I'm just happy that you're here with me still. I couldn't believe that I'd lost you so cruelly that time... If the robots hadn't..." she hugged her daughter tight and tears flowed gently down her cheeks.

"It's all right, mum, I know, I'm just so glad to be here still, Jake too. We were so happy that day... But (brightening up) here we are now! Nothing is going to take us away again, I promise." She smiled and kissed her mother.

"Jake! I think we're ready now." Kia called as they picked up their bags, glad to be leaving those memories behind.

The bunker was almost empty of its inhabitants now, its purpose in future would be to house supplies and weaponry for stocking up the garrison in years to come. A skeleton staff would stay in rotation to maintain the building, otherwise all the people who lived here now had new homes near the army barracks. All built by the robots, a veritable town was emerging around it. As there were many new recruits in the barracks there needed to be housing for their families, so a town evolved at the foot of the Blue Mountains. It was to be called Bluewater.

***

Nobby had almost become a mascot for the army, through his valiant effort to defend the Bunker community in their time of need against the rogue AIs. They named their barracks after him, it was called Camp 159 after his Checker number! Nobby had VIP status and had free admittance at all times to the camp grounds. Nobby felt great joy in having the camp named after him and decided he would help them however he could. He had helped build the perimeter barrier around the camp and installed their perimeter alarm for them, even if it went off several times whilst he was installing it , he felt proud!

The army had a direct line to Nobby should they

need help in the future and Argo almost burnt a circuit when he discovered that Nobby was their first port of call if a disaster should occur in the future!

Towns were evolving across the globe from the remnants of society that had survived the Alien Wars. The robot armies built and renovated with the aid of the Mechs and businesses were stocked with goods produced by the Blues in the domes around the world. Life was returning to a kind of normality once more.

An announcement was relayed via the home computer screens that Captain Grey was going to present information on their long journey back to civilisation and discuss their findings. Everyone was eager to find out the story behind Earth's renewal and people talked of nothing else for days before the broadcast.

New Names

The gathering was arranged by Bill, who was now elected town mayor. All homes had received notice of the gathering via their home computer screens for a week before. Now the whole town was gathered together to discuss issues concerning the community.

The meeting hall had been built right in the centre of the town and it had been used as a gathering point for dances and weddings and any community events that required lots of space. The hall was now filled beyond seating capacity, people stood at the back and sides eager to attend this first meeting of the town.

Bill stood up. "Welcome to all of you this evening. I'm glad to see such a turn out. I hope tonight to cover any issues that have arisen since your arrival in the town. I know that some of you are still awaiting your vehicles from the dome and I'm suitable assured by the Blues that production has been increased and you should all have had your vehicles by the end of next week." A mutter of approval went through the crowd.

"Anyone who has any old music CDs or DVDs that were scavenged over the years, we would encourage you to bring them to the town hall so that we can upload them onto our home computers so that you all can enjoy a bit of your past favourites once more."

A voice called out from the crowd."I've found all the old Star Trek series DVDs, will they do?"

People laughed and Bill added that they certainly would. A lot of other people offered up the items they were intending to contribute, much to the satisfaction of the town as a whole.

"Next, I'd like to have a list of people who would like to offer their skills to help the community but have not yet got themselves a job. I intend to try and get you working in your own field of expertise if at all possible, so if you could fill in your details on the way out tonight that'd be great."

Another voice called out angrily. " And what about the scavengers? How do their skills fit in now? Not exactly needed are they? What do you propose to do with them?"

Bill shifted uncomfortably then spoke calmly. "We owe our lives in many ways to the scavengers. Without them we may not have survived. Without their skills we would have been lost. Just because we don't need to scavenge any more doesn't mean we don't need them. Their ingenuity, strength and persistence are valuable skills in many fields. Their bravery second to none. It is up to the individual how they wish to use those skills in their future . I welcome their input and I will help them to achieve their goals, whatever they may be. Please come to see me at the town hall for help and advice if you need it."

The crowd muttered agreeably at Bill's words.

"The robots have told me they would like to train some people to operate some of their transports and machinery, so if there are those who are interested in doing this please give me your details at the end." The crowd became excited at this news and many nodded their heads in agreement.

Several small agenda items were dealt with, involving jobs in the Mall and training for construction and engineering. There was even a call for people to offer their time for farm work, which some seemed particularly interested in.

"Are there any other issues that you wish to be brought up before I state my final item on the agenda?" Bill asked. The crowd looked at each other, muttering.

A voice called out. "Are there still places on the training scheme for nursing staff at the hospital? I'd like to put my name down for that." Wren stated clearly.

Bull and Robyn looked astounded at her, unaware that she'd been contemplating such a thing.

Bill replied. "Yes, there are some places still available, and if any of you wish to train as doctors, please apply at the hospital. Any more issues? No? Well then, my final item on the agenda is choosing a name for our town. Are there any ideas?"

People voiced a few opinions, but others rejected them. A couple of people suggested they give it the same name as before, but that was rejected also on the grounds that nothing remained but ashes of the former town that their homes stood on.

"That's it!" Remarked Robyn animatedly, standing up. "This town has arisen from the ashes just like in the story! Let's call it Phoenix!"

The crowd cheered and clapped in agreement.

"Phoenix it is then! Welcome to your new home,

Phoenix, arisen from the ashes." Bill stated and the crowd stood up and cheered before dispersing.

The Journey

It was eight o' clock in the evening and all were gathered around their computer screens to find out the story of their salvation. The image of Captain Grey appeared on the screen and he began his introduction.

"My fellow humans, welcome to our report on what led to this day, the day of your salvation and Earth's renewal. It all began over fifty years ago, when as a young astronaut I was trained to carry out special missions into deep space to gain information on what was basically out there. The government had been intercepting strange transmissions from outer space for a decade and we finally discovered where they were coming from. We were trained to travel vast distances to get there through the use of hyper sleep as the transmission came from the other side of our galaxy." (A map appeared on the screen with a distant star highlighted.)

"A team of brilliant scientists worked on creating artificial life forms that would guide and maintain the spaceship that would take us there. These are the Blues that you see working at the domes and on board our ships today." Grey called up video images of the robots at work around the ship, maintaining machinery and guiding the ship on its course through space.

" Our first efforts were the Whites, the checkers that you saw marching through the countryside gathering objects and creating the domes. They turned out unsuitable for our purpose and were used mainly in construction later on. We travelled asleep through space until we reached the vicinity of the planet that the transmission was coming from. The Blues woke us up in time before all hell broke loose! We had emerged at the edge of a full-blown war between two alien life forms! Here we have some video images of the battles we witnessed from a distance."

The spectators watched in anguish as they saw the widespread destruction of several spaceships in space, to be followed by the pummelling of the planet surface below the fight. Grey continued.

"We realised it was only a matter of time before we'd be spotted so we got out of there as fast as we could. The Blues guided us to a large asteroid out of the view of the forces battling it out. We decided that we would need powerful weaponry to defend ourselves if these aliens ever came our way.

We set the Blues to work on a plan to produce weapons. There were plenty of raw materials we could use on the asteroid and the robots gathered what was needed and started work on their project. Meanwhile, our team of scientists, led by Professor Kingsley, now deceased, persevered to produce super intelligent beings to help advance our technology. " (The screen portrayed the Bronzes and Silvers).

"At first the AIs worked well, seeing flaws in some of the Blues' plans and amended them. They decided we needed more manpower so a mass production of robots and AIs was developed, and with that the construction of several new ships took place. The asteroid was an invaluable source of raw metals and minerals."

Images of the construction on the asteroid filled the screen. There were dozens of shuttles and ships being constructed and fitted with weaponry. The robots and AIs moved with ease along the astcroid's surface, building the fleet of ships to suit their needs.

"On board the mother ship, Professor Stark created a hybrid AI with far more skill and intelligence than the other AIs and gave him the ability to fly too. We called him Argo. Lots of you have met him."

Mutters of recognition passed between members of families and neighbours in the public houses who were watching the transmission. Professor Stark's picture and Argo's image, flying through the skies was seen on screen.

"Argo was the first in the production of our Gold AIs, the supreme, which we called the Argonauts. They had ideas beyond our comprehension. They produced such advanced weaponry that we were sure would protect Earth from any invasion by such alien species... But it was already too late! Transmissions from Earth took a long time to reach us and fifteen years after we left Earth we were told in a transmission that Earth was being attacked by an invading force and the planet was being annihilated, could we come home to save our planet..."

The people sat there stunned as they realised the truth of the statement and how far away their salvation would have been.

"Of course, we knew that by then Earth was already doomed. We didn't even know if there would be any survivors to save, but Argo persuaded us that there was a way. He went away and came back with a plan to create a machine that would renew and clone items, even people if we had enough DNA. We were persuaded to let the Argonauts build their machine, even though it would take some time, time we didn't have.

"Eventually it was ready. We tried it out with inanimate objects at first and it worked! But we needed to try it out on humans too..." Grey bowed his head sadly before continuing. "Professor Kingsley, without our knowledge, decided to use take his own life so we could try out the machine...." There were gasps amongst the audience. "We placed his body in front of the machine... but instead of renewing him the machine disintegrated him instantly.." Grey paused, upset at recalling the memory.

"Argo was devastated too at his loss, but turned it around and developed the technology to be miniaturised as weaponry for each individual AI and robot instead. You probably recall the tanks and guns being vaporized by the robots early on."

"It took several more attempts to perfect the machinery for its purpose and that took several more months. Then we needed a guinea pig, I refused to let anyone else on board try it out so we headed back towards the planet where we had found the alien battles raging earlier. To our complete horror we saw it was still raging on. Well, it was an opportunity to test our weapons and our renewal machine so we set off into the heart of battle.."

Audiences everywhere were stunned by this revelation and awaited nervously the next event Grey had endured.

Destruction

On the computer screens the mother ship zoomed through the asteroid belt with precision evasive manoeuvring by the Blues, away from collisions. The alien planet looming larger on the horizon, battle still raging between the two tenacious rivals. It would be hard to figure out who to engage with, or perhaps the alien focus would be diverted to the new enemy on the block? They approached from a high angle into the battle, waiting for acknowledgement in one form or another from the aliens.

"Engaging shields, Captain." Argo stated.

"We have shields?" Captain Grey remarked with surprise. He had left the Argonauts free rein with preparations for the ensuing encounter, the technology being way above his understanding on the whole.

"Shall I take her in, Captain?" Argo enquired as

he linked with all supporting ships, now numbering in excess of five hundred.

"Yes, take her in, Argo. Let's see what unfolds. Defensive positions primarily until we know what we are dealing with."

"Aye, Captain." Argo related the order to the fleet and they set off towards the fray in box formation.

Several curved spaceships swooped up towards them, encircling the formation.

"We are being hailed, Captain." reported a Blue officer on the bridge.

"Acknowledge." Grey commanded and on the screen in front of them appeared a uniformed person of human appearance, but whose skin colour was grey.

The person started to speak, but in an unknown language to the captain.

"I shall put the translator programme on, Captain." Argo informed Captain Grey.

The grey alien spoke again. "Who are you and what is your business here?"

Grey thought carefully before speaking. "My name is Captain Grey and this is my fleet. We are travelling through the galaxy and happened upon your battle. Is there anything we can do to help?"

The alien replied. "I very much doubt it. This war has raged on for a decade. We are too evenly matched for either party to win. But we will not give up our fight to protect our planet."

Grey asked. "What is the war about? Perhaps we can help you?"

The alien was taken aback. "My name is Commander Glian of the Scenaran fleet and the planet being bombarded is where we are from. These invaders arrived trying to plunder our resources and began trying to lay waste to our cities when we refused. Many people have died in this war, but giving up would be far worse. If there's anything you can do to help we would welcome it."

Grey immediately accepted the challenge, eager to try out his weaponry.

Glian's ships led the way into the battle and Grey's ships followed, piloted by one thousand AIs, still in formation. The invaders' ships were larger and slightly slower, but their weapons had a longer range. Very soon Grey and his fleet were encountering fire from all directions. The battle was on! The shields held and no damage was incurred by the fleet, bullets and missiles absorbed by the shields.

The smaller shuttles detached from the Starfinder mother ship and began decimating the invading forces in their paths. The ships swarmed into the melee, blowing up the lead invaders without hesitation. Their weaponry was far superior to the invaders' and soon numbers were being depleted at a fast rate.

One of the large invader ships emitted scores of small craft, like bees swarming out of their hive, pursuing an agitator. They swirled around the Starfinder mother ship, intent on causing havoc and to damage the ship's weapons at close range. They were small and agile and fussed around too quickly for the mother ship's weapons to lock on them.

But the Argonauts flew out of the docking bay, helmeted with radar vision screens. Each Gold flew to attack its own prey, matching the agility of the small craft with their advanced flying capabilities. The invaders laughed at the sight of these flying robots, but their laughs didn't last long when the robots emitted lethal rays in the direction of the craft that disintegrated them instantly. As they began to see their comrades reduced to stardust they began to retreat as fast as they could, none a match for the superior Argonauts.

Grey watched events unfolding from the bridge.

He saw the invaders' depleted ranks gather together in a group and waited for the explosion of firepower that would follow. But to the left, emboldened by Grey's success in the battle, Glian's forces pursued the remaining ships and instead of fighting back they fled at hyper speed into the abyss beyond!

Grey could not believe how easy it had been to defeat the invaders and how these had been pummelling Glian's planet for years. Glian's face appeared on the screen, with shouts of joy in the background on the monitor.

"Captain Grey I really must congratulate you on achieving such a success in such a short time! I wish we had met a long time ago. I would like to invite you and your crew to visit our planet where we will offer you a feast to reward your efforts on our behalf today."

Grey was taken aback. He wasn't expecting it to be so easy, but he accepted, saying he would be only bringing a small number of his crew onto the planet. He didn't want to reveal the fact that most of his crew were in fact artificial.

Chapter 18

Scenara

The planet's surface was of blue and yellow hues, but wrecked by large bomb craters in all directions. Large cities lay in ruins, Grey noticed as he descended from the mother ship via shuttle. On board were four of the ship's scientists and Argo as protection. Just because they helped defeat the enemy temporarily didn't automatically mean that this species was trustworthy. It was better to be safe than sorry. They descended, following Glian's lead, towards a large opening in the ground, which seemed to be an entrance into an underground dwelling.

Argo led the way out of the shuttle, producing stares from all around. It seemed that nobody on the planet had seen anything like Argo before. Captain Grey followed behind, with four Professors in tow. Glian was there to greet them, with an entourage of six more grey men dressed similarly in purple and grey uniforms.

"Greetings Captain Grey. Welcome to Scenara." Glian spoke first.

It would have been impossible to have a conversation with them without the translator chips that Argo and his team had set in their collars on board ship. Argo himself was adapted to decipher language patterns in order to deduce meanings no matter what the language, so he had no difficulty.

"We thank you for the opportunity to visit your home planet. It looks like Scenara was once very beautiful. I wish we could have met sooner."

Glian smiled, he and the other Scenarians were all of similar height, around five foot tall, all with grey skin and grey hair. Apart from the colouring they were very similar to humans from Earth.

Glian looked at Argo and questioned Grey. "I hope I'm not rude, but you seem to be very different from this person (pointing towards Argo). I haven't seen anything like him before. Is he the same species as you?"

Grey smiled and replied. "No he is a superior species, living alongside us, his name is Argo."

Argo responded. "I'm pleased to meet you, sir."

Glian was taken aback on hearing Argo speak and smiled nervously. "Please, if you'll follow me I would like to treat you all to a feast for your part in our victory."

Glian led the way, along a tunnel decorated with magnificently extravagant designs made of something similar to mosaics. They depicted fantastic creatures that Grey had never seen before, with alternate scenes of beautiful landscapes in blue and yellow hues. The small company marvelled at the intricacy of the designs.

"These are beautiful. You have great craftsmen in your community." Grey remarked as they walked along.

"Oh, yes, I'm proud to say that my son was mainly responsible for the designs. They depict our animal life and our ancient cities, Unfortunately some of those beautiful cities are now reduced to dust because of this endless war. I'm sorry that you aren't able to see Scenara in its former glory."

They continued on as the company took in the splendour of the designs, each over seven foot tall and at least ten foot long.

"Perhaps you will be able to restore your planet

now that the war seems to be coming to an end. I'm sure the invaders have had enough of being pulverised themselves by now. I shouldn't think they'll be back, do you?"

Glian shook his head. "I'm afraid I don't share your faith, Captain Grey. The war has gone on for so long I cannot assume that this one defeat will stop it altogether."

They entered into a hallway which had large ornate doors at one end. The doors seemed to be made of a bluish wood carved with people's faces all over it. Two guards stood either side of the doors. As Glian approached they opened the giant doors to allow entry. Beyond was an enormous room, decorated exquisitely with lavish furnishings and blue plants in enormous pots were dotted around the room's perimeter. A woman dressed in a long flowing silver gown came up to Glian. She had sparkling jewels in her hair and around her neck. She was very beautiful.

"Ah, gentlemen, meet my wife, Kicha. My dear, these are the people who saved us today. They are to be our guests at the feast tonight."

Kicha smiled broadly, which made her even more beautiful, "Gentlemen, welcome to Scenara. What planet are you from? I don't think we have seen people like you before."

Grey replied that they were from Earth, a long way away and that their mission was to explore the galaxy and learn new technology on their way.

They all sat down at the comfortable seating and drinks were brought in on trays by two men dressed in black robes. The drinks were black and cold, but Grey could not imagine what they could be made from.

"I hope you will like our guara juice." Kicha spoke, as she sipped hers.

Argo quickly scanned the contents surreptitiously and gave a slight nod to Grey, confirming it was safe to drink. Grey took a sip and was surprised to find it tasted quite delicious.

"Ah, lovely! It tastes rather like a mixture between blackcurrants and lemons, which grow on our planet. Very refreshing!" He drank some more and the others followed suit. Argo however, just pretended to sip then put his drink down.

They all spoke at great length about their respective planets for some time then it was time to eat. Glian led the way to a dining room, where a large table was set with places enough for everyone. On the table there were large platters of fruits, but not like any at home! These were oddly shaped and either coloured yellow or blue. Some had blue leaves attached to them, others no leaves at all. The plates in front of each seat were however empty. Perhaps they were going to be waited upon thought Grey.

They all sat down and more drinks were poured for them, then another black-robed man, which Grey had now decided must be a waiter of some sort came over to take Glian's plate. He asked Glian what he would like today and Glian replied listing items Grey had no idea what they were. He watched curiously as the waiter went towards a hole in the wall, set the plate in it then repeated Glian's order as a door slid shut on the opening. A few seconds later the door slid open and a plateful of food appeared , which was then placed in front of Glian. He began to eat straight away. Obviously the Scenarians did not entertain the same manners as on Earth. Kicha was asked what she wished next and again whatever she had ordered appeared on the plate and was served!

Grey was approached next and he was unsure what to say, so he simply asked for chicken and rice with a lemon sauce, hopefully! The waiter seemed unperturbed and went over to the hatch and repeated

Grey's order and , sure enough, his food appeared exactly as he had wanted! Amazing! He tasted the food and found it to be exactly as it should be! Such a technology he would have to obtain somehow.

When it came to Argo's turn he said that he was on a diet and did not eat on certain days but was happy to sit with them. Glian thought it very strange, but of course he did not know human customs so he accepted it.

The meals were enjoyed by all, followed by the delicious fruit presented in front of them, Grey tried a blue fruit that resembled a tomato in shape and texture. It turned out to taste just like a plum! So far, everything they had tried was tasty! After dinner they were all given a smaller drink that was yellow in colour. Grey watched as the Scenarians sipped it carefully. One of the professors hadn't noticed and downed it in one, thus erupting in a coughing fit and turning red faced. It was very strong alcohol of some sort.

"Oh, I'm sorry. I should have warned you that luthiol is quite potent, you must sip it just a little at a time. I hope you will be all right professor?"

Stark gave another cough then nodded bravely. "Silly me, I should have thought a bit more. It's very nice though." At which point the waiter topped up his glass a bit more.

Music filled the room abruptly and the companions saw a troupe of dancers glide into the room. all dressed in the finest silkiest blue materials, covered with glittering gems here and there. The professors marvelled at the flexibility of the dancers and gasped in surprise as some were tossed into the air only to land gracefully on their partner's hands. They writhed expressively to the hypnotic music and seemed to have endless energy. The company enjoyed the floor show immensely.

Argo asked if he could investigate their food machine as he was fascinated by it and Glian asked a waiter to show him the operating centre in the next room while the rest of them continued to enjoy the evening.

When the visit drew almost to its close Grey asked about the casualties they had suffered and had they lost anyone close.

"Why do you ask, Captain Grey?" asked Kicha worriedly.

Grey replied." Well, you have been very hospitable to us all and we would like to do something for you as a thank you if we can."

"Oh?" Glian interrupted. "I thought your help in defeating the enemy today was a big enough thank you. What did you have in mind?"

Captain Grey spoke again, looking at Glian and his wife seriously. "I have a machine on board my ship that might revive a lost relative if they died recently enough. It has not been tested yet, but we would offer to do this for you if you have someone you hold dear that has suffered in this war."

Kicha and Glian looked at each other astounded. "Are you serious?" Glian asked again.

Grey nodded and Kicha fell to her seat in shock.

Glian looked evenly into Grey's eyes. "If you could do this it would be a great thing... Two days ago Kicha's brother, the king was killed in action. He lies in the hall of mourning awaiting entombment. Would this work for him?"

Grey was worried now that the king's body was to be the guinea pig. "I cannot guarantee it, but I think it is worth a try, don't you?"

Kicha began sobbing, but happily and her husband nodded. "Do it, please, do it."

Resurrection

As the king got up from the bed the small company surrounding the machine gasped in shock, then bowed in respect to the king. King Khali looked around him confused then touched his stomach where a gaping wound had been the cause of his death, but it was no longer there!

Servants approached with fine robes to cover the king, then Kicha ran over to her brother and bowed before him, kissing his hand. He bade her to rise and embraced her. He was told what had happened and how these new people from Earth had saved the day in the battle, then performed this marvellous resurrection. The king turned to Grey and his entourage and bowed to them adding.

"I am indeed in your debt, twice, by all accounts. If there is anything you require I would gladly offer it to you."

Grey thanked the king, bowing to him, then added he would like to learn the technology that provided them with their meals earlier. The king laughed and agreed willingly and the company returned to the planet below to investigate further the mechanism of the gadget.

The King regarded Argo with great interest, just as the other Scenarians had done, but accepted that he was a superior species and allowed him full access to the serving gadgetry. The King asked Grey if they would like to visit the domed city that was protected from the bombing. Grey of course jumped at the chance, giving Argo time to study the gadget in detail.

The King took them into a shuttle running on a railway next to the dining room. They all sat down then the shuttle sped off, seemingly without a driver. They passed through a long, dark tunnel then out into another see-through tunnel, where they could see the ruins of towns to either side and the blue and yellow countryside decimated by war. They travelled for about ten minutes when Grey saw in the distance the domed city they were headed for. It seemed to have a shimmer all around it and when Stark enquired what it was Glian replied that it was their shield that protected it from the bombs. They had developed the technology after seeing all their cities being torn apart by the alien bombing.

Stark conferred with Glian and found their technology similar to their own spaceship shields. Stark had begun to develop smaller shields for individual AIs to use in battle in the last few weeks and found it to be very successful. But he was not about to share that information just yet.

They arrived at the domed city and marvelled at the height and spread of the dome. It seemed to be constructed via a matrix of panes of transparent material, sturdy and reflective, with pipelines and ducts bisecting the quadrants of the dome to provide air and warmth to the atmosphere inside. It was the size of a small city on Earth, full of low-rise smaller domes, interlinked by short tunnels which contained rails for travel by shuttle from A to B.

Several taller buildings dominated the skyline. They were of conventional rectangular construction with most of the exterior surface made of coloured glass, it seemed to Grey. Larger arched buildings were dotted around the dome, presumably they were areas of commerce and gathering, Grey reckoned by their size.

Around the buildings the plant life was lush. a grassy substance was in many areas but coloured blue and here and there they saw different-shaped trees of many yellow hues dotted around the buildings. A lake was seen in the centre of the dome, sparkling and pale blue and surrounded by parkland where people milled around enjoying themselves. Several vivid flower beds adorned the park, with the flowers limited in colour to orange, yellow and blue tones. No animal life was in evidence under the dome, not even bird-like creatures could be seen. The humans enjoyed the scenery and wondered at the limited colours of the planet's natural plant life.

A carriage stood in front of the railway terminus and the king boarded the ornate blue wooden structure. Four footmen controlled the vehicle and the king indicated for the humans to board the other carriages behind his. When all were aboard the footmen wheeled the convoy around the city towards a palatial structure, which turned out to be the King's official residence.

Several blue and yellow flags waved in the gentle breeze created by the ducts at the turrets of the palace. The King dismounted and led the way along a blue carpet inside the great arched doorway of the building. Heralds dressed in uniform on either side of the arch blew into great silvery horns to herald the arrival of the king. All around bowed low to the king as he passed them.

The human party were stunned by the extravagant wall hangings and vast golden mirrors gracing the walls of the palace interior. Treasures stood in alcoves along the corridor leading to the throne room. The thrones were magnificently carved out of a gold and silver marble type material and deep blue embroidered cushions perched on each throne for comfort. Spiralled pillars of silver and gold held up the vaulted roof of the throne room and it was a breathtaking sight to behold.

A young man dressed in fine garments came rushing into the room from a side door, his face showing sheer astonishment at seeing the king alive and well. He stopped in front of the king and stared briefly into his face to see if it really was him and then bowed down low to the ground in front of him.

"Majesty!" The man uttered reverently. The king bade him rise then hugged him in a bear hug, laughing broadly. The king turned to Grey and said.

"My friends from Earth, meet my son and heir, Prince Cruza." Then, looking at his son, began to explain what had happened.

Prince Cruza had been fighting in space in the battle when the humans arrived, but had to perform his duties as leader of his troops before being able to join his mother, Queen Laifa and the humans. He had not heard that the King had been resurrected, so it came as a complete shock to him when he saw his father just then. The Queen had rushed to meet the King with Prince Cruza when she had heard of his resurrection. She was overwhelmed with gratitude for her husband's swift return and held her husband tightly with relief.

Once the company had been escorted around the palace, Prince Cruza took the humans to a large balcony overlooking the whole city so they could see it all in its glory. The prince was eager to hear about Earth and how they had defeated the invaders so easily, so once more the guests were to be treated to a fine dinner in their honour. They would stay at the palace as the guests of King Khali overnight.

Grey had gleaned a lot of information about resources on this planet and Stark in particular was interested in obtaining a piece of the material used for the dome structure to use again back on Earth when they returned there. It would be useful as temporary shelters perhaps for survivors, he thought. They could easily feed it into their cloning machine as it would be analysed for its molecular structure then cloned into whatever quantities and shapes they required. They did not share their purpose or methods with the Scenarians, but Prince Cruza happily obliged by providing them with a sample of the structure.

Grey's Conclusion

Captain Grey pointed out that these resources were developed for use in the construction of the domes here on Earth and the shields for the robots and domes were also tweaked with the technology they encountered on Scenara. The planet was bombarded again by the invaders for a week afterwards, but Grey and his fleet helped the Scenarians again to defeat the enemy and very quickly the enemy's ships were so depleted that the war finally did end .

They stayed months on Scenara as guests of the King and Queen and spent the time creating their vast fleet of ships and supplementing their robot army using their cloning facilities. When they thought they had sufficient numbers to help Earth in its renewal Grey was able to continue on his mission. It was now time to head home to Earth, and on the long journey home they developed their defence shields, weaponry, dome materials and their food gadgetry, all to benefit mankind when they returned to Earth many decades later.

On their long arduous journey they encountered other life forms and planets which were able to sustain life, but nowhere did they find a place that matched Earth's diverse beauty and resources. Sometimes they had to engage in fighting again to continue on their mission, but their superior firepower was their saviour each time.

During the journey some of the professors died of old age, happy in the knowledge that they had done good for their planet. They did not want to be rcsurrected, they had had their time and had learnt a great deal, now it was time for new generations to take over. In the end, Grey and Stark remained as the only two humans left on the ship. Argo had produced a companion for Grey from DNA on Scenara of a cat. It was of course grey like its owner, but Grey was happy and touched by Argo's sensitivity.

One particular time on their journey home they were bombarded by fragments of asteroids that had collided with something earlier and spun them into the fleet's path. It was a testing time for their shields, many held particularly well, but some of the smaller craft were lost by colliding with large segments of an asteroid. They had to spend time on one of the planets' moons to create new craft to supplement the fleet to bring it back to the number they required to help out Earth. That delayed their journey even further, but it was necessary if they were to complete Grey's Grand plan to restore Earth to its former glory.

On their final approach to Earth Grey sent out scanners, groups of orb-like droids to scan the Earth's surface to determine the type of problems they were likely to encounter and would need to resolve if Earth was to be saved. They were also used to try and ascertain if there were survivors on the planet too, something that would be essential in kick starting the Earth back to life again. There was also the possibility that the aliens were still around to be considered.

The orbs showed the true devastation the planet had suffered over the decades, because from space the Earth's atmosphere was shrouded in dust storms and largely shut out much of the sun's energy. There was no way of seeing the Earth's surface from outer space at that time. The Argonauts had to develop a way of ridding the planet of its pollution and they worked on a method of achieving that, eventually coming up with a satellite system that sucked up the dust clouds, like tornadoes into outer space, to be disintegrated by the mother ship's light beams. It took a long time to fully restore the Earth's atmosphere, but the Argonauts achieved it as the survivors found out to their surprise and gratitude.

"As you can imagine, you people of Earth, it was rather disappointing to find, when the robots were down on Earth, trying to establish the new domes to solve your problems, that humans still fought with weapons just like before. It seemed there would never be an end to war. I thought you might have learnt from that, but you attacked anyway, without trying to find out first what was going on." Grey continued, with his captive audience stunned into silence and embarrassed by their actions.

"That was why it was necessary to destroy your weapons, to prevent further attack as we endeavoured to put right what had gone wrong on Earth. I hope you can all understand that. When we discovered rogue AIs in our midst we took you away from your homes for your own safety and I hope you find your new homes to be much more satisfactory. We have worked hard to rein-vigorate Earth, it will take a long time to re-establish your lives, but we aim to help you as much as we can.

"You need not fear further attacks from outer space, because we have permanently deployed an Earth defence system around the globe so that if any intruders try to invade again they will find our weaponry a great deterrent. Space stations are set up all around the Earth to protect you, manned by our AIs. They will stay there for the future years to come to keep you safe."

The people sighed with relief at this news and nodded happily at each other. It was welcome news. Now they could focus on living.

***

Grey and Stark stood beside each other on screen and said they were both going to be staying on Earth, to live amongst humans again. But their fleet was going to continue on a journey to deep space to search out the invaders that had decimated Earth, to find their home planet and make sure they got the message never to return again. The fleet would be leaving in two months, but the Earth's defence stations and a few shuttles would remain here with some robots on Earth to protect it. They thanked the audience for watching and listening and wished them a happy new life.

People around the globe that had survived were overwhelmed by the journey Grey and his scientists had made and would remain ever thankful that they had made it back to save them all.

Chapter 19

The Date

Reed had made sure he had put on his nicest jacket, not too formal, casual but smart. He had tidied his stubble and hair and worn his first pair of jeans without holes at the knees for a long time! He kept looking out of the cafe window, watching people go by, wondering if she'd come. He had liked her from the first time they met, they seemed to have a connection somehow, not just connected by the War and loss of partners, but on a more personal level, they just clicked.

He became nervous as she crossed the road towards the cafe where he sat waiting for her. His heart beat loudly in his chest and he was worried she would hear it. He hadn't been this nervous in a long time. He got up as she entered the cafe. She beamed a smile at him and approached the table.

"I'm not late. am I?" she asked worriedly as he pulled the chair out for her to sit.

"No, not at all, it's just me, I like to be early so I could get a nice table near the window for us."

Bull's mother sat down and lay her handbag upon the empty chair next to her. It was new, she'd only bought it yesterday, it was her first handbag ever, black with silver buckles either side of the handle. It's not something that she would have needed in the Hub!

Reed handed her a flower and asked if she was happy with her new flat.

"Oh! It is lovely!" She exclaimed. "But it does

still seem so unreal having my own space and my own kitchen. It'll take a while I guess. How about you? Is your flat finished now?"

Reed passed her the menu and looked into her eyes. They sparkled so beautifully, He thought her very pretty. "Yes, I moved in a few days ago. I'm still trying to find out where things are or where they go!" He laughed easily.

A waitress came up to take their order and both opted for a latte and a piece of chocolate cake. As the waitress went to fetch their order Mary remarked, "It looks like we like the same things! You can never get too much chocolate I say!"

Reed added, smiling." After being on rations for years we deserve to spoil ourselves don't you think? I'd never even tasted chocolate before Grey got here."

They chatted easily, comfortable in each other's company and enjoyed the chocolate cake so much they decided to return there to have another dose later in the week! People passed by the window on their way to shop or meet friends, life had become easy again.

There came a little tap on the window next to them as they sipped their coffee and as they looked they saw Bull wave as he passed by.

"Your son, isn't it?" Reed asked.

"Yes." Mary replied, putting down her cup. "He's such a good boy, well, he's a man now! But to me he'll always be my little boy. He has always taken such good care of me when we lived in the Hub, always bringing me a little gift of some sort, if he could. I don't know what I would have done without him. It was hard when Phil died, that's his dad. But Bull always made me smile. Still does!"

Reed held her hand gently. " I can see how much you mean to each other. Will there be a problem if I keep seeing you, do you think?"

Mary blushed at hearing he wanted to keep seeing her, then answered. "No. Bull only wants me to be happy. I think he can see that I am."

Reed kissed her hand gently. "I intend to continue to make you happy, if you'll let me." He offered, looking into her eyes searchingly.

Mary nodded her head shyly, but happy to have Bull's blessing. In all their fifty years in this world neither of them had had such normality in their lives before. They had been small children when the War broke out and had only known hardship. Now it was their time. Time to enjoy living again.

As Bull walked along the street he smiled, thinking how happy his mother had seemed at the cafe. Reed seemed to like her by all accounts and he hoped he would be there for her if he decided to leave... He thought carefully about it. Yes, he seemed determined that this way of living was not for him. He pondered his options. They all led to him leaving, one way or another. How would his mother react? That was his main worry, but he hoped having Reed in her life would soften the blow

The Tower

Finch took her by the hand and led her up the ramp carefully.

"Finch! Why have I got to have this blindfold on? Where are you taking me?"

Star asked full of curiosity as she was led into the shuttle. The Silver nodded to Finch as he entered the seated area, indicating the laden table set in front of the seats. Perfect! He thought that Star would be blown over by it. He sat her down on the comfy chair by the table then took off her blindfold gently.

Star looked in amazement at her surroundings.

She was seated in one of the space shuttles, but it was decorated with little silver stars everywhere, hanging from the bulkheads and spread across the white cloth covering the table. Star-shaped silver balloons floated at the top of the room with silver ribbons dangling in a twisted pattern from each one. The table had been set with red roses and there were strawberries, chocolate and cream neatly arranged in bowls in front of her. There was a magnum of champagne sitting in an ice bucket beside the food and Finch started to pour some in the sparkling glasses for both of them.

Star was totally caught by surprise and was almost unable to speak!

"What...Finch? What is going on here? Did you organise all this?" Star spluttered the words out in her shock. She'd never had such a beautiful surprise before.

Finch gave her the glass of champagne and touched her glass with his. " A toast! To both of us. To our new life together."

Star sipped her champagne. She had never tasted it before and she giggled as the bubbles fizzed up her nose.

"This is so lovely!" she remarked, holding his hand in hers. She kissed him softly as he sat beside her. She felt the aircraft lift off and nervously looked around.

"We're moving! Finch, what's going on?" she asked nervously.

Finch smiled as he replied. "The food and drink is only part of my surprise for you. We're going on a little day trip too, somewhere I've been told is very nice, romantic! I wanted to give you a treat, so sit back and enjoy the ride!"

He picked up a juicy strawberry and dipped it in the chocolate and cream and held it to her lips. She had never had strawberries before, but they looked delicious so she took a small bite. She enjoyed the taste so much she ate it gladly. She did the same for Finch and he ate his first strawberry too.

"Yum!" they both agreed they were delicious and drank their champagne and continued with their romantic meal.

The Silver led the shuttle over the towns that had been newly built, then crossed over many lush green and yellow fields before approaching the sea. Finch held Star in his arms as they travelled and when he saw the sea through the shuttle window he showed it to Star. Neither of them had seen the sea before.

"Oh, it's so big!" Star exclaimed.

The Silver turned his head slightly to talk to them. "This is nothing! Wait until you see the ocean! I'll take you over the Atlantic Ocean if you like?"

Finch decided it was definitely a great idea and they watched in awe as they saw the magnificent ocean below them some minutes later.

"Oh! What's that moving in the water?" asked Star, pointing to the ocean below.

The Silver replied. "It's a couple of whales enjoying the air. Look! They are spurting water, can you see?" He arched the shuttle sideways so they could see more clearly.

"Wow! They look huge!" Finch remarked, impressed. "What are the smaller ones in a group, going faster alongside them? Are they baby whales?"

The Silver looked briefly then answered. "No they are dolphins, a different species, they are both very intelligent species though, so I believe."

Finch and Star watched enthralled at the sight of the immense ocean below them, but soon they returned to fly above land once more. There seemed to be fields upon fields of large yellow flowers for miles.

"What are they?" Finch asked the Silver again.

"In the fields?" the Silver questioned. "They are called sunflowers, they grow very tall, as tall as me. You can produce oil to cook from them."

Star looked at Finch and asked again where they were going.

Finch looked to the Silver, who nodded to the right.

"Well, if you look to the right we're going to be landing very soon." Finch replied, full of mystery.

Star looked over Finch's shoulder out of the window and gasped as they approached a tall golden tower with gardens and fountains surrounding it. They descended to land near the tower.

"What is this place?" Star asked. "It's so pretty."

Finch pulled her upright and held her in his arms and kissed her tenderly.

"We are in Paris, France, right next to the Eiffel Tower." Finch replied finally. As the shuttle landed the ramp opened up and Finch tied a silver star balloon to her arm and led her outside.

It was a glorious autumnal day, with the sun shining, the sky still blue, but the leaves on the narrow trees nearby turning into beautiful shades of amber and gold.

Star took in the glorious sight.

"It's sooo beautiful!" she whispered, turning full circle to look around her. She turned to Finch again and kissed him passionately, melting into his arms, then spoke softly.

"Thank you. It's the most beautiful surprise ever! It is wonderful! - You are wonderful!" Star kissed him again.

He took her by the hand towards the tower, a few people watching them nearby, smiling at the young lovers. It was beautiful to see Paris being restored to its former beauty once more.

Faster

Blue 90 had primed the engine to perfection, its movement almost soundless as it turned over in its vast enclosure. Blue 75 had attached the last leads to the booster and it was ready for use. Captain Grey would be surprised they thought. He had not known about their plan to amend the engines, but as it was now completed they would have to try it out, so that meant owning up to the captain. Blue 90 decided he would go to broach the subject with him right now and hope he would be pleased.

The Blues closed the engine compartment and Blue 90 went up to the bridge to see Captain Grey.

"Blue 90 reporting, sir!" The Blue spoke as he saluted the captain.

Grey turned from his monitor to face the Blue. "Yes, 90? What is it? Something wrong with the engines?" he inquired curiously.

"No sir, far from it, Captain Grey. We Blues have been working on a project to alter the engines in the mother ship, and if successful we could very quickly adapt the other ships to match this engine's powers."

The captain looked rather perturbed and asked. "Alter the engines? In what way ? Were they faulty?"

The Blue shook his head and answered. "Oh no sir! It's just that it has taken us a long time to complete our journey back to Earth and we Blues were concerned that it shouldn't need to take so long. So on our journey home we have been designing a method of adapting the engines to enable us to travel through space in a much shorter time. We have spent the last few months on board ship amending the engines to perfect them to our design specification. I hope you don't mind, sir?"

Captain Grey digested the information slowly. He stood up to think. Was he hearing correctly? Faster space travel?

"Just how much faster are we talking about, 90?" asked the puzzled captain.

"Well, sir, I could demonstrate to you if you wish; the engines are ready to be tested. Basically, a journey that would have taken a year before would now only need to take a month sir."

The captain fell back into his seat, astounded. "So, you're telling me that with this new engine we could arrive at Scenara, for example, in just a few months now, whereas it took us years before?" The captain looked awestruck.

"Yes sir." replied the Blue. "Would you allow us to do a test run now, Captain?"

***

The ship's crew prepared for the test flight, not sure where they would end up, but hoped they would be back in half an hour after set off!

The captain watched in disbelief as they zoomed at hyper speed through the galaxy, passing the closer planets one by one in the space of minutes rather than days. He was astounded, as were the AIs on board ship. If only they had been able to do this before! He marvelled at what the scientists had created, the technology that they had produced via the Blues and the AIs, and now this! It was a dream come true. The next crew of the Starfinder would be able to travel back and forth to Earth much more easily if they wanted now. Now that would be an even more attractive proposition to put to the proposed new crew .

They returned to Earth in the half hour as planned and Captain Grey congratulated the Blues on their success, giving them full permission to alter all the fleet's engines to match the mother ship in the space of the coming months docked here. The Blues set to work at once, pleased in the knowledge it had worked.

Stocking

Nobby was busily unpacking the cargo containers as they emerged from the dome and was loading the contents onto the transports bound for the shops in the town centre not far away. He and five other Checkers sorted the contents into various trucks lined up in front of them. They were new supplies for the main stores in Phoenix. He was carrying the clothing items into one truck and the other Checkers each were allocated a different truck to be loaded, each with different types of goods.

Nobby liked this job because it was easy, he couldn't get things wrong. His construction work had turned out to be a bit beyond him, so Nobby had returned to his cargo work at the domes. If it was clothing or footwear it was bound for his truck. Checker 130 was loading sports equipment for the truck going to the gym, Checker 122 was loading entertainment discs for the new music and film store. Checker 143 was loading furniture for the new Habitat store. Checker 162 was loading children's toys into another and finally the last truck was loaded with jewellery by Checker 120. They were all bound for the high street in Phoenix.

Nobby's truck was filling up fast. He seemed to have more stock on his than the others, but he wasn't worried about it. He opened another box to see the contents. "Ah, yes, definitely clothing." Nobby talked to himself as he eyed the black diving suits in the box. He hefted the box into the truck then went to get the next container. He rifled through the contents until he found more clothing.

"Hmm, these look like clothes too." He muttered as he picked up the cricket whites and the football outfits and stuffed them near the back of the truck. The trainers followed close behind them.

The other Checkers seem to be taking ages to find their things, thought Nobby, but he was sure he'd be rewarded for being the first to complete his job at the rate he was going. He knew he was allowed time off to visit his friends in the new barracks when his job was complete, Argo had arranged it as his ongoing reward. He opened another box and thought hard. The contents were rather strange, very sparkly, so he read the labels carefully. They said diamond tiaras. He didn't know what a tiara was so he accessed his cranial database and saw an image of it being worn on the head. Therefore the box of tiaras were stacked in his truck too.

Very soon there was hardly any room left. He went over to the container and saw there were still more shoes to be loaded. He thought they were rather small and uncomfortable looking. They seemed to be made of sparkly plastic, very pink, with heels, so he loaded the children's toy costumes onto the truck. Now it was full!

Nobby smiled to himself as he went to the commander to report he had completed his truck loading. The commander was very impressed and couldn't quite believe it, but he told Nobby to tell the driver he could set off for the store now. So Nobby was first to finish and went to hide before he was given more work. The other Checkers looked astonished to see Nobby's truck being first to leave. They were having difficulty finding enough goods to load onto their trucks. There seemed to be still lots of space left inside their trucks yet, there were very few of their goods left to load from the containers. It was a mystery.

Hours later the commander received an irate

message from the store manager where Nobby's shipment was sent. Apparently half the clothes he had ordered hadn't turned up, but instead he seemed to have lots of items belonging to the jewellers, the sports shop and the toy shop in the truck! The commander ended the transmission and said to himself.

"I'm going to kill that Nobby if it's the last thing I do! NOBLACZEC!" he bellowed at the top of his voice. All the other Checkers stopped what they were doing to look. But Nobby quietly and discretely went to hide in a container where nobody would find him...

Chapter 20

Homecoming

The Mechs shifted and lidded all the cargo containers as they arrived via the conveyor belt, ready to be shuttled back to the mother ship. They stacked the containers high on top of each other as they entered the docking bay at the other end, ready for filling later with manufactured supplies for the ship's next journey into space in a few weeks' time. Nobby lay completely unaware where he was as he had put himself on sleep mode inside one of the containers.

Captain Grey took his personal belongings from his room on board ship, few though they were, and went towards the shuttle with Smokie his cat in his arms. He was looking forward to seeing his newly constructed home. built to his own specifications by the Mechs and robots below. He had longed to settle back down on Earth, happy in the knowledge that Argo was more than capable of running things until a new captain was appointed.

Beside him in the shuttle sat the last remaining human on board ship, the last of the scientists who had journeyed with him through space for over forty years searching for a solution to Earth's problems. Together they had achieved their goal. Now they deserved a rest from all the travelling and were both looking forward to life on the land once more.

"I see you've got as much as me in terms of personal belongings." The captain said to Stark jokingly.

"Yes, to think this is all we own personally from over forty years in space, sad isn't it!" Stark replied smiling at his old friend.

"At least we'll be neighbours once more, old friend." Grey surmised. "We'll be able to continue our chess games at each other's houses quite easily. I'm looking forward to sitting out on the patio in the fresh air once more. That's what I miss most about space travel, with all that confinement indoors there's no outdoor pursuits."

The two men laughed as the cat meowed in agreement. Grey wondered what the cat would make of the great outdoors. He had not been out of the spaceship much since he was created. He hoped the cat wouldn't run away in fright.

"Shall we celebrate our homecoming with dinner at my house this evening?" asked Stark hopefully. He wasn't sure how he'd adapt to being alone in his own home for a change.

"That sounds an excellent idea." Grey agreed willingly. The same sentiments were uppermost in his mind too. It would take a lot of adjustment for both of them.

The shuttle soon landed in the town of Phoenix, where Grey and Stark had decided to settle. The two companions walked side by side down the ramp to head for their new homes. As they walked down the small street where they were going to live they saw in the distance a large crowd. They wondered what was going on.

"Oh no! Do you think the survivors have grievances already?" Grey asked his friend worriedly.

"I shouldn't think so." Stark replied, pondering what was going on. "I wonder what they want?" he added as they approached the crowd.

When the two men were close to their homes the crowd had hushed into silence. Grey began to get worried, as did Stark. All of a sudden the crowd erupted into shouts.

"Surprise!" they all called out, brandishing balloons and banners on which "Welcome Home!" was written in bold colours. Streamers flew through the air above them as the crowd gathered around the two men, patting them on their shoulders happily.

Travis stepped forward from the crowd to speak. "Captain Grey, Professor Stark, we would all like to welcome you to your new homes here in Phoenix. We are so glad you decided to live here amongst us. All of us owe you so much for what you have done here on Earth. We are all so grateful. We never believed it possible for us to have a normal life again, but you made that happen. We hope you don't mind, but we have arranged a Welcome Home party for you at your new homes."

Grey and Stark were overwhelmed by their welcome and agreed willingly to accept the party. Travis led them to Grey's house, which now brandished a huge banner with THANK YOU written on it in large letters hanging from the balcony above the porch. The same was seen on Stark's house next door he noticed.

Grey and Stark walked through the doorway into Grey's house and found it decorated beautifully with fresh flowers, banners and balloons. A large table was laden with buffet food and drink and music was activated by someone on the music screen as they entered. The crowd followed them in and Grey and Stark were handed champagne. It was beautiful. Grey was home. The cat seemed unperturbed by the noise and the music and left Grey's arms to settle down to sleep on a comfortable fluffy cushion on a seat nearby. Grey was overwhelmed by happiness.

The party had extended into Stark's home too, having also been treated in the same way as Grey's, full of food and decorations. The whole town had turned up to welcome the two men home. It was a wonderful party. Everyone enjoyed themselves.

Finch held Star close as he topped up her champagne.

"I could get used to this partying lifestyle!" Star remarked laughingly. "But it's not as good as the one you arranged for us." She smiled knowingly, then kissed him tenderly.

Bull shifted uncomfortably nearby as he saw the kiss. He tried to get her out of his mind, but nothing seemed to work for him. *In time maybe*, he thought to himself. *Give it time.*

Aftermath

The party had gone on all night. Everyone had enjoyed themselves so much they stayed on to party long after Stark and Grey had retired with their blessing. They enjoyed having company to warm the houses up. It seemed befitting somehow.

There were bodies slouched across the lounge early next morning, the worse for wear after being deprived of alcohol for so long. Robyn had taken her daughters home with her around midnight to put Chaff to bed and Wren had helped her mother carry Chaff home.

Star slowly regained consciousness, she was aware of bodies next to her and across her. She freed an arm and rubbed her eyes to focus. His arm was wrapped around her waist and she looked in shock to discover it was Bull's arm! Just at that moment he stirred and looked straight into her eyes. His gaze made her blush. He became suddenly aware of how he was holding her, how he had held her all night. She didn't know what to say, but at that point Finch, who was lying next to her also stirred and Bull quickly moved his arm away and sat up embarrassed.

"Oh god! My head!" Finch moaned beside her and stretched his arms out of their stiffness. "That was one heck of a party!" he groaned as he rubbed his head to stop the pounding.

Star and Bull sat more upright to wake up. They both looked around to see who else was around them. They both saw Travis staring directly at both of them, from the sofa opposite, he'd obviously seen everything.

"How's your head this morning?" Travis asked Bull directly. "Do you remember much of last night?"

Bull then judged he'd behaved inappropriately, but he could remember nothing!

"Bit hazy, can't remember anything." Bull offered shame facedly.

"Me neither." Star added, just for good measure.

Travis got up and went into the kitchen and eyed Bull to follow him. Star held Finch's hand and kissed him on the cheek as he tried to stir off the sofa to get a drink.

"Oh, stay here a little bit longer." Star tried to persuade Finch in case he overheard Bull and Travis talking. She pulled him close for a cuddle, to which he responded gladly.

"What the hell are you playing at?" Travis launched into Bull as he entered the kitchen sheepishly.

"I don't know what you mean." Began Bull. "I actually remember nothing from last night." He protested, truthfully.

"Then I'll tell you." Travis spoke in a half whisper, half bellowing. " As soon as Finch passed out last night you were all over Star! You danced with her, if you can call it dancing! It was more of a lover's embrace. She was too drunk herself to protest it seemed to me. What were you thinking? You were kissing her when I came into the room! " Travis was quite angry.

Bull cursed and held his head in his hands. He didn't remember doing that, although it's something he had long wanted to do!

"Oh my god! What must people think? I had no idea that happened! What the hell's Finch going to say when he finds out?" Bull was beside himself with worry. He didn't want to ruin their friendship.

Travis paced up and down the kitchen.

"I think you might have been lucky enough not to have been seen by anyone but me and Bill. Everyone else was either asleep themselves or were in too much of a drunken stupor to remember. I'm as sure as anything that Star's not going to say anything, she wouldn't want to upset Finch. If I were you I'd steer clear of them for a while."

Bull nodded, clinging onto the hope that nobody saw anything. Travis walked out of the house and headed home.

Bull stood in the kitchen for a while thinking. He was shocked by what he'd done. He wondered if Star realised what had happened.

"Penny for them." A voice at the door made Bull turn around. It was Finch. Bull was sure he knew but couldn't say anything.

"It was a great party last night, it's a shame I passed out when I did. I hope you enjoyed yourself." Finch spoke cryptically, but without revealing his true thoughts.

Did he know?

"Yeah, It's a shame that we're not used to the alcohol. It tends to ruin things if you have too much of it." Bull probed carefully.

"Hm, my thoughts exactly." Finch remarked. He knew! Bull was almost sure of it!

"Did you hook up with anyone at the party?" Finch asked innocently, half-yawning.

Bull didn't know what to say."No, I don't think so. I was too drunk to remember!" Bull decided to say, which was the most truthful.

Finch tapped him on the back playfully and went to make a coffee.

Bull breathed a sigh of relief, it seemed he'd got away with it, after all. "I think I'll go home, see if mum's all right." Bull stated and headed out the back door so as not to pass Star.

Star came into the kitchen a few moments later. "Did he remember anything?" Star inquired, touching him tenderly.

"No, it seems not." Finch replied as he turned and handed her a cup of coffee.

Restlessness

Days later. "Shall we go for a walk down to the river?" asked Finch as he held Star in his arms on the balcony of their new flat.

Star eagerly agreed and they set off hand in hand, passing the new homes in their street before turning down towards the fields where the river flowed just beyond. They enjoyed the smell of the freshly renewed air and saw red berries growing in the hedgerows that bordered the fields where the horses frolicked along. Sparrows flitted along across their path and Star and Finch watched them hop along from one bush to another.

Children were splashing about in the water, paddling in the shallows in their Welly boots, laughing and giggling at this new experience. Star listened to their voices, they were having fun. It brought back memories of a dream she once had, a dream she never thought would become reality. Now here they were. It had come true!

The horses were grazing close to the river and some were drinking from it when the two arrived at the newly repaired bridge. It now spanned the entire river whereas before, the bridge had been blown up at its centre. Finch leaned onto the wall of the stony bridge, looking down at the river below, watching the children playing, deep in thought.

Star watched him for a few moments in silence. It was strange not to see him with a quiver at his back and a bow over his shoulder nowadays. Gone was the tatty, ripped old leather jacket that he practically lived in previously, now he was dressed in a black hooded jacket with a white shirt underneath. It all smelt so clean and new.... not like the familiar Finch smell she was used to. It was disconcerting.

"What are you thinking about?" Star inquired, curious to know what was troubling him. He hadn't been himself for days now, quiet and pensive most of the time.

"Oh, nothing much." He replied half heartedly. "I just can't take in all these changes. It all happened so fast. It takes some getting used to. I feel like I've lost my purpose in the world I guess. I always knew what needed to be done before the robots came. We all had our jobs in order to survive, but now..."

Star looked into his eyes as he turned to face her. "I know exactly what you mean." she began. "I've been feeling much the same for a while now. I don't feel needed anymore.... Oh , not by you. I don't mean that!" she quickly added as he began to look hurt. "Needed by the community. All our needs are catered for by our robot invaders now. There's nothing for us to do anymore! It feels wrong somehow."

Finch held her tightly in his arms and kissed her

tenderly. "I have been thinking about something...I don't know how you will feel about it, but I need to say it. I want to see what you think." Finch held her at arm's length to see her reaction...

***

That evening Bull stared at the sparkling street lights. They were solar powered apparently, so Bull had been told. Here they were, brightening the whole street, people no longer had to live in the dark. The houses and flats on either side were all lit up too, full of people enjoying their new comforts, no longer confined to the dark and cold habitats they once called home. Bull strolled along the street slowly and watched as a ginger cat wandered ahead hunting for mice. *Who had a cat already?* he wondered. He heard the sound of footsteps behind coming towards him, so he turned to see who it was. It was Finch.

"Hey there! I thought it was you." Finch walked up to him.

"You out admiring the night skies too?" Bull asked.

Finch shook his head. "Everything's changed, hasn't it? It's so different, our lives now. We've become redundant, us scavengers. It feels strange not having anything to do any more."

Bull was hearing his own thoughts reflected back at him. "I thought it was just me. I was thinking exactly the same. This new comfortable world isn't for me, but what can I do?"

Finch smiled and told Bull of his idea. Bull's eyes lit up.

"That sounds like a great idea! How does Star feel about it?" Bull inquired, hopeful.

"Oh, Star feels the same , she's all for it! What do you think?" Finch questioned with a touch of excitement in his voice.

Bull grinned broadly. "I'm in! It's just what I need. People will think we're mad, but who cares. It's our lives, we should live it the way we want to."

Finch asked ."What about Wren? Will she be up for it do you think?"

Bull declared evenly. "Wren and I have gone our separate ways. It just wasn't working out. She's all excited about this new world. She doesn't feel the same as me."

"Oh, I'm sorry to hear that. Are you ok?"

Finch felt a bit embarrassed to have brought up the idea. Bull replied that he was more okay now than he was half an hour ago and the two strolled on down the street to talk about their plan and find a robot.

***

When Argo heard about their plan he thought it was an excellent idea, so he pleaded their case to Captain Grey.

"You think this would work out?" Grey asked Argo, although he himself was full of doubts.

"I think so, sir. There are bound to be some of the survivors finding this new life difficult to adjust to. Their sense of worth has been affected. They are at a loss as to where they fit in to their new life. I think this is a way out for them, until they are ready to embrace the new Earth."

Grey replied thoughtfully. " Well, if you think you could cope, as I'm sure you could cope with anything, then I will agree."

"Thank you, sir. I will report back to the people involved as soon as I can." Argo saluted and left the house.

Professor Stark appeared from next door and

asked. "Is everything all right? Why was Argo here? Has something gone wrong somewhere on the planet?"

Grey replied cheerfully. "No, nothing wrong, far from it. I believe we have acquired some prospective new crew for the Starfinder!"

"Oh? New crew? Have the AIs created a new handling unit?" Stark enquired, slightly puzzled.

"No, we are going to train a new generation of human crew on board the Starfinder, my friend!"

Stark took the news happily. "It seems right that the next voyage should have someone to take over the human role on board ship, seeing as we won't be accompanying it anymore."

"My thoughts exactly!" Grey added.

***

When Argo found the humans he related Grey's reply to them. He explained they'd have to undertake rigorous training first. They hugged each other with glee, full of a new found happiness and hopes of new adventures.

Chapter 21

Trials

The notice went up on all home and mall computer screens.

"All those interested in training for space travel please enrol for classes at the gym on Friday 6th November." It was signed by Captain Grey.

Many people saw the sign and wondered if space travel was for them. Nobody much had even contemplated it, but others welcomed it gladly and enrolled into one of the classes starting the following week. The classes were run by the gym staff and advised by the Golds. They liaised with the Space programme trainers and informed of the type of exercises necessary to ensure fitness and endurance to qualify for the space programme. The Argonauts oversaw the classes to make sure of the quality of fitness of individuals.

Several classes had to be set up due to the number of interested parties, but the numbers began to dwindle over the period of a few months due to the gruelling exercises causing large numbers to drop out. By early December only fifteen people had survived the trials in the Phoenix area .

Amongst these were Star, Bull. Finch and Guy. Gale, Lin's mother, along with two soldiers from Sergeant White's regiment also made up some of the numbers of interested parties that passed the trials. They had all received training in military assault and techniques as well, led by Major White and his son. They were then assigned to the last step of training at the Space programme centre. Argo was impressed by the candidates' perseverance and endurance. He reported the findings to Captain Grey when the trials were finished.

"Well, have we got a new crew that will hold up then?" Grey asked Argo as they sat in his lounge, relaxed on his comfy settees. Argo was surprised at how the humans arranged their homes, but he liked it very much. It was cosy, relaxing!

"Yes sir!" Argo replied, "Very capable bunch. We have seven who have made it through with flying colours."

"Do we have a clear leader amongst them, do you think? Does any one of them stand out?" Grey inquired hopefully.

"One that will make a captain? Yes sir! I think we have found our man." Argo reported happily.

Grey was impressed and relieved. He was told the person's name then Grey told Argo it was to remain a secret until the flight's departure, He would speak to the individual beforehand to check all was well then announce the captain to the community at lift off.

Argo agreed, then he went to tell the successful applicants they had passed their training to crew the Starfinder when it departed just after Christmas. They could celebrate the festive season before they left for their long voyage through space. Their mission, to find more allies for Earth and to ensure the annihilation of the Earth's alien invaders!

***

Finch and Star were delighted they had both made it through to crew the Starfinder. It would be the beginning of a new life for them, a life that would be filled with excitement and purpose once more. It was what they had hoped for and also they could celebrate the festive season amongst friends before departing.

They were disappointed when they saw on the list that Bull hadn't been chosen, he'd been so keen to take part, They wondered why, but when they asked , he kept very quiet about it, perhaps he was worried about leaving his mother. Although she seemed to have developed a new relationship with Reed and seemed very happy. The two would be sad to leave Bull behind, they would both miss him. Somehow they'd always imagined that they'd always be together.

Lin was excited that her mother had passed the trials, but she seemed to know she would. She knew also that they both were going, her mother wouldn't leave her behind and Argo had told her she would come too. Lin had always known the journey that lay ahead of her and was excited to be a part of the journey through the galaxies. She knew she would be needed.

Sergeant White was sad to see two of his finest soldiers leaving on this journey, but he understood how they felt. They were attracted to the unknown, the adventure and the experience it would give them. Meera Khan's parents were obviously upset that she wanted to go, but they would not stand in her way, it was her life and she must live it. They knew there was a chance of seeing her again now that the Blues had accelerated the travel time through space with their newly hyped-up engines. They took comfort in the fact that her boyfriend, Private Kian Furze was going to accompany her too. At least they had each other. It was as it should be. It didn't make it any easier to say goodbye though. They weren't looking forward to that.

Kia was sad to see her friend Guy go, but she understood why he wished to leave for this adventure. She made him promise to come back safe and sound, which he did, laughing.

The candidates all knew they would be leaving

shortly on a long journey through space to find the alien invaders' planet and persuade them forcibly that they should never return to Earth again. Their other mission was to find new technology and resources they could use back on Earth one day and hopefully form alliances with other life forms in the galaxies. A visit to Scenara was scheduled on their journey too, so it would be full of adventure for the new recruits.

All were looking forward to their new adventure and , although sad at leaving their friends behind on Earth they now had the technology to be able to return to Earth much sooner once their mission was complete.

Christmas Celebrations

Snow had fallen on schedule a few days before Christmas and, far from dreading the onset of cold weather like before, this year was different. This year everyone had a warm home to call their own, with all the comforts required for a happy holiday. The streets of Phoenix were decorated with Christmas decorations in the old style, with Santa's and reindeer adorning many a front lawn, accompanied by sparkling Christmas trees brightening up every window.

The town square had a massive Christmas tree, laden with lights and trinkets, donated by the robot army from the dome to the inhabitants of the town. Even the robots had taken to celebrating the Christmas season by adorning themselves with tinsel around their necks.

Robyn, Wren and Chaff, dressed in warm coats and scarves, stood in the square admiring the enormous tree, as did many other inhabitants of the town. A man was roasting chestnuts on a brazier in one corner and there was a small queue of people gathered around it ready to sample the food. All of a sudden sweet music started playing nearby. Robyn and her daughters turned to look where it was coming from. They saw around the other side of the tree a group of people stood, dressed in warm navy coats, some brandishing brass instruments and others singing along to the tune they were playing. At closer inspection she saw Sergeant White was one of them, playing one of the instruments. She also recognised other faces, more people from the Bunker community and a few surprise faces too!

Star and Finch smiled as they watched Bull's mother Mary and her new beau Reed singing in the choir. They looked very happy together, side by side singing the Christmas Carol. Bull watched nearby too/ They wondered if they should go over to him, but were unsure how he felt about them going on the journey in space without him. It was so unfair, they thought. He had seemed the most capable of them all in the trials, but Bull didn't seem too worried. They walked over to him, arm in arm, snowflakes in their hair, glistening before melting into droplets of liquid.

Bill and his family hummed along to the tune and behind them in the snow some small children were playing snowballs , throwing them playfully at each other. Bull rushed to a snowdrift and formed some snowballs and began a snow fight with Star and Finch and Wren. It was the most fun they'd had in a long time. They savoured every moment.

Up in space the Mechs continued to pack more and more containers into the cargo hold, ready to be filled before the journey. Unbeknown to them Nobby was still entombed in one of the containers, completely surrounded by crates on all sides, unable to free himself. He decided it was best just to keep himself on an extended sleep mode until he was freed once more.

At the home of Travis later on, the family and close friends sat down for their Christmas meal, prepared without the hassle of having to cook everything themselves. The food gadget was indeed the best invention ever! Bill and his wife enjoyed sharing this special occasion with their oldest friends and the wine flowed freely as they celebrated their first Christmas in their own homes together and in comfort. All over the town people were appreciating what they had been given, a new home and a new life of comfort and hope. It was a good feeling.

Grey, Stark and Argo sat in Stark's lounge enjoying this new found peace. The men had asked Argo to join them, even though he didn't need food or drink. They wanted to enjoy their time together before Argo left on the long voyage into space without them. They wanted to be briefed on the preparations for the voyage and check that the new crew were all up to speed on their duties.

"Tell me Argo." began Grey. "How is the new captain coping with keeping his identity a secret? Has he had any problems?"

Argo replied. "No problems sir. He tells me that only his closest family know and they have been sworn to secrecy too. May I ask sir, why is it to be a secret?" Argo asked quite puzzled.

Grey smiled as he answered. "Well, Argo, in my experience, if you choose a younger guy for the job, the older ones can cause trouble. If it is a fait accompli then there's less chance of them being able to argue the point with me when I'm a million miles away! They will just have to accept it this way."

Argo wasn't sure he agreed with that, but he accepted that's the way Grey wanted it so he changed the subject.

"Captain? Have you by any chance given Checker 159 a special mission lately?"

The captain was puzzled by this and answered. "You mean Noblaczec? No, why?"

Argo was a bit uneasy on hearing this news and added.

"Well, it's just that I haven't seen or heard about him for a few weeks now. I don't know if that's good news or bad news!"

The men laughed and reassured Argo that he was bound to be up to no good somewhere and he'd soon turn up.

"That's what worries me captain." Argo remarked, adding. "I'm not sure that it's a good idea to leave Nobby behind to help the Army in Blue, he'll be more of a hindrance than a help I reckon."

Stark replied. "Don't worry, Argo, we'll keep an eye on him. You enjoy a Nobby free trip for a change!" They toasted to that and laughed again.

The Final Day

New Year had been celebrated in style, with the whole community enjoying a fantastic display of fireworks put on by the Blues in the town square. Most of the community had never seen fireworks before and revelled in the colour and excitement of the show. It was their last chance to celebrate together as a whole community before the Starfinder set off in the morning for the voyage that had been long anticipated.

A shuttle had parked up at one corner of the square ready to take the new crew up to the mother ship in the morning, in front of all the town to wave them off. It was guarded by the Silvers and all supplies and luggage of the new crew were already on board stowed away.

"This new year is going to be full of new beginnings!" Finch mused as he held Star in a warm embrace. "I wonder how we're going to adapt to life on board ship?"

Star thought about the long journey ahead. "I think the hardest thing will be not having the warmth of the sun and fresh air to invigorate us." She continued. "I hope we're doing the right thing, leaving our friends behind."

Finch looked worried for a moment. "Yes, that's worried me a bit too. For so long it's been the four of us, you, me, Bull and Wren out together on scavenging duties. We made a good team. Now it's just you and me girl. It's such a shame the others aren't coming."

Star felt it too, but she was so glad that Finch had been chosen with her. She would never have gone without him.

The next morning arrived, with a hint of winter sunshine in the sky and the snow had all gone a few days earlier. The community were all out to see them off. Some had made banners and flags to wave. They waved them frantically as the crew arrived with Captain Grey and Professor Stark leading them. It had been hard to say goodbye to everyone, but they all felt they would be back in the not too distant future. So their hearts weren't too heavy.

Star had hated saying goodbye to Bull. It was like leaving a part of her behind. He had hugged her and turned away abruptly. She suspected he didn't want her to see him cry, so she said goodbye last night and wished him well before leaving his house. Finch had told her he was funny with him too, but that he'd wished him well and told him not to take too much crap from their new captain. They shook hands before Finch left.

Both Star and Finch were tapped on the back as they passed through the crowd towards the shuttle. Everyone wished them well. Lin and Gale were also hugged and wished well, despite some feeling a sense of relief that Lin was leaving with her mother. They were still rather afraid of her.

Robyn and her daughters were sad to see them go, but felt they hadn't seen the last of them. Chaff gave her friend a friendship bracelet she'd made especially for her and Lin put it on immediately. Lin handed Chaff a box, saying it was a gift for her to remember her by. When Chaff opened it there was a snow globe inside, but the snow were little stars instead, against a black background and floating in the liquid was a little astronaut that looked a lot like Lin, floating above the surface of a rocky planet. Chaff laughed as did Lin and they hugged goodbye.

Star looked at the crowd in front of her, seeing all the familiar faces smiling back at her. She tried to see Bull in the crowd, but there were so many people it was hard to find him .She hoped he'd be ok. She would have loved to see him one last time before leaving.

Grey stood half up the ramp to address the crowd as the crew formed a line in front of the shuttle, all now dressed in their blue and black crew uniforms, each with their name embroidered onto the suit.

The Silvers stood either side of the shuttle standing guard. There seemed to be no sign of Argo yet. Grey spoke.

"Friends and neighbours, the time has come to let the new crew of the Starfinder board the shuttle to start their new adventure. We wish them all a safe and bountiful journey. I know they will be missed, but take heart in knowing that you will see them again in the not too distant future!" The crowd began to clap and cheer, waving their flags and banners of Bon Voyage. Grey raised his hand to speak again and the crowd hushed,

"Argo, who is to be the new fleet commander, tells me that the new crew excelled in their training, they are a credit to you all." The crowd cheered again, then Grey continued.

" As you all know a crew has to have a captain and we believe we have found a truly remarkable person to take over that role. This person has not only excelled in all of the trials but has shown strength of character, wisdom and ingenuity to boot." Everyone looked at the crew, wondering who it was to be, the crew all looked at each other too, as if pretending they didn't know who it was."

Captain Grey waited until the crowd had hushed until speaking again.

"I would like you all to join me in wishing our new captain the best of luck..." Grey pointed to the upper part of the ramp, where Argo was leading a person out, dressed in the captain's stripes.

"Everyone, please welcome Captain Carter... Captain Bullfinch Carter."

He began to clap to gasps in the crowd as Bull descended down the ramp! But very quickly the whole crowd erupted to cheers and loud applause and the applause and cheers were loudest coming from Finch and Star!

"Oh my god! He knew all along! No wonder he was funny about it! " Star announced laughing with glee.

Finch shook his head in disbelief, adding.

"You wait 'till I get hold of that bastard! I'll kill him!" Finch laughed, remembering what Bull had told him last night. [don't take any crap from that new captain of yours].

The crew marched up towards their new captain and fleet commander and saluted them, then they all gave a final salute to the crowd and Grey before heading inside the shuttle for lift off.

The crowd watched as the shuttle sped up into space and many a tear fell from eyes as they watched it disappear from sight.

On Board Ship

The crew arrived at their new quarters and un-packed their belongings as Bull was briefed by Argo on the bridge about the schedule for the day. Bull was happy now that he'd seen Star and Finch's reaction, they really were happy he'd been chosen as captain. It was a great relief not to have to keep the secret any longer.

"Blue 7, set the course for Saturn." Bull com-manded.

"Aye, Captain Carter." the Blue replied with a salute. He was going to have to get used to not saying Captain Grey in future. That would be embarrassing!

The mother ship sped off into deep space, fol-lowed by the reduced fleet. Only a small crew of Argo-nauts stayed behind in the fleet to protect the Earth from the new space stations dotted around the globe. Earth would hopefully be safe until they return. Several robots on the planet acted as peacekeepers in every town or city and a few Silvers and Bronzes remained as shuttle pilots for Grey to oversee Earth's progress in the coming years. The creation of new Silver security squadrons had been started to patrol the globe.

Down in the cargo bay the Mechs were lifting and shifting the cargo containers to be filled with sup-plies for the journey from the cloning room nearby. The Blues had been busy manufacturing the foods and sup-plies they would need for the foreseeable future and now it was passing along conveyor belts to be stored in the huge containers. When they opened the fourth tier of crates and opened one to put in supplies of uniforms they stopped in surprise to see a robot lying inside. It seemed to be disconnected. The fleet commander was hailed to offer advice.

"What is it?" Argo asked as he entered the cargo bay. "Don't tell me there's a problem already?" He walked over to where the Mech was pointing and looked down into the container where Nobby had just switched himself back on.

"Nobby? What the hell are you doing here?" yelled Argo, dumbfounded. "On second thoughts, don't answer that!" Argo added turning on his heels, yelling "Just keep away from me, just keep away!"

Nobby looked up at the Mech and asked "Can I go down to the dome now?"

Chapter 22

The Rockies

Deep in the Rocky mountains, where trees had returned to cover the vast mountain range once more, even though the area was devoid of humans since the War, a figure moved along the craggy heights looking into the distance at the developing world. He had not thought that the Earth would return to its former mantle and wondered what it meant. He returned to his people, who resided in the caverns below and decided it was worthy of investigation.

He entered the large cave where his colony had established themselves around forty years ago, intent on staying in this land and raising generations of his people here amongst the crevices and ravines embedded in the mountain range.

The dark crevices and caves resembled their homes back on their home planet Viba, but here they did not have to suffer constant tremors and suffocation from poisonous gases leaked from underground as they did back home. When their comrades had fled those many years ago he and his unit had decided to colonise this area for themselves. They had been left alone here all that time as no humans lived anywhere for hundreds of miles. Now it seemed the Earth was changing again and Sarf needed to find out why.

Sarf gathered his weapons and supplies and with a group of his best warriors set off to explore this new Earth to find out what was going on....

END OF PART ONE

To be continued in Part 2, *The Voyage* available Spring 2015.

Part 2

The Voyage

Chapter 1

Warning

Lin felt the danger running through her body. All her senses warned her to act quickly as though all of the crew's lives depended upon it. She communicated telepathically with Argo, the AI fleet commander on the Starfinder mother ship. Argo and Lin had a strong telepathic connection and they trusted each other implicitly, even though Lin was only six years old.

"Argo! Danger ahead! Veer the ship away from it quickly! We have very little time!"

Argo heard Lin's message loud and clear even though he was on the bridge of the ship and Lin was laying in its depths in her own bedroom next to her mother Gale.

Argo scanned the sensors again, but there was no sign of anything in front of them!

"Say again Lin. I cannot see any danger. Where is it?"

The captain leapt to Argo's side on hearing the urgency in his voice. Argo related quickly to Captain Bull Carter what Lin had said. Bull looked ahead through the window on the bridge. The sensor had shown nothing and as far as Bull could see, there was nothing to be seen but stars for thousands of miles around.

Suddenly the sensors on the Starfinder began blaring an alert all over the ship. First officer Kian Furze reported urgently-"Hull breach, Captain. In Sector Five."

Bull thought quickly where that was, he was quite new to the spaceship, having taken over from Captain Grey a few days earlier. Grey had retired after his long mission through space to find resources to save the Earth from its devastation after an alien invasion forty five years previously. He had to travel for so long in space because the technology for faster space travel had only just been created by the Blues on board ship in the last few months. Now the Starfinder and its fleet could travel in a fraction of the time it used to take when Grey was in command.

Whilst Argo, an advanced AI, checked the safety of the fleet, Bull, realising that Sector five was where the girl he was in love with was sleeping, rushed to hail Star on his mic.

"Star! Star! Are you there? There is a danger in your area somewhere, be on alert! ......Star, can you hear me?"

But there was no response at all from Star's room.

Bull rushed out of the bridge to the beamer, where he could beam himself down to the sleeping quarters in Sector five, where Star's room was. As he left the beamer on the fourteenth level he nearly crashed headlong into Finch, who was on security duty near the engine rooms below and had rushed towards his girlfriend's room to check that she was all right when he heard the alarms sounding.

Finch and Star were lovers, both part of the ship's crew from Earth and they were friends of Bull's, so Bull was honour bound to never act on his love for Star, out of respect for his friendship with Finch.

"What's happening?" Finch asked worriedly as they both ran towards the sleeping quarters. "Is Star in any danger?"

Bull replied that he'd not been able to hail Star when the alarms set off and that there was a hull breach in her sector somewhere. On hearing this news Finch ran even faster towards his love, calling her name urgently.

"Star! Where are you? It's me, Finch. Star can you hear me? " He called on his collar mic repeatedly, but again there was no answer.

The sizzling energy cloud had engulfed Star completely, probing her thoughts and controlling her mind, looking for something it had never encountered before. It held her in its grip and she was unable to move or respond to her lover's calls. *How he must be worrying about me,* she thought in her stricken state.

The sizzle of the energy hummed in her ears almost making her wish she was deaf. It was overpowering and intrusive. She tried to move her legs but her body could not respond. It held her in a vice-like grip. She tried to speak but her lips seemed fused shut. Anyone else might have totally panicked and given in, but Star was made of sterner stuff, she had been one of the Earth's Scavengers in her past, a vital role that helped her community to survive the devastation of her planet.

The ship's human crew, numbering only eight were all survivors of the Apocalypse of over forty-five years previously. They had their lives turned around when a robot army landed on Earth last year and revitalised their world with their advanced technology, returning it to its former beauty. The rest of the crew, numbering in their thousands, were all artificial intelligences from that very army that saved them.

Argo was the supreme Gold AI, possessing many skills, highly evolved and trustworthy, he was the fleet commander now, based on board the Starfinder mother ship. Now the ship had been breached by this intrusive energy cloud. It had been invisible to all their radar equipment, only Lin had felt its presence.

The two friends kicked open Star's bedroom door, guns in hand ready to defend her, but when they entered the room they were shocked by what they saw. Half of the room was engulfed by the energy cloud, sizzling and moving around Star, holding her in its grip. Her whole body seemed to glow with electrical energy. They ran towards her to try and save her from the energy field's grip, but as soon as they came close the spikes of electrical energy knocked them back viciously, stinging their bodies like sharpened knives!

"Star, can you move?" Finch asked urgently. But Star could not respond, it seemed.

Bull again ventured closer to the energy cloud but Star's eyes, the only thing she could move, glared in warning at him. Bull understood her well, having partnered her on all their scavenging patrols in their past lives, they had made a good team. They complemented each other. He had fallen in love with Star over the last year, but could not act upon it due to her love for Finch, his best friend. Now both men felt helpless to rid her of this menace.

Blue 7's voice hailed the captain on his earpiece. "Captain, we have lost control of the Starfinder, all systems are non responsive to our commands. We are locked in position from when we suffered the hull breach, we are not moving!"

Bull responded quickly." Are the life support systems being maintained?" The Blue replied that they were, but he had no control over them. " Are the rest of the fleet affected by the same problem?" Bull added.

"No captain. The fleet report no problems with their ships. What would you like to do, Captain?" Blue 7 enquired, awaiting the new captain's decision on how to resolve his first problem in his new career.

"Get one of the support ships to focus on our position to see if they can rid us of the problem. There seems to be some sort of energy field inside Star's bedroom, holding her prisoner. We can't get near to it from here. See if they can find the problem from the exterior. Captain out."

Blue 7 hailed the Silver commander in one of the fleet support ships to investigate how their ship was being held and to offer advice on moving the obstacle if possible. All the fleet support ships were piloted by Silver ranking AIs, below Argo and the Golds in skills, but still extremely skilled at manoeuvring their ships in times of battle. The Silver commander turned his ship around to head for the mother ship, but still keeping a safe distance from the danger. The rest of the fleet awaited just ahead, unmoving, ready to offer support when needed.

Silver 1 circumnavigated the mother ship from a safe distance, looking for the danger. On turning into the starboard quadrant the commander saw the problem clearly through his control window. A large energy field, like a sparkling cloud of electricity abutted the hull of the ship at that point, as though it was half in and half outside the ship at the same time. It was substantial in size, writhing along the hull of the ship. This would be a tricky operation to try to move it. He reported the details and awaited orders.

***

Meet our Author

Beth Schluter

Beth Schluter was born as Bethan Frances Jones, in Chester, North Wales, in the United Kingdom and lived in the beautiful small town of Bala, North Wales until she went to College in the early seventies.

Having qualified as a Late Primary teacher of Art , Music and Languages at Newcastle-upon-Tyne Polytechnic, Beth went on to teach in Harrow, London, following her love of the Arts and Literature. In Harrow, she married and had a daughter, Helena, who inherited her mother's love of Literature.

Beth has always dreamt of writing a novel, since she was sixteen when she attempted to give it a try. But exams and work gave her little opportunity over the years, to complete her project, and she only resumed her passion when she received early retirement in 2012.

Beth's love of everything Science-Fiction led her to begin writing novels in this genre. Indeed, she had so many ideas that her debut novel became the first part of a trilogy, with books two and three being written in quick succession behind the first, *The Hub*.

Having enjoyed her first experience of writing, Beth hardly stopped to breathe, and by the end of 2014, she had written nine novels, two of which were children's Fantasy novels!

She continues to enjoy writing, embarking on both children's and adults' novels in Science Fiction and Fantasy genres. If her debut novel's reviews are anything to go by, *"an exciting and evocative novel. The danger feels tangible"... "the characters are brilliantly written, feeling completely real.." (Essex Life Magazine),* then the reader should be in for a real treat.